P9-DMR-241

Venus and Lysander

Yoshiyuki Ly

ALL RIGHTS RESERVED

No part of this book may be reproduced or transmitted in
any form or by any means, electronic or mechanical,
including photocopying, recording, or by any information
storage and retrieval system, without permission in writing
from the author, except in the case of brief quotations
embodied in reviews.

Publisher's Note:

This is a work of fiction. All names, characters, places, and
events are the work of the author's imagination.

Any resemblance to real persons, places, or events is
coincidental.

Solstice Publishing - www.solsticepublishing.com

Copyright 2017 Yoshiyuki Ly

Venus and Lysander

By

Yoshiyuki Ly

Dedication –

This is for my readers who have followed me since my fanfiction days.

Chapter One

Reign of Fear
(Val of Lysander)

Every day, I risked death for living as I wanted.

As if going about my life beyond the familiar was cause for honest offense.

Unfair as it was, there were others in society who had been born with the scales tipped in their favor. For a time, I believed that those blessed individuals would work to tip the balance in *everyone's* favor. Fresh-faced and wide-eyed as a child, I begged my father—an esteemed lawyer—to teach me about his valiant battles in the courtroom. I worshipped the tales of other virtuous lawyers who labored to right our society's wrongs. Between fistfights and running from worse dangers, I prayed for acceptance beyond my family. Yet by the time I reached adolescence, I fell into a deep despair once I saw that the world wasn't going to change for me.

Already they had decided that I was less than nothing.

I came to understand that if I wanted change, I had to seek it out myself. As I neared my mid-twenties, I found my confidence. Living in this supposed gutter of non-acceptance helped me to view life from the bottom up—ever looking at the stars, ever chasing after my goals while most others remained complacent, sleeping with their eyes open. At last, the imperial city of Eden I lived in grew to tolerate my 'strangeness,' as they called it. Only when I had been shy and weak had they felt brave enough to tear me down. Now that I was older and more capable, they turned to other ways to discredit me. While they wasted their time shrinking themselves for the approval of others, I snuck in the shadows of their gossip and lies to carry out my goals.

On this early spring day, I awoke at nine in the morning. I had scheduled a vital meeting with Emperor Xavier's Privy Council. They wished to listen to my proposed solutions to our empire's latest military crisis. As commander of my family's private army, I was hopeful that they would listen to me. It was rare indeed for the council to bring someone to speak before them unless they had all agreed beforehand that the proposal was worth their time. This long-forgotten optimism swelled within me anew as I embraced this rare opportunity.

The estate I lived in with my family had been passed down through generations. Lawyers, doctors and philosophers were among those valued as nobility. My father, the Magister Pathos of Lysander, worked his hardest to uphold the family business. My twin brother, Lord Yosef of Lysander—older than me by nine minutes—was responsible for following in our father's footsteps. From twelve years of age he had been betrothed to the Lady Gabrielle of Eidos—daughter of the most beloved baron in the northwestern islands. Gabrielle now lived with us as Yosef's wife and my dear sister-in-law: supportive of my endeavors and my truest confidant.

And I, Valerie of Lysander, named the second-born son of the Lysander estate, had been given leeway to do as I pleased, as were all noble second-born sons in our Empire of Tynan.

I was no man, of course. Not by flesh. Not by mind, heart or spirit. I was only content to dress as any gentleman of my stature would. I wore my dark hair as long as any maiden's. I made no efforts to hide my womanly figure, the richness in my voice, or the natural sway of my hips when I walked. Dressing this way was merely a personal preference—not a transition. Even if I wanted to pass as a man, my face alone would have given me away too easily. I suspected I still would have preferred to dress as I did if I were not legally male.

This controversy had all begun with my mother's maddened despair. She had given birth to my twin brother and me during a terrible recession and famine. Our family had lived with but a façade of wealth at the time. When faced with the possibility of true poverty after providing a daughter's dowry in my supposedly inevitable future, my mother had tried to suffocate me. My father had managed to save me and swiftly divorced her. No one believed she'd attempted an act of such cruelty; she'd fled anyway.

I knew nothing of where she was now—if she was a beggar on the streets or dead. I didn't care enough to find out. In a way, I was grateful to her for inspiring the life I now lived.

To avoid the shackles of a dowry, my father had written a new reality for me. In the eyes of the law, I was the second-born son of the Lysander Estate and commander of our private army, allowed to attend the emperor's court in whatever manner of dress I so desired.

My family's estate was on the fringes of the Empyrean Palace grounds in the imperial capital. Outside my bedroom window, I saw the rising towers of onyx, more powerful than stone in our region. The imposing black glittered in the morning light, serving as a show of strength to anyone crossing over the Eidos Sea along the horizon. Not far off, the rising mountains of Nyx Mons pierced the cloudless skies.

Once it was time for me to walk across the vast grounds to the palace, I found my sister-in-law pacing in the sitting room. Gabrielle was dressed in her fine gown and jewels for court, her long, auburn hair fanning behind her as she moved about. She seemed panicked; short of breath. I grabbed her shoulders to make her stop; she wouldn't calm down.

"Gabby, what's gotten into you?" I asked her. "Why are you up this early? I thought I told you I need to do this by myself!"

"As much as I admire you for this, I must go with you," insisted Gabrielle. "What if this is a trap? The council was too quick to heed your request! It took your father three weeks to secure his last meeting! For a magister! Not to belittle you…"

"Yes, I am but a lowly second-born nobleman who licks the boots of her betters."

"Your sarcasm isn't needed!" she protested. "Val, you know how much I care… I'll not let you leave without me!"

Once my sister-in-law made up her mind, there was no arguing against her. "What of Yosef?" I wondered. "Will you abandon my poor brother to his studies for the day? He already complains to me that you don't spend enough time with him."

With a scoff, she said, "You already know my answer to that." Gabrielle grabbed my hand, pulling me along to the door in a hurry. "This is far more important than him! You're the only one who can do what needs to be done."

We left across the grounds at a brisk pace to the Empyrean Palace. Melting snow scattered about the paved walkways and manicured greenswards. The dragging of Gabrielle's dress along the paved paths and the urgency of her hand in mine made me see how surreal this felt. *What needed to be done* felt as monumental as ever. Our empire was on the brink of war with the Kingdom of Tibor to the north, and I had a solution to our shortage of soldiers.

As Emperor Xavier was a citizen of the kingdom, with the royal capital Tenrose as his birthplace, he legally held claim to the lands. Queen Beatrys of Tibor wished to formally secede from the empire, while Emperor Xavier wanted the kingdom to surrender, thereby enveloping all the world of Tellus into his possession. Tynan was an empire of fractured lands that the emperor's predecessors had conquered over time. Tibor remained as a united front, as they had been for several centuries.

The people knew that this was but a show of power for the emperor to see if he could conquer the world. Tynan's men were hardly interested in being Xavier's pawns. And so there remained but one solution: allow women to join the imperial army. Allow them to prove themselves as fighters, as equals in the eyes of the law. For countless years, men had excluded women from positions of power—forbidding them from reading or writing, forbidding them from joining the temples as members of the clergy, forbidding them to think for themselves. All to control them, to keep them in line. And if any of them dared to deviate from these defined social norms, such as myself, they were to be defiled and shamed and banned from society.

As with most backward forms of thinking in our dear empire, this abhorrent practice was deeply rooted in religious superstition.

The holy *Hallows* of our Anathema religion detailed a mythical apocalypse that had destroyed the world centuries ago, forcing human survivors to begin civilization anew. This apocalypse was purportedly brought about by a group of maddened thaumaturges and sorceresses. Thaumaturges, separate from sorceresses, were regular humans who required a catalyst to perform their spells—a sword, a staff, a book. Sorceresses could manipulate the elements and human minds, making them far more treacherous. This blind, make-believe witch hunt spread the belief that it was too dangerous to allow a woman to have power. Too dangerous, and yet it was all too easy for people—men and women both—to decry that we were too passive, incapable of accomplishing anything on our own. Which was it, I wondered? Were we to be feared for our destructive potential or ridiculed for how little natural clout we possessed?

Both made no sense to me, but sense was not so common here in our Empire of Tynan.

If an army of women were to achieve Emperor Xavier's goals, however selfish and grandstanding, those women would pave the way to the equal rights they—we—deserved. I was in a rare position to give that opportunity to them. My privilege as the legal son of a noble family of lawyers was all that kept my ethos relevant. This meeting with the Privy Council attested to that privilege. I would have been a coward not to take advantage of this opportunity.

Passing through the crowded halls of the imperial court was never simple for me. Sour anxiety and self-conscious illness crept through my throat and down to my stomach. Everyone watched me walk by. They scrutinized my black military officer's uniform, my silver chain of service and my hair that I kept in a long tail down my back. They gossiped about the scars across my eyebrows that had healed as thin gaps of hair, how they hardened my *'otherwise pretty face.'* They criticized the way I refused to smile as a woman *should have.* Their scandalized whispers and judging faces made up the sharp decorations in the palace, the stony paintings on the onyx walls, and the dark shadows across the gleaming marble floor.

After so many years of this, I should have been used to it. I should have known how to rise above their judgments. Each time this happened, I felt my anxieties grow worse than the last.

Gabrielle squeezed my hand as we continued on to the council's assembly room.

When we arrived, she waited for me outside. I entered to the wide-open space occupied by two rows of long tables. The morning sun shone through the windows, filling the room with rays of light specked by thick, floating dust and old age. At the tables sat the Privy Council in their velvet robes of violet, each of the chairs filled except for one. The emperor's onyx throne at the end of the room was empty. And the nearest chair to the throne, that of the emperor's trusted adviser, was also unoccupied.

The Privy Council pretended to ignore me, chatting away among themselves. I was quite difficult *not* to notice. Ever did they perceive me as a woman stepping out of line, yet they did not stand when I entered the room. Only now did the council wish to treat me as a man who was required to boldly make himself known to a room full of authority. Their rudeness was but yet another tired game of court; it did not bode well for this meeting.

"Good morning, Your Graces," I said, making certain my voice carried loud enough.

Holy Oracle Wells, the most amicable of the emperor's council, *appeared* glad to see me. "Ah, Lord Commander Val!" he greeted. Wells gestured for everyone to quiet down. "We're to hear your proposal today! As you know, the empire is in desperate need of military support in our latest dilemma against the kingdom. Please, proceed! You have the floor."

I had a terrible feeling about this. The other holy oracles, judges, doctors and theologians of the Privy Council barely disguised their leers. Yet I'd put so much work into preparing this speech. I couldn't squander this opportunity. Not for anything. But those empty chairs worried me the most. I'd counted on the lady chancellor Lucrezia of Azrith to be here as a vague form of support. She was the only woman on the Privy Council. Her absence—and Emperor Xavier's—disappointed me as much as it fueled this ill feeling.

"Thank you, Holy Oracle," I replied, bowing. "Well, then, allow me to skip any further formalities and get straight to the heart of the issue. As our empire has not waged a full war in well over a hundred years, our military is fractured. Not to mention—the last war was made up of several civil wars in region to region. Since then, each

nation has been sovereign in spirit only to itself...
Reuniting our men in each country will prove difficult. If
the Privy Council would pass a simple piece of legislation,
we could have the largest military in global history."

"And what legislation would that be?" asked Wells,
eyes bright with interest.

"Allow our women to join the imperial forces. Train
them well. Pay them fairly. Treat them as equals and they
will prove that they are worthy of defending Tynan's great
lands."

I went on to explain why this would benefit us all.
The added value of doubling our imperial army, the
increased productivity in our towns and cities with more
women safely employed, the boost in morale from our
greater numbers that would offset the public's historic
disapproval levels with our emperor... I detailed all of
these, the logistics, the causes and the effects. I spoke from
my heart as well as my mind, putting to use all the lessons
my father had taught me on how to command an audience.

I'd expected them to be shocked or outraged. I had
prepared any and all counterpoints they could have brought
up, and I'd intended to argue with them until they conceded
to my views. Instead, they listened with empty, glassy
expressions. Through that glass, I saw the transparency of
this game they played with me.

They didn't believe a word I said. Their bigoted
beliefs had cemented their decision already. As I realized
this, my speech slowed... stopped. Mirth burst through the
silence as the Privy Council laughed in my face. Anger
steamed at my neck. Hot, prickling sweat slithered down
my back. Hatred blinded my sight red. Were my skin as
white as the majority in the room, they would have fully
seen the crimson heating my face. Through their howling, I
heard the lady chancellor's heeled boots clicking hurriedly
down the hall and into the room. She was late. She could
have spoken up for me. *She was too late.*

With learned control, I bowed to the men cackling at their tables. I turned on my heel and left the room, storming past the lady chancellor. I cursed her magnetic beauty for managing to make me *look* at her at a time like this. Irresponsible as she was, I carried on.

"Lord Commander!" called Lucrezia, boots clicking anew. "My lord, please, wait—"

I whipped around, hissing at her, "I'll not wait anymore! I swear, your indolence knows no bounds! Were you so preoccupied with another sex party with your *friends* that you could not arrive on time?!"

Lucrezia matched my glare. "Your foul accusations are unwarranted!" she fought back. "How dare you speak to me with such ignorance?! You should know better than to believe those *baseless* rumors!" She looked as if she had more choice words for me. At the last second, she held them back, disarming me instead: "... I understand that you are angry, Lord Commander, but I was not notified of this meeting until minutes ago. The council loves excluding me whenever they can. Even so, this is highly unprofessional on my part... I must apologize."

An apology from the lady chancellor was as rare as a snowless day in Tynan's winters. She had earned a reputation for being callous and single-minded, acting only when it benefitted her. Lucrezia's intimidating and attractive manner of dress contradicted the sympathy I saw in her heart-shaped face; in her smoky makeup that brought out the green of her eyes. The long tresses of her brown-blonde hair soaked in the morning light of the hall, making her seem amenable to me.

For these few years I'd known Lucrezia at court, I detested how she allowed her power to rot in this palace. *She* should have done what I came here to propose. I had no patience for her excuses; I yanked my wrist from her hold and went to find my sister-in-law.

Gabrielle and I left the Empyrean Palace amid the whispers, amid the judging, the stares. She had heard the laughter, and my argument with the lady chancellor, and guessed as to the outcome of my meeting with the council. There was no need to discuss my dishonor.

We went out into the city, into the heat of the afternoon where I could blend in with the crowd. Horse-drawn carriages passed through the bustling cobblestone streets. Tall, jagged architecture of Eden's all-black buildings decorated this district nearest the Empyrean Palace, where the upper-class just short of nobility all lived and thrived. The wide, intersecting avenues elongated along the horizon at midday, eclipsed by the panorama of Nyx Mons looming behind the city. Further beyond, the plains, forests and rivers stretched onward and outward to the rest of Tynan's lands, whose overworked citizens envied the quality of life here in the capital.

I saw a fire nearby. Gabrielle guided me through the crowd so we could get a better look. There in the city courtyard, a group of oracles stood praying before a burning sorceress. Or someone who had been in the wrong place at the wrong time and accused of sorcery. I knew nothing of this woman except for her supposed heresy. I was powerless to stop the burning of her flesh, the stench and the spectacle of it all. No one else cared the way I did.

This silence stung. That echoing laughter wouldn't fade away.

The Privy Council, this burning, and the lack of empathy for other human beings, everywhere—it was expected and allowed. That didn't make it right. I had sworn to myself years ago that I wouldn't let these issues boil into hatred within me. Yet the memory of the council's laughter burned me too much to set aside. My breathing grew pained, labored from the weight that had been building for too long. I felt I could have gotten away with anything so long as I planned it right…

And if I were caught, no one would believe a woman had pulled off such a crime of passion. It simply didn't happen in this day and age.

What could I do with this invisibility? Who or what could I target?

The council were nothing without their power. Their influence. Their money. Stripping them of their money was one way to make them feel as worthless as those they looked down on. I turned my gaze across the street, narrowing my eyes against the sun. There was the Imperial Bank between the city's onyx masonry. Within the heavily guarded vaults were the council's piles of coin, sitting there as trophies while the poorest people in Eden starved in the streets.

A sudden idea flooded me. This inspiration felt as a manic rise through the skies. I told my sister-in-law to return home. Gabrielle didn't ask what I was up to, but I had a feeling she knew already. I hurried through the busy streets. I passed through as I pleased here, given a certain invisibility: the citizens of Eden were too self-absorbed with their own goings-on during the hectic business day to stop and get a better look at my androgyny. This ironic solitude still did not quell the rage I felt.

Across town in the smog-ridden industrial district, I reached the foundry where a group of my soldiers worked. Two of my long-time friends shared a shift today: Sebastian of Svärd and Lee of Valdivia. They both passed as men, far better than I, and chose to identify as such. I snuck past the guards to tell my friends the news. The three of us came up with a plan to carry out later that night. We knew that the Privy Council wouldn't listen unless they could see the world from the eyes of the underprivileged.

Staying quiet and playing by the rules wasn't an option anymore. The only way I could incite any meaningful change was to take away the council's power. Destroying this bank was the first step. If they arrested me,

I had an easy way out: by their logic, no woman was capable of committing a crime. I planned on taking full advantage of that. I wanted them to squirm in the rotting sick of their hypocrisy, poor and powerless. I wanted them to hate me even more.

I needed them to learn firsthand not to underestimate me.

***

By nightfall, our plan settled into motion. We had agreed that we needed several distractions in the city to divert the authorities away from the bank. Sebastian planned to steal an officer's uniform and enter the bank to plant explosives near the windows. Lee was responsible for starting a fire some miles away—avoiding any casualties—to make sure the horse-drawn fire carriages could not make it to the bank in time. Once the fire was in full force, Lee was to mobilize a riot in the streets over Emperor Xavier's tyrannical war on the horizon.

I made my way to a residential complex in Venus' Embrace nearest the bank. I was forced to take my time as I went up to the highest landing, slowed by my asthma. Once I caught my breath, I knocked on each door to see who was home. With my head covered in a cloak, I muttered empty apologies to those who answered before going to the next door. I needed an empty home to access the windows facing the bank across the plaza. Already I heard the stringent sirens from the fire carriages leaving the station nearby. After more apologies and more irritable tenants answering their doors, I knocked on the last door. No one answered. I looked about to make sure no residents were nearby and knelt down to pick the lock. With a satisfying click, the door opened. I entered and locked the door behind me. I kept my steps quieted, muffled along the rugs, avoiding the bare strips of wooden floor in case they creaked.

I scanned the modest home for anyone asleep in the bedrooms. As the riots built in the streets below, I knew I had little time to pull this off. Expediency over caution—my instincts would save me if needed. I found the bedroom whose windows faced the Imperial Bank across the way. Two small beds and several toys strewn about the floor. The children's room...

I locked the door and removed the heavy prototype sniper rifle from over my back. Both Lee and Sebastian had worked together to craft this for me as a gift. As they were alchemists in my private army, they were able to create technology beyond even the swords and shields of Tynan and Tibor's forces. They also supplied the rest of our soldiers with similar weapons. Only a few privileged people in all of Tellus had access to guns and muskets, let alone a fine rifle such as this. The council knew not what they'd turned down in denying us.

I opened the window to get a better look outside. Security officers fled the bank in droves to help quell the riots across the street. Through my rifle's scope, I saw Sebastian near one of the windows. He left explosives on the candlelit tables where I could see them through the night. Down below, a few officers remained outside the building, debating on whether they ought to go help with the riots. I waited until Sebastian exited the building. The officers still did not leave their posts. I didn't want to cause any casualties. All I wanted was to burn the money in the bank. Normal citizens weren't allowed to keep their coin in the vaults there. They had no need to worry once this was done. I couldn't wait for the officers to make up their minds.

With measured focus, I guided my scope to each of the windows. I blocked out the enraged shouting from the protestors and police down below. I found the first explosive sitting on a desk by the open window. I lined up the centers and fired. The kickback from the shot startled me more than the burst of flames beyond. The cacophony of the riots overpowered this first explosion. I pulled my rifle's bolt handle and lined up the next shot. I set off another, and another, until finally everyone noticed.

The Imperial Bank went up in flames, smoke billowing thickly into the night sky. I breathed a sigh of relief. My tension left me. I couldn't wait until the council learned that all their money had disintegrated as smoke in the sky, as ashes sprinkling in the winds.

My heart stopped when I heard voices in the next room. A panicked mother urged her children to hurry into their bedroom—this bedroom—to collect their things. I slung my rifle over my back, covering it underneath my cloak. I couldn't jump from this high up to the street below. There were too many people there packed together, fists and voices raised in protest.

"The door's locked!" cried a young girl on the other side. "I can't get in!"

The mother huffed, impatient. "We haven't got time to look for the key!" she said. "The fire will reach us soon if the firemen don't hurry!"

"But what about our toys?" worried another girl.

"Forget them! The city's in danger! This is important, girls! Now off we go, come on!"

I held my breath as I waited for them to leave. Once they were gone, I hurried down the stairs with the other tenants. I stayed detached from the panic all around me, keeping my focus clear. I blended in with the thick crowd out in the streets. By the time the fire carriages arrived, the Imperial Bank was ruined. I imagined the council's faces upon receiving the news that they were bankrupt. Their money and power were all that had distinguished them before. Without those, they had nothing, *were nothing,* just as they believed me to be.

Could they wrap their minds around someone such as me organizing this? I returned home to await the Privy

Council's decision. There I found Gabrielle and my twin brother Yosef staring out the window with our servants, talking about all the commotion.

Yosef smirked, morbidly amused. "The emperor can't go to war now," he boasted. "Where will he find the men for it? Are we to battle against the kingdom with the few souls stupid enough to die for His Imperial Majesty's greed? He's pathetic if he thinks we'll go!"

Gabrielle sighed. "They would have had a solution if they'd listened to Val," she said.

"Their egos can't handle an army of women making history like that. As if that's any reason to keep you in chains! Val will prove them wrong somehow. If anyone can, it's her."

"I'm glad you understand…"

She trailed off when she noticed me nearby. Gabrielle's eyes widened in shock. She knew what I'd done. In a rush, she pulled me down the hall into my room. I removed my cloak and returned my sniper rifle to its hiding spot behind my bookcase.

"*You* did this!" she accused.

There was little point in denying it. "I did."

"Why? *Why* would you do such a thing?! You targeted the Privy Council's money—their families' money! They'll have your head cut off for destroying their fortunes!"

"Now that they're in poverty, they can see what it's like! Maybe they'll have a bit of sympathy for those they've neglected… That's the only way anything will change!"

Gabrielle held my face tightly in her shaking hands. "Justice *isn't worth* losing you!" she cried. "Val, don't you see?! You're sacrificing yourself needlessly for this cause! The council will force *more* tax money to fill their vaults and you'll end up dead—for nothing!"

"I will live as recklessly as my goals demand. I won't give up—not for anything."

"You make it sound as though I'm a fool to care for you so…"

Just as I tried to empathize with her, I heard the front door burst open. Heavy, armored footsteps and rattling chains sounded down the hall. I heard Yosef and the servants shouting.

The imperial guard smashed my bedroom door in. Burning fires from torches brightened my room; black steel, sharp helmets and muskets rushed through. The guards dug their gloved hands into my limbs and apprehended me in chains. Uncaring, unfeeling, the guards dragged me out of my home and across the palace grounds.

The Privy Council knew damn well that I did this. They had no evidence whatsoever except for my clear motive for revenge. And yet here they were, unlawfully arresting me out of spite and anger. As the guards attempted to intimidate me with talks of prison and my beheading, I looked up at the night sky and stars above. I laughed at the smoke there from the fire. The guards thought me mad, yet I was anything but.

This was glorious hypocrisy at its finest.

These were my final hours. Laughter was better than fear or tears. It was all I had.

Chapter Two

Pyretic
(Lucrezia of Azrith)

For the first time in days, I had the freedom to sit down for a lovely dinner with a guest. I smiled over my meal, laughing easily while the rest of the Empyrean Palace was up in arms over the latest crisis. Outside my window, the council's piles of riches burned away as the most beautiful clouds of smoke our city of Eden had ever known.

As the Privy Council enjoyed keeping me out of their privileges, their prejudices against me had at last worked in my favor this time. I had my funds stashed away in my own private holdings. The emperor's personal money had also gone untouched. My only loyalty in this court was to Xavier alone. This problem didn't affect us, thus I could take the time to enjoy these simpler pleasures amid the panicking outside my door.

In my cozy dining room down the hall from my chambers, I sat with my dear friend James of Eden, a fine lieutenant-colonel in the imperial army. The fireplace crackled away near the table as we spoke over dinner and wine.

For sadistic reasons, I found myself attracted to soldiers, to people of principles. Inflating their heads with compliments on their character during the day was all good and well. Stripping their egos down and humiliating them for my pleasure at night was most satisfying. Their shift in behavior showed who exactly held the power in our relationship. Lieutenant-Colonel James was more than willing to play these games with me. He learned about his own limits while I witnessed that learning firsthand.

Yet being around James served as a reminder of all I had left to do as chancellor. Any efforts I made to reform this city had been blocked. It was too easy for me to blame the Privy Council's inaction as well as their untold influence over the emperor. And yet that was the truth.

I could not act without Xavier's approval, nor would he without the Privy Council's say-so. This battle of influence had caused a rupture in my lifelong friendship with our dear emperor. In keeping me away from Xavier, I could not advise him as I should have for fear of being thrown out of court—or worse.

I also had a responsibility to Xavier. I had to represent him in the best way possible within these constraints. I could not stay by his side if I spoke my mind and turned the Privy Council against me completely. I also could not accomplish my own goals if I was no longer chancellor. I'd had to set aside my pride and pick my battles accordingly.

Witnessing the council's destruction gladdened me—for the moment. I raised my wine glass each time James and I heard another aide stumbling over himself in the hall, or another member of the council shouting in a crazed panic over his monumental losses.

"What a time to be alive!" I said, toasting with James yet again. "I wish I could kiss whichever madman is responsible for this pandemonium. He did us a great service indeed! I must say, this is the best dinner I've had in years."

James grunted in his charming way. "Almost makes up for this morning," he pointed out. "Leaving in a hurry like that… You missed out on the long hours we could've had together."

"Oh, don't you start," I scolded. "You know they withheld the details of the young lord commander's meeting from me. I'm making up for it now, aren't I?"

"Mm, depends on what else the night has in store."

I laughed softly. "You're incorrigible."

As handsome and easygoing as James was, I knew the limits of our friendship with one another. I enjoyed the appeal of an older man such as him: his grizzled features, the breadth of his experiences, and his disregard for the fussier details in life. But despite James having five years over my thirty-two, there was something that his age couldn't make up for. James and I didn't challenge one another to grow.

And so we had an understanding: we were to remain friends with benefits. Nothing more. Our minds were elsewhere while I had him against the wall or face-down on the bed. I refused to open my legs for him or anyone else. He accepted this without protest... unlike others I'd known.

This would end once either one of us found the destination of our mental and emotional wandering. I wanted to believe that this day would come soon. I wanted to hope that my instrumental approach to politics would pay off. Settling for James was one thing. Gritting my teeth and dealing with the council's blatant sexism and xenophobia was another.

They suspected I was a witch who had ensorcelled my way into Xavier's heart.

After all, why else would he make me—a woman—his right hand here in the empire? Never mind my academic credentials as a worldly scholar, my fluency in different languages, or my diplomatic skills. No... none of that mattered to them because of what they believed I was.

Yet I was, in fact, a sorceress. Only Xavier knew. I was wise enough to keep my identity hidden from everyone else. The people's ignorance would have driven me out of court if they knew. Oracles around the world—regardless of their faith—had the power to disable sorceresses at will. But one incantation from them, and a sorceress' powers would self-destruct within her flesh. If not for that, I wouldn't care if anyone other than Xavier knew about my abilities.

The burnings at the stake were merely for spectacle. If they were truly threatened by one of us, their incantation would have been far more effective. Of course, using it would have been an outright admission that we did actually exist. The possibility of dying in such a way kept a great many of us in hiding.

I wished to improve the world's perceptions of magic users. I could not improve anything without the influence I had here at court. I had grown used to having to hide. I had also learned not to hope for much by way of my own happiness. Yet being used to this did not make it any easier. Bearing my cynicism was unhealthy, but it was all that protected me from the thinly-veiled daggers at court.

Having this dinner was all I allowed myself as a way to forget, to relax. And tomorrow I would be back to the same numbing routine. The fine men of the Privy Council would find some expedient, corrupt means of restoring their wealth. This scare was but a temporary one.

All would soon return to normal.

Nothing would change.

My servant Rosa entered. "Pardon me, lady chancellor!" she said in a rush, giving a curtsey. "Magister Pathos of Lysander is here to see you. He says the matter is urgent."

"Yes, of course," I replied. "Have him wait in my office. I'll be there in a moment."

"Understood, my lady," answered Rosa, taking her leave.

James sighed in disappointment. "Guess that means we have to postpone again."

"Come now, James," I said. "We have finished our meals. You weren't so naïve to think that I would be *completely* excluded from ongoing matters, were you? Duty calls, as usual."

"Your *duty* has a habit of interrupting us at the worst times."

"And were I an ambitionless woman, you would not care for me nearly as much."

James' entitlement to my time grated on my nerves. I sent him on his way with vague promises to meet again soon.

I could not attend to the Magister Pathos in this revealing dinner gown I wore. I returned to my chambers to change into something more appropriate: my black jacket that fanned out behind me as a skirt, a violet collared shirt underneath, tight trousers tucked into my leather thigh-heeled boots, and my silver chain of service. I brushed hair and made certain that my makeup was as it had been during the day. Intimidating dress was but one way to maintain my credibility here in the palace and abroad. Not *too* intimidating. I enjoyed creating my own brand of feminine appeal and power: a concept that too many people found confusing. Instead of saying as much to my face, the nobles at court enjoyed spreading false rumors about me.

My self-expression reminded me of Magister Pathos' daughter—legally, his son.

Lord Commander Valerie and I had at least one thing in common. We just so happened to challenge general conventions each day with our preferences. I respected her bravery, yet I had never communicated this to her since Xavier and I arrived here in the Empyrean Palace four years ago. Because Valerie tended to avoid parties at court, she and I had only spoken a handful of times. And even those times had been mired by the company of others around us.

Valerie was a woman that the world could not touch, could not understand for fear of burning. I doubted that my words would have reached her had I said anything. The lord commander was ever preoccupied, ever on the move with her breadth of ideas for changing this world. She had amassed the largest personal army in Eden's history—nearly five hundred strong—all from her own personal connections and networking. Most of Valerie's soldiers had once been impoverished women or wives who'd needed to escape their abusive husbands. They found their purpose again under her command.

In a way, Valerie set the standard for all others to follow. It was odd for me to admire another in this way, let alone someone younger than me. Seven years younger, in her case. Odd indeed…

As I made my way to my office to see her father, I wondered if I should have amended my apology to the lord commander. Passing on a message through the magister seemed too impersonal. Waiting until she was next at court was unreliable. I had to find her myself and continue our conversation in person.

Yet her assumptions about me still left a terrible taste in my mouth.

I found Magister Pathos standing as still as a statue in my office. His violet lawyer's robes blended in with the décor. In this dim candlelight, I noticed the aged lines over his rugged face and the strands of white showing in his short, dark hair. His family's trademark—those storm-grey eyes—were filled with pained thoughts I could not discern. His sorrows tonight felt pronounced even in his collected stoicism.

I'd heard the story of why he'd had to divorce his wife in Valerie's infancy. Given the magister's distance and dourness, I suspected that tale was true.

"Magister Pathos?" I asked, cautious. "What's happened? You look unwell."

"Lady Chancellor Lucrezia," said Pathos, bowing slowly in his weariness. "I must apologize for interrupting your evening. I knew not where else to turn."

"You needn't apologize. Will you sit? Would you like a cup of tea?"

"No—no, thank you," he replied. Pathos swallowed his anxieties, speaking clearly. "They have my son—my daughter. They have Val. They've taken her."

"Who has taken her? What do you mean?"

"The imperial guard. They've taken her to the gallows…"

I could not contain my astonishment. "*What?* His Imperial Majesty gave no such order! Granted, things between us are…" Giving too many personal details about Xavier was unwise. Still, I would have heard if he'd ordered Valerie's arrest. "Never mind that. Please, tell me what happened."

"Not an hour ago, they barged into our home and arrested her while I was in the city. Charged her with arson, inciting riots. They believe she is responsible for burning the Imperial Bank and all its treasures. No one was inside the building. When I asked them for their arrest warrant or any evidence against my child, they threatened to silence me by pain of death."

"Do you have any idea why they would suspect her?"

Pathos reminded me: "They are threatened by her. That is reason enough."

"Is the lord commander capable of such a thing? Setting fire to the Imperial Bank?"

"My child is tired of being treated as a second-class citizen," said Pathos. "She won't allow revenge to go ignored. My Val leapt straight through the loophole of the crimeless, fragile lass. They arrested her anyway."

"Do you mean to tell me that she is guilty?" I asked in disbelief. "You word yourself as though the lord commander did in fact commit this crime."

"No, my lady. I only know my child well enough to understand why she would have."

The magister's assertion chilled me.

"And what would you have me do, Your Grace?" I went on. "I am no lawyer. I cannot negotiate her charges on your behalf."

"For a crime of this magnitude, only those on the Privy Council have the authority to assess her guilt. However, due to the nature of the situation, everyone affected by the incident bears a conflict of interest. Except you, Lady Lucrezia. By default, you must speak with her."

Magister Pathos was right. I bade him farewell and left with a few guards for the gallows.

I felt responsible for this. If I'd been present for Valerie's meeting, the council wouldn't have laughed her out of the room. And if she *was* responsible for the burning, she would have stayed her hand, had I been there to support her. But perhaps that was naïve of me to believe.

The gallows underneath the Empyrean Palace were a cesspool of maddened cries made louder by needless torture. The Privy Council held the lord commander in solitary confinement as if convinced of her guilt already. I hated this foul stench, this false justice. I could do nothing about the corruption in our system until Xavier wanted to act.

That in itself was complicated. Xavier was not himself. No one except me understood this. The strains of ruling a divided empire had taken their toll on my childhood friend. He didn't wish for me to see his suffering. Naturally, his refusal to allow me to care for him had added to the rift between us.

With these recent rumblings, Xavier and I couldn't carry on like this.

I needed to visit him soon.

I had the presiding guard unlock the lord commander's door. Creaking wood sounded, and there I saw Valerie knelt upon the cold, sullied floor, her wrists chained to the ground at her sides. She did not move or make note of my presence. I signaled for my guards to wait outside. I entered the room alone, listening to the door close behind me. Being locked in here like this, the room felt as a much smaller, more intimate world than the outside.

Valerie stared at the ground in silence. Those storm-grey eyes of hers held within a chilling calm. Still in her military uniform and chain of service, she maintained her dignity. Far-off moans and screams from other inmates didn't faze her.

I pulled over a chair from the corner and sat down in front of her. I crossed my legs, watching her for a while.

Harsh as they were, Valerie's alleged actions lined up with my own ideals. She had the courage to do what I couldn't—assuming these charges were true to begin with. Yet there was no denying the severity of what she may or may not have done. Burning the Imperial Bank was extreme. Beyond extreme. Through Valerie's apparent stoicism here in front of me, I sensed a world of anger within her heart. Within that rage, I saw how dangerous she was. And yet I didn't *feel* as if I had a reason to fear her.

I wondered if I should have feared her as much as the council did. If Xavier or I had been the ones to cross her, would she have acted similarly against us?

Eventually, Valerie bowed to me. "My lady," she said, chains chiming.

"My lord," I replied. "This is quite the predicament you've found yourself in."

"So it is," she observed, monotone.

No sharp wit. No stinging sarcasm. This imprisonment had stolen Valerie's character.

"Well, then," I said. "Since you are not up for conversation, I shall get straight to the point. Are you guilty, lord commander? Did you burn the Imperial Bank?"

"Yes, it was my doing."

Valerie's honesty shook me terribly. Anyone else would have denied their guilt. They would have pointed to the lack of evidence and demanded to be released. But

Valerie knelt here before me, calm and composed as ever, despite the searing anger I sensed within her. Did she not care for herself? Did she care at all if she was released or sentenced to death?

I saw the truth there in her eyes, as colorless and unyielding as her father's, and it disturbed me.

"You could not have acted alone," I continued. "There were distractions in the city. Officers were led from the premises to quell the riots in the streets. Firemen could have put out the blaze in time had they not been guided to another disaster miles away. Who helped you?"

"I take full responsibility for my actions."

"That is noble of you to say. But it won't get you anywhere. You know that."

"This is all a farce, lady chancellor," she said.

"Oh? How so?" I asked.

"The Privy Council would be loath to admit that I committed anything of this scale. This goes against the public opinion that we are incapable of careful planning and execution. If they start to believe that, then what's next? Theologians will have to stop writing texts about our mental capacity being equal to children. Terrible consequences, indeed."

"This is true. You've a sharp mind, my lord. I wish you weren't so disobedient. I don't wish to see anything happen to you."

Valerie turned her nose up in scorn. "Then you care for my well-being more than I do."

"Apparently," I agreed.

"Let them kill me," she said. "Or don't. If I die, whoever would miss me would move on. The rest of the world won't concern themselves over me... I don't matter."

If anyone else held her future in their hands, they would have been careless with it. I felt responsible to handle this correctly. Though I knew she was guilty, her confession alone was not enough to convict her. There was no evidence. No eye witnesses. No accessories she would name. Valerie was near the point of breaking. She was exhausted. I knew that she wasn't a true danger to anyone. She was simply tired of fighting without the right kind of help.

I would have readily offered my assistance if she hadn't made those obscene remarks about me earlier that morning.

"Quite frankly, I am not interested in sending you to your death," I explained. "But, as long as we are both here, we might as well make the most of our time together."

Valerie scowled, suspicious. "Speak plainly," she said.

I took a moment, puzzling over how to word myself. I could not tell Valerie that I felt we had much in common. Nor could I tell her how odd it was for me to hold my tongue outside of politics. I was... afraid she wouldn't understand these sentiments. I had known her since she was twenty-one, when Xavier first took the imperial throne after our arrival. Since then, I had watched her mature into a fearless, peerless woman with the utmost resolve. She would not believe me if I told her I had been hesitant to speak with her for fear of her inner fire burning me.

This was my one opportunity to get to know her. As intimidating as most thought me to be, appearances were deceiving. I hoped that the same was true for her.

"Our altercation this morning has left me rather sour, you see," I began.

Valerie let out a dry laugh. "Has it, now?" she wondered. "And why in God's name would you care what I think of you, my lady? Our paths never cross unless a whisper of gossip about me passes your desk, or another about you passes mine. That is all we are to one another—mere whispers."

I sighed over how difficult she was. "Yes, gossip... I have heard my fair share of tall tales about you. But I do not give those stories much weight. It disgusts me that you haven't the decency to do the same for me."

"These are not mere *stories*, lady chancellor," claimed Valerie.

"What *stories* do you mean?" I asked, dreading her reply.

"They say you are a sadist who enjoys punishing men. Kicking them in the balls and fucking them mercilessly with *toys*. Is that James man one of your playthings? The lieutenant-colonel? He follows you around at court as a puppy would."

"Those are half-truths," I allowed.

Valerie seemed surprised by my response. "Then what is the rest of it?"

"I am not the crazed woman they paint me as. Have you ever experienced that type of relationship, my lord? The reality is just as normal as this conversation, I assure you."

"I don't doubt that," she said, averting her eyes.

The sudden shyness in her gesture left my mind free to wander.

I had always found Valerie beautiful. Though she likely knew how gorgeous she was, she didn't seem to put much stock in her looks. Most women I knew enjoyed flaunting their appearance, comparing themselves to others, and so forth. Such things couldn't have been further from Valerie's mind. Her priorities were elsewhere. Many aligned with mine, in some respects.

That was what made her stand out to me more than anyone. Certainly more than James.

And the tales of her preferences for women over men: I had spent more than enough time pondering if they were true.

I reached out and touched her face, softly. Through Valerie's honeyed complexion, I saw traces of heat there. She would not look at me. I felt her jaw harden beneath my touch. Her breaths blew harder, warmer against my wrist over time.

Valerie and I knew one another at a distance. Yet that space was wide enough, influential enough to open these realms within me. The promise was there. The hope was there. Everything I'd denied myself was right there— in the way she glanced at my boots just under her torso.

I was but one impulse away from pushing Valerie's head down, to have her kiss the leather over my legs in apology for her rudeness that morning. She wouldn't have been able to resist me. Valerie had nowhere to run in these chains. But… that was too much, too soon. Much too soon. As much as the possibility tinged me with long-forgotten excitement, I couldn't take advantage of my position over her. After all, I had no idea how she felt about me.

With anyone else, I would have been bolder. I would have asked. Or I would have taken them for myself and asked questions later. Despite my issues with her, Valerie remained an exception for me. Making me hesitate. Making me wait and observe…

"You owe me an apology," I reminded her. "Do that, and I shall let you leave."

Valerie studied my face. I sensed she was about to do as I asked. At the last second, her pride decided otherwise. Her pride, or her pessimism, made Valerie scowl and turn away from me. Or perhaps that was neither of those. I'd had a terrible time reading her so far. The longer I stared at her, the more doubt I noticed in her eyes. She seemed uncertain of herself again.

I waited for a response that would not come.

"Mmm, is that so?" I pondered. "An apology isn't too much to ask for. Especially when it is deserved. Your silence feels personal. Do you dislike me that much?"

"I do not *trust* you," she said in a low voice.

"Nor I you for committing arson and inciting riots, regardless of your intentions. Then again, I'm beginning to think that you did none of these things. You were too quick to confess. Why would you take the blame for what's happened? For glory, perhaps? I've no idea now. It would be irresponsible of me to take your words at face value."

"I've already confessed!"

"And I've already told you I would set you free with but two simple words," I said, standing up. I left for the door, possessed by an idea: "Sit tight while I find out just how true your claims are. When I return, I expect a little hunger and fatigue will have loosened your tongue."

Anyone else would have shouted for me to wait, to reconsider. Valerie said nothing as I left her cell. As the guard locked her door once more, I again waited for the words she refused to say. Disappointed, I left the gallows, left the palace, en route to the scene of the crime by myself.

***

At nearly midnight, the streets of Eden were empty. Too empty, as if haunted. I walked through the central plaza in Venus' Embrace, the city's most well-off residential district. I headed toward the burned Imperial Bank. Everyone had fled their homes by official decree. They were not to return until the ashes had cleared from the skies. Thick smoke and soot in the air couldn't reach me by the faint spell I'd cast over my face.

Just in case anyone had avoided the decree by staying in their homes, I thought it best to keep up with this habit of mine.

I stopped in the center of the roundabout street. I stared at the bank across the way, marveling—in a morbid way—how capable Valerie was. She'd obviously had help with this. I needed to know who had helped her, and how. I clasped my hands together, focusing on my memory of her. Swirling at my feet, the shadows of her presence here summoned ghost-like images all around me.

There I saw two curious-looking young men. They whispered to one another amid the crowd of shadows around them. The conjured people and horse-drawn carriages mirrored the same moment from earlier in the day. Another pulse of power, and I heard the men speaking:

"Lee, listen!" said the first. *"Whatever the hell's on your mind can wait! This is more important. The council kicked us out of our homes! And for what? All because we don't buy that Anathema bullshit the oracles shove down our throats! It's time they paid for it!"*

This Lee person frowned, angry. *"I didn't forget!"* he retorted.

"Then what are you hesitating for?! Val told us the plan. She's our commander. When she gives an order, we follow. We owe her for this! I'm glad to help! Aren't you?"

"'Course I am! I wanna do this, yeah... some shit's just hard to set aside."

"Well if you don't get a move-on, we'll lose this opportunity. You think I want to work in a fucking foundry for the rest of my life? We pull this off, and the imperial army will have to let us in full-time. Then we can quit this sorry job! In a few years once people learn what's what, we won't have to hide anymore! Come on!"

"We're always gonna have to hide, Sebastian... that won't change."

Sebastian pushed Lee along. *"Enough of that! It's time to move! Let's go!"*

Both men ran off to their respective posts. I held onto their essences: a long thread of black weaving through my hands as a tether. Sebastian went to the Imperial Bank, sneaking around to knock out one of the guards and steal his uniform. Lee left in a taxi carriage, going several miles away to start another fire, another distraction.

All the while, Valerie hid in plain sight in the crowd nearby. I held onto this tether, staring into her eyes—the only distinguishable ones in this mass of faceless citizens passing through me. Valerie looked up at one of the residential complexes across the plaza. Beneath her cloak, I saw a concealed weapon protruding over her back. I wove the tethers quicker, speeding up time.

Enraged riots broke out in spots along the city just as the trio had planned. The shadows moved faster as smoke. When the ones in the sky grew, and the sun set in this pixel of the past, Valerie at last moved from her spot. I weaved her tether tightest around my hands, holding steadfast. I could see her walking up the stairs of the building behind me, unusually taxed for breath. She knocked on each door of the landing, one by one, until at last no one answered.

When Valerie took her spot at the window, I didn't recognize the weapon she held in her hands. That rifle was far more advanced than the swords and shields both Tynan and Tibor's soldiers used. Guns and ammunition weren't yet effective enough for distribution among our armies. She must have known an alchemist or two who could have crafted such a relic for her. Alchemy was strictly forbidden in the empire by the Anathema scriptures, much like traditional magic was...

I had my proof of her confession as I watched her fire the rifle with exactness. The explosives Sebastian had set inside the Imperial Bank detonated on impact. With the firemen distracted on the other side of Eden, there was ample time for the fire to reach the council's funds in the underground vaults. The blaze burned in the past as three of them—Lee, Sebastian, and Valerie—each escaped their situations as if they had not been present in the first place. They had learned to embrace society's habit of erasing their existences to fit their own needs, turning into phantoms at will.

I stared in awe at the aftermath of their teamwork. I couldn't remember the last time I'd been this impressed by anyone.

**

By the time I returned to Valerie's cell, I expected her to have her apology ready. I took my seat before her once more. Her body leaned forward, jolting to stay awake. I didn't want to have to resort to this. But after witnessing what she and her friends had done, I'd made up my mind. I wanted them on my side, on Xavier's side. I couldn't trust them to be out and about on their own. If they were determined to cause a storm, I needed them to work in my favor.

Valerie had nothing to say. She stared at the ground, breathing harder than before. Hunger no doubt clawed at her stomach. She kept licking her lips as a poor quench for her thirst. Valiantly, she resisted her weakness, jaw clenched in concentration. I shifted in my seat, moved by her efforts. Her breaths in particular echoed through the small cell, clouding my ears with my imagination. Was her need for food and drink the only reason she was like this?

"Well?" I asked.

Still nothing.

"Such a difficult woman you are," I said with a sigh.

I noticed then that she was distracted by her thoughts. Valerie appeared fixated on the images in her mind, staring at the ground to give a canvas to the colors. Now I was curious. I waited until she looked into my eyes. The intensity there acted as the avenue for my exploration. Non-intrusive, undetectable, I weaved my way into her mind to see her thoughts for myself.

There I saw Valerie's fantasy: of her ripping the chains from the ground, of her grabbing me by my waist, shoving me against the wall and kissing my neck, hard. The suddenness of it all startled me. I fought not to recoil or react in any way. In her thoughts, I cried out in mixed want and denial; tried and failed to push her away. She overpowered me. She pinned my wrists to the wall over my head, hissing in my ear: *"How I've wanted to rip this control from you…"*

Fantasy and reality blended together the longer I watched her ravage me. Never had I allowed anyone to touch me like this. To have me in such a way. My ego had kept me away from that. Yet here I watched Valerie do what I'd denied myself for so long. I watched and watched; wanted to keep watching; wanted to keep burning in this building heat. But it was too much—too much for me to handle.

I ended the link and looked away. It took everything in me not to give away what I saw. It felt so *real*—her fingertips digging into my body, her lips on me with such urgency. I held my breath to slow this quickening within me.

Even if I hadn't seen her thoughts, I would have sensed the energy about her.

Valerie's aura was but a misty reflection of the scene in her mind. Angry, rebellious.

If I allowed this silence to linger, I feared Valerie would notice my *control*. Revealing my cards now felt safer. More practical than fantasizing about her fantasy right in front of her. As much as I could, I bottled up this desire, setting it aside for later.

"Sebastian and Lee—are they part of your family's private army?" I inquired.

Valerie glared up at me with weary eyes. "How do you know about them…?"

"I have my ways," I responded.

"Leave them alone," she blurted out, hoarse. "Leave them out of this!"

I hummed, intrigued. "Oh, I will. Unlike before, my promise comes with strings attached. You could have saved yourself this trouble if you'd done as I asked the first time."

"All of this… for an apology?"

"It's the principle that matters," I clarified. "Now that I know what you are capable of, I cannot simply allow you to leave." I held up three fingers. "Three conditions. If you object to any one of these, your only option will be to wait here until you change your mind. Considering what you've done, I believe this is more than fair."

"… what are the terms?" asked Valerie.

"First, you are to apologize to me. Second, you are to report to me when I have need of your talents. Once I tell the emperor what's happened, he will want to put you to work."

"For the empire…? Do you mean to punish me further? I am not patriotic in the least."

"Fortunately for you, neither is His Majesty. You shall learn why in due course."

Valerie was too tired to note the contradiction there. "What is the third condition?"

"You're to wear a device that will allow me to keep an eye on you. Not literally. But if you act against the emperor, or me, I'll be the first to know. If we grow to trust one another in the future, I will remove the device. In short, it is in your best interest to behave from now on."

"And you'll give me your word… that you will leave my friends—my soldiers—alone?"

"You have my word."

I waited for her to finally do as I said. Whether Valerie chose to do this for herself, for her friends, or for me, it didn't matter. Hours ago, proud and defiant, she would have refused my terms outright.

Now, here she was, bowing to me once more. Her fatigue had dulled her senses. Valerie rested her head along my boots. Such a small, accidental move from her made my heart swell. Any other time, seeing Valerie with her guard down would have sated my sadism. Instead I felt protective of her. Listening to her slur her words, sleepy as she was, made me smile. This was such a contrast to her thoughts moments ago.

"I apologize, Lady Lucrezia... for my rudeness earlier—yesterday—every day. You are an impeccable woman. I did not think... that my words would have such an effect on you. I did not think that you cared for me at all, yet you have chosen to be generous. I am at my lowest before you... and you've not laughed or dismissed me. I must have misjudged you..."

I wanted to tell her that I was not impeccable at all. Valerie only thought me so because that was how I wished to appear, to protect myself. I did appreciate her sincerity.

"Pledge yourself to Emperor Xavier," I went on. "To me."

"I am at your disposal," droned Valerie, drunk with exhaustion.

"You're not to forget this promise," I stressed.

"I won't..."

"I'll make sure of that. Give me your hand, my lord."

Valerie placed her left hand over my lap. I locked a pair of black handcuffs over her wrist. Hidden magical properties in the metal allowed me to check on her whenever I pleased. I'd be able to tell where she was, who she was with, and, most important, what she had in her hands at any given time. I would know to be on alert whenever she handled that rifle again.

Feeling her rest against me like this, it was difficult to believe that she held any anger in her heart at all. No matter how proud she was, Valerie was still human. The Privy Council *had* hurt her feelings by laughing at her proposal. I understood the deeper reasons—the causality— behind her reaction to them. That was why I couldn't punish her any more than this.

I told the guard outside to release her.

Valerie and I said not a word as we walked from the gallows out to the grounds. I didn't want any of the guards to overhear our conversation. We stopped once we were outside in the chill of night, away from overhearing ears. She seemed embarrassed to have let her guard down with me. She couldn't know how much it pleased me to see this rare side of her.

"Expect to see me at court this weekend," I said. "Once I have a better feel for you, His Majesty will want to have a private audience with us. Let's give it a few weeks first, shall we?"

"Yes… that's fine," replied Valerie, blinking hard to stay awake.

"For now, you ought to return home. I'm certain your family misses you terribly."

"My sister-in-law will never let me hear the end of it…"

I smiled over her misfortune. "Have a good night, my lord."

Unexpected, Valerie bent down to kiss my hand. She lingered there, uncertain, staring down at my boots. She then left across the grounds to her estate, oddly subdued. This transformation in her from defiant to demure was beyond fascinating. I'd always known Valerie as a private person who expected danger around every corner. But I sensed she was also deeply sensitive, as I was. She was multi-faceted, as she needed to be to survive.

I wished to see more of her faces—if they were just as beautiful as the one she wore each day.

***

I went to visit Emperor Xavier in his private den. His caretaker mentioned that his condition had improved somewhat after hearing about the Privy Council's monetary demise. I found him sitting in a warm chair by the fireplace, his head covered by a blanket. When we were children living in the Kingdom of Tibor together, I recalled his ears growing unusually cold in the night. I sat down at his side, knowing that he wouldn't acknowledge me—not right away.

The silence of the moment pained me even more, knowing that he couldn't comprehend my presence in his current mood. His light brown eyes had been dulled by his struggles to rule an empire that saw him only as the bastard child of Tynan's previous ruler. Xavier and I were the same age, and yet each time he fell into another of his despairs, he seemed several decades older than his strong, stern features suggested. But a few shades darker than Valerie, his mixed race—imperial and royal—marked him as an enigma to the empire.

After a few moments, Xavier turned to regard me. "I am ashamed," he said. "I allowed the council to take advantage of my weakness… Speaking for me. Making me sign legislation while in the insipidness of my nightly depression, knowing full well I cannot understand a thing… Why didn't they consult you?"

I rubbed his hand closest to mine. "You know why, my friend."

Xavier appeared as a lost child. "No, I don't… I told them you are to speak for me when I am debilitated. Why couldn't they follow but one order?"

"They do not have the empire's best interests at heart. To them, Tynan was but a playground in which they could exercise their wealth and influence. Queen Beatrys of Tenrose grows impatient with these talks of war. She'll no doubt prepare her armies soon."

"The council had the gall to claim *I* wanted the queen's lands," said Xavier with a sneer. "They did this because I am weak. I shouldn't have inherited this empire from my father. The Privy Council insisted on it because they knew they could control me. Isn't that right?"

"Unfortunately, yes…"

Xavier drew a powerful fist beneath my hand, veins webbing beneath my touch. "I will conquer this illness," he vowed. "Whatever it is, I'll not allow it to hinder me further."

"What do you believe started this?" I asked. "What ails you, Xavier?"

He smiled wistfully and said, "I miss our childhood, Lu. Those days were easier. Simpler. Running around the countryside in the rain with you; pretending to be sick the next day and skiving off our studies... And then, all of a sudden, the father I never knew I had was dead, and I was expected to lead in his stead. I didn't know what to do... I still don't."

"Set aside your pride and let me help you, dear. I know that we have had... certain disagreements over the years. Do you see now that the council pitted us against one another? They know that I am the only one who encourages you to use your voice."

"Yes... forgive me. You are my only friend in this world... Can we start over?"

I held his covered head close to me, sighing in relief. "Of course we can."

Xavier's caretaker called from the other side of the door. He slipped a missive beneath the opening and went on his way. I opened the seal and read the letter. This was a detailed account from a young man who'd heard sniper rifle shots at the time of the fire. I laughed, showing the parchment to the emperor. He, too, laughed for the first time in ages. I then explained what I'd witnessed on my own after recreating the scene of the crime.

"So it appears the lord commander isn't all talk," observed Xavier in fascination. "She knows how to take action. This brings me much joy. I trust that you allowed her to return home?"

"Yes. She pledged her loyalty to us in exchange for her freedom. We could certainly benefit from her many talents."

"Then let us discuss the plan moving forward," said Xavier. "Lord Valerie is an extraordinary woman indeed for helping to mend our friendship. I would very much like to see what other surprises she is capable of. She could be the missing key that we need."

"We are in full agreement, my friend," I replied, dropping the missive into the fireplace. Xavier and I watched the parchment curl with black burns until it disintegrated into ash.

Chapter Three
Giving Up
(Val)

On the evening before Emperor Xavier's next party at court, a few of my soldiers urged me to spend some time with them. Word had spread to my regiment about my anarchy against the Privy Council. I couldn't blame them for wanting to celebrate my freedom. I wasn't normally one to go out. I only did it for my soldiers. Many of them had suffered a great deal before I recruited them. I wanted my troops to keep their spirits up through this fight for our rights.

I had about an hour yet before I was due to meet them at our usual drinking hall in the city. I needed to get away from Gabrielle fussing over me, from Yosef's constant jokes about me blowing up more buildings, from Father's concern over Lucrezia's handcuffs chained to my wrist. As much as they had every right to be concerned about me, I felt trapped at home. More so than I had been at the gallows.

I escaped to the top of Eden's tallest clock tower overlooking the goings-on that night. I could think freely here, sitting next to the backdrop of the ticking clock with my sniper rifle. Here I had the perfect view of the Empyrean Palace glittering in the moonlight, its grounds rife with hedge mazes, lakes and flower beds. Closer to me, the city's Lyceum glowed with slow-burning lights as a bastion full of scholarly textbooks and historical records of Tynan's bloody history. Near the Lyceum, I heard citizens yelling over the latest planned provisions.

The council wished to place a tax on the city's Grand Cathedral in order to restore some of their wealth.

The clergy's oracles tried and failed to quell the crowd with promises that they would think of a solution to the issue.

This was the second time the well-to-do citizens of Eden had revolted against the Privy Council's plans. The first had to do with the talks of war and the inevitable tax increases needed to pay for soldiers and weapons. Now that *their* pockets were affected, they suddenly cared about right and wrong. Small strides.

Their anger phased out from my ears as I stared at the palace beyond.

Lucrezia's compassion had surprised me the other night. I had assumed she was a selfish, emotionless woman, focused only on her own goals. As much as I cared for Lee and Sebastian, she cared for Emperor Xavier in the same ways. If anyone else had gone to assess my guilt, I would have been dead by now. My bravado from the day of the fire now melted over me as pools of regret. My mood had more to do with Lucrezia than I was aware of. Seeing her in this different light impacted me just as much as getting to live another day.

I stared down at her claim over me—these handcuffs chained to my left wrist. The chain sounded friendlier than the ones in my cell had. Engraved over the black steel was Lucrezia's name. This reminder of my serendipity kept her on my mind.

I had a view of her on one of the palace's balconies with the emperor himself. Sniper rifle in hand, I peered through the scope to get a better look. There I saw Lucrezia sitting across from Emperor Xavier, both of them laughing over glasses of wine. I hadn't seen His Majesty smile in some time. There had been rumors spreading around that he was ill; his scarce appearances at court were meant to stave off the gossip. I knew that he and Lucrezia were childhood friends, yet they did not spend much time together these days. That seemed to have changed now that the Privy Council was all but destroyed.

Had I done them a favor without knowing?

Lucrezia glanced in my direction. She stared right at me through the scope of my sniper rifle, the striking sharpness of her eyes softened by her sly smile. Startled, I fumbled my gun, hiding from her view. This steel over my wrist was unnatural. She shouldn't have been able to track me. I knew enough of alchemy from Sebastian and Lee to know that those magicks weren't at work here. Yet I suspected Lucrezia wouldn't give me solid answers if I asked her about it.

I collapsed my rifle and made my way down the tower. I couldn't bring this to the drinking hall. Even though I felt safer with my prized weapon over my back, I didn't want my soldiers to think that I had cause to be paranoid. I went home first to return the rifle to my hiding spot. I prayed that Gabrielle wouldn't corner me and notice what was really on my mind.

* * *

About twenty of us packed into Eden's busiest—and friendliest—drinking hall near Maleficus, one of the more questionable areas of the city. The hall's owners didn't mind our eccentricities so long as we paid our tabs on time. Here we could wear our military uniforms as women and not be bothered by rude remarks about why we weren't at home raising our families. The rest of my soldiers who passed as men didn't have to worry over someone possibly seeing past their clothes and starting a scene.

This was a safe space.

This particular drinking hall had a reputation of serving as an old trafficking site down to Elysium, the haunted lowtown underneath Eden's roads, where all sorts of outcasts resided. Legends told of the scorpion's empress who remained in the streets of Elysium as a ghost, pining after her fallen lover: a paladin by the name of Ser Videl. The empress' *scorpion* from Eden had died defending her and the lower city from an imperial invasion in ages past.

Many of my soldiers had once lived down there, having been homeless with no place left to go. The empress, Raj Mangala, had tended to their needs as best as she could.

Elysium's history was largely ignored in children's schools, passed down instead through word of mouth. Staring down at the device Lucrezia had locked over my wrist, I thought back to all I'd been taught to forget: the one my father had said would make more sense to me in time.

The paladin who had defended the city below had been part of the Excalibur, a group of magical knights. The corrupt Holy Knights Thirteen had ruled over Tynan when it had been a mere city comprised of both Eden and Elysium. After a battle of diplomacy, the Empress of Elysium and her paladin secured her city's independence. When the empire expanded to the lands beyond, the Holy Knights Thirteen fell out of favor for the Imperial Crown. The first emperor of Tynan knew that his throne could have been taken from him at any moment by a skilled thaumaturge or sorceress. To protect the new world order, oracles learned certain incantations that would inflame a sorceress' magic within her blood, killing her. The erasure and fear of death by clerics kept sorceresses scattered and afraid to live out in the open.

New Testaments of the *Hallows* circulated then, of the oracles of yore condemning sorceresses for bringing the world to ruin. Mass burnings and witch-hunts drove thaumaturges and sorceresses into hiding. Women were kept from positions of power in case they were sorceresses-in-hiding. Their rights were stripped from them over the years, a little at a time, to keep them from rioting with too much effectiveness. Alchemists were forced into hard labor to revive the technology Tellus had lost in the supposed apocalypse centuries ago, creating the buildings and machinery that adorned the Empire of Tynan as a whole. And once the cathedrals had no more need of the alchemists, the oracles had cast them aside, claiming them as heretics on the level of other thaumaturges and sorceresses.

It was too simple for those in power to change the truth to suit their own needs.

I stood at the long wooden bar with a mug of ale in hand. A few of my soldiers drank with me. Most others had wandered off to find a lover for the night. Sebastian and Lee in particular were at my side, their arms draped around my neck as they sung my praises over the loudness in the hall. I smiled with ease, as was rare for me. They teased me about my time with the lady chancellor in the gallows. I hadn't told them of how my mind had strayed in my fatigue and resentment; how I'd lost myself to thoughts unfamiliar. Thoughts I'd repressed for longer than I realized.

I couldn't forget those images, more powerful than anything I'd imagined in recent times. Resentment had spurred those foreign feelings within me. Resentment that Lucrezia had had my life in her hands, and that I had been powerless to resist. That resentment spun into aggression. And the only aggression I knew how to express in that moment was sexual. Lucrezia's face, her body and her mind were divine. And her attitude—that poised perfectionism, that ego, with the promise of compassion underneath it all...

Too often these past few days, I felt stuck in my thoughts of having her. Lucrezia couldn't know. No one else could know. Not even my friends who seemed to have picked up on how distracted I was.

"Don't be shy, Val," said Sebastian, grinning next to my face. "It's clear she's taken a liking to you... Why, if you don't get to know her better, I will!"

Lee took a thoughtful drink of his whiskey. "Ain't it strange how *pretty* Lady Lucrezia is?" he asked.

"Strange how?" I asked, trying not to sound too interested.

"I dunno. It's kinda unnatural, don't you think? I mean, it's no wonder that James fellow is head-over-heels for her. Then again, she's from Tibor. Heard the women over there are goddesses next to the ones here. Maybe that's got somethin' to do with it?"

"Foreigners, goddesses!" shouted Sebastian, the alcohol taking its effects on him. "If we weren't warring with the kingdom, I'd want to take a visit and see them all!"

"Idiot," scolded Lee. "We ain't warrin' yet."

"*Yet*, gentlemen," I emphasized. "Assuming His Majesty allows it, we may be in for a trip to the Kingdom of Tibor quite soon. Just please, promise me you'll be prepared for combat... I don't need you fantasizing about the women there during a fight. That's the surest way to get yourself killed."

Sebastian gave me a sloppy salute. "Aye, aye, commander!" he said, pushing himself from the bar. "Now, if you'll excuse me, I believe my betrothed is here. I should go find her..."

Lee and I watched Sebastian push his way through the crowd, legs wobbling.

"His *betrothed*," I mocked. "I swear he's delusional about her."

"Hey, go easy on him," scolded Lee. "We're short on options 'round here..."

I took a bitter swig of ale and said, "You're right."

We passed a while in silence. I only had the one mug to drink. Anything more was beyond my tolerance levels. It would have been irresponsible of me to have more.

Lucrezia was still on my mind. More than I felt comfortable with. Drinking didn't make me forget.

For a time, I tried to focus on the cacophony of conversation around me—drunken laughter, shouting; the deadbeat husband who hated his wife and unfairly couldn't stand his children; mild brawls and rhythmic fists smashing against the tables as onlookers cheered for their favorite contenders; the pair of women pondering over where they could have some private time together without anyone spying on them again… I could pretend to listen to them all I wanted. It was no use. These stubborn thoughts about Lucrezia weaved through those distractions.

I remembered the natural authority in Lucrezia's accent: steady, attractive.

I remembered the nerves that had collected in my throat each time I spoke to her.

I remembered the smell of her perfume cleansing the dirt and sick in my prison cell; the smell of her leather boots right next to my nose.

I remembered the feel of her hand along my face.

I remembered how my face had heated in response, despite myself.

And I retained in my face the pain from each punch I'd suffered from some ignorant fool who couldn't stand the sight of me. I recalled these details about Lucrezia with the same clarity. This was a blessing and a curse.

As if Thanatos himself had heard my thoughts, an unfamiliar group of women entered the drinking hall. They were already drunk, cackling loudly about the night they'd just had on the town. Lee and I exchanged glances. We just *knew* that the ladies would somehow find their way over to us. Sure enough, they saw us sitting here, minding our own business, and found reason for offense. Out of the corner of my eye, I watched their scandalized reactions, their mouths moving quickly with gossip. Grandstanding, two of the women came over to us while the rest went to find a seat somewhere.

Lee muttered under his breath, "Here we go."

"I'll deal with them," I promised.

"Wish you didn't have to. I'm really sick of this shit, Val… You've got no idea."

Right as I was about to ask Lee what he meant, one of the ladies bumped into him on purpose. "What've we got here?" she said at the top of her voice. Other people turned to stare. "You're too pretty to be a lad, boy. You got tape wrapped round your chest? A plastic prick in your trousers? And for what?!"

"Passing as a man, are you?" accused the other. "Well, it's not working! You should follow your friend here. She knows she's too delicate to walk around in oversized clothes. You can't hide with that face!"

"Pardon me, ladies," I said, hoping to distract them from Lee's growing ire. "We're only here to have a drink. I suggest you leave us alone."

"Or else what?" asked the first. "You'll beat us 'til we do as you say?"

I rolled my eyes. "Hardly. If you think we want to be men, you're mistaken."

"Then what's this about?!" shouted the second, waving her hand at us. "No daughter of mine would walk out the house dressed like that! Stop pretending you're something you're not! Cretins like you give us a bad name. How are the oracles to take us seriously when we ask for more of a say in the cathedrals? They look at you and think none of us can be trusted to behave!"

"And instead of pickin' on us," snapped Lee, "you could go to your fucking cathedral and *do somethin'*! It ain't our fault your oracles are sexist. They're gonna be that way unless *you* take a stand. So don't waste your time tryin' to school us. Get lost, will ya?"

The ladies scoffed and went on their way. As impassioned as Lee's protest was, it fell on deaf ears; the women muttered more insults as they walked off. Too much like everyone else in this city, they were set in their ways.

I noticed Lee scribbling a note on a sheet of parchment. When he was finished, he folded it up, looking uncertain of what to do next.

"Val?" he said.

"What do you have there?" I asked.

Lee handed me the note. "You can't read it until you get back home," he declared. "Promise me, yeah?"

"Yes, all right," I agreed, tucking the note away.

"And... thanks—for everything. You've been a great friend to me. Took me in when I had nothin'. Put clothes on my back and a roof over my head. You did that for nearly all of us. You're a saint, you are."

I smiled, puzzled over his sincerity. "This isn't like you, Lee."

"Yeah, well, there's a first time for everything... You deserve it, lord commander."

As unusual as Lee's declarations were, I very much appreciated them—and him. We spent a little longer talking about our hopes of making history in the coming war. It appeared Sebastian wasn't returning any time soon. He must have convinced his 'betrothed' to spend the night with him again. Lee and I decided to leave without him.

After we parted ways along the quiet avenue, I had a terrible feeling of a sudden. It *really* wasn't like Lee to thank anyone or express his gratitude, ever. The mystery surrounding his letter bothered me as well.

Though I'd promised not to, I opened the letter then and there. Lee's messy scribble was short—short enough to break me.

I give up. Tired of feeling like shit every day. I don't matter. Nothing's gonna change.

I give up, Val.

Sorry.

I ran down the street in Lee's direction. I knew—*I knew*—exactly how he felt. I couldn't let him to go through with this. I couldn't let him go. I couldn't let him give up.

"*I don't matter.*" That was what I'd said to Lucrezia just days ago. I had believed it in my moment of weakness. I had seen my inevitable beheading in the future and I'd pined after it, giving into the lies almost everyone tried to force upon me. Now Lee wanted to bring about his own demise—because of those same lies, that ignorance, that undue hatred.

No—they couldn't win. We couldn't let them win.

I couldn't let my best friend go like this.

Relief swelled within me once I spotted Lee down the next street. He was in the middle of the wide road, speaking with a strange man. Lee had his jacket open, revealing his chest wrapped with gauze as concealment. I hid behind the building at the corner. The man had his back to me. I saw a small revolver at his waist; he held his hand over it, stepping closer to Lee, threatening him. My friend stood there stone-faced. Lee had given up. He wanted this man to end him in a blaze of intolerance.

I snuck toward them. If I moved too quickly, I risked the man acting sooner than he intended. I had some time while they exchanged words.

"Your kind deserves to rot in hell," spat the stranger. "Bunch of freaks!"

"If that's what you think, then just shoot me," said Lee, much too calm. *Closer…*

The man gripped his revolver. "Are you mocking me?!"

"Nah… maybe I want you to kill me. If it'd make you feel better…"

A bit more—"Don't bullshit me, girl—"

Just as he pulled out his gun, I moved in front of him. I twisted his grip. The barrel of the revolver pointed right at his temple, with his finger over the trigger. I shoved him up against the nearest wall. He sputtered against me, resisting, his whole body trembling in fear.

"Val, what are you doing?!" cried Lee.

I ignored him, hell-bent on making this stranger pay. "Fucking coward," I hissed.

"L-Leave me be!" he wailed. "P-Please, don't kill me! Don't kill me! I-I've got a wife! Children!"

"Stop!" shouted Lee. "Don't do this, Val! Don't!"

"Come back as a sissy!" I said to the man, tightening my hold on his finger over the trigger. "Or as a woman who doesn't fit in her body. Come back as someone who's sick of these rules on what's allowed! Come back as one of us! *Then* you'll know how it feels!"

"Wait—STOP!"

I forced the trigger down all the way. Blood blasted from the side of his head, spattering thickly along the wall. I stepped back, watching his corpse slump to the ground. I saw in him every person who had brought me to that worthlessness Lucrezia had witnessed. Lee stared in horror. That could have been him instead. Panicked screams sounded from the homes above. I grabbed Lee by his arm, hurrying him along. We escaped before anyone spotted us.

***

Training with my troops in the valley outside of Eden the next morning wasn't the regular affair I'd come to expect. Last night, I'd escorted Lee back to the safehouse most of the other soldiers shared. He didn't want to discuss what had happened. There were just over five hundred of us out here in the crisp dawn of the spring morning—my full regiment. Instead of watching all my soldiers during target practice, I was focused on Lee, on his morale. I let everyone follow the usual routine. They led themselves. I was but a specter spending too much time on one person, shadowing him—reminding him without words that I was here for him, and that I wasn't going anywhere.

For all of Lee's pride, he seemed to appreciate my presence. I hadn't said a word to anyone about the incident. Not even to Sebastian or Gabrielle. My guilt wouldn't let me. I had seen myself in Lee's decision last night. As much as I acted as if I had broken free from society's shackles, I knew how wrong that was. I should have been stronger than this. I should have risen above this.

The sad truth was that I was just as susceptible to these things as anyone else. Every time someone had told me that I was less-than, that I was worthless, it stayed with me.

I couldn't fight this shame.

Burning the Imperial Bank hadn't rid me of the memory of the Privy Council laughing at me. Killing that man hadn't exterminated every other person like him from the world. Winning this upcoming war against Tibor wouldn't change *everyone's* views. There would always be some prejudiced person who got off on putting others down.

Listening to the firing of our advanced muskets, I couldn't help this pessimism. I was only capable of going wherever my impulses took me. And even then, those wouldn't fix everything.

I had a difficult time spotting any progress. To know if this was all worth it.

Yet seeing Lee alive and well, smiling as he hit the bullseye—I knew *this* was progress.

We finished training late that afternoon. My troops and I returned home on horseback. I had to get ready for dinner at court that evening. Lucrezia would be there... She expected to see me. She expected us to speak, to get to know one another. I lingered overlong in the bath. I spent too much time deciding on which of my military uniforms to wear. I settled on my white coatee, dark breeches and boots. And once I was dressed, with my hair pulled back in my usual tail, I stared at myself in my bedroom mirror.

I touched the thin gaps across my brows, recalling how Lucrezia had done the same a few nights ago. I hadn't expected her hand to be so soft. Was I a fool to want more of her? I must have been.

For years, I had believed the rumors about her. In my contempt for Lucrezia's inaction, I had convinced myself that every terrible piece of gossip about her was true. But now, hearing of the untold power and influence the Privy Council had had before, I knew the truth. Lucrezia hadn't been able to do anything for fear of being overruled. Now that I was sympathetic to her, and she to me, it made perfect sense.

How odd that my opinion of her changed this much after a simple shift in perspective.

Gabrielle burst into my room. "Come now, Val!" she said, pulling me out to the hall. "What's gotten into you? We'll be late if we don't hurry!"

Yosef waited for us by the front door. "There you are! Finished daydreaming about your next explosion to set off?"

"Not now, brother," I muttered.

"What? Don't deny it! I know you crave the anarchy, the thrill of it all!"

"I'm not in the mood for your jests," I told him, leaving through the front door.

Yosef sighed. "Fine, fine," he relented. "You're grumpier than usual today."

"Will you not walk with us, Val?" called Gabrielle. "We should go together!"

I waited for them to catch up. With Gabrielle's arm in mine, and her other in Yosef's, we left across the palace grounds. The last shred of the dusk's light peeked across the darkening sky. All across the grounds, other noble families from other estates left their homes, on their way to engage in the predictable games at court. I felt my eyes glazing over at the thought.

Soon we arrived at the decorative ballroom where Emperor Xavier held the palace's dinner parties. The brightness here ever reminded me of the heart of a diamond compared to the stark onyx black elsewhere. Glittering chandeliers hung over the groups of couples, family and friends dancing together to the bards' music. Along the sides of the room sat the long dinner tables covered in the finest cloth, supporting the weight of endless meals— enough to feed the starving and sick in the slums for weeks. To the emperor's credit, he did have excess food sent to the poor after each of these occasions. From what I understood, this was one of the few charitable provisions the council had allowed, as they didn't have to pay the volunteers.

Yosef and I guided Gabrielle over to our father speaking with his colleagues.

"Father!" called Yosef, getting his attention.

"There you are, my twins," he greeted. "And my dearest Gabrielle, I see quite a few of the neighbors leering at your gown with envy. As they rightfully should."

Gabrielle beamed at him. "You're too kind, magister."

Father gave us a tired smile. "Enjoy the party, won't you?" he said. Yosef and Gabrielle went to socialize with their friends nearby. "Val, my sweetheart, how are you? I admit I've not been able to sleep since your arrest earlier this week… I find myself paranoid that it will happen again. Are you staying out of trouble?"

"I'm doing my best," I lied, my eyes scanning the room.

"What's that supposed to mean?" he worried.

I spotted Lucrezia over with Xavier at his onyx throne. Like last night, the two of them seemed to be getting on quite well. I grew distracted when I considered that Lucrezia likely knew what I'd done to that man. These handcuffs over my arm had since been warm with her awareness. She didn't glare at me with disapproval as I'd expected.

Seeing Lucrezia smile warmly at me spoke volumes. She had the most beautiful smile. One that radiated across the room. It radiated within me, just as she enjoyed.

I noticed her subtle laughter. She knew I couldn't take my eyes off her.

"Honestly, Val," said Father, sighing. "Your mind tends to be elsewhere whenever we have these discussions. I know you are angry. I only wish you'd have a modicum of restraint."

I wondered how he would react if he knew I'd killed a man last night.

"You needn't worry for me," I explained.

"As your father, I *must* worry."

"I know."

"You also owe the Lady Lucrezia a great deal," continued Father.

I tore my sight away from her at last. "I—*what?* Well—yes, of course I do…"

He smiled anew, rephrasing: "You are in her debt. I expect you've settled whatever ill feelings existed between the two of you before. Would you like my advice?"

In my periphery, I noticed Lucrezia and the emperor watching me still, whispering.

"All right," I said.

Father touched my shoulder, leaning in to say, "You crave to change this wretched world that looks down upon you for your mere existence. I wish for the same—without risking the consequences you suffered the time before. Do as the lady bids you to do. Treat her well. She is His Majesty's right hand. Please her, and she'll no doubt extend your reach in this court."

"I understand…"

"Good. Now go to them. I shall be here if you need me."

I steeled myself when Emperor Xavier hailed me over. I made my way to him, to Lucrezia. Of course Father believed it was in my best interest to do this. Any other time, I would have refused these calls to make nice with other people. Yet I knew that I had misjudged the emperor and Lucrezia both. If our goals did in fact align together, then there was no harm in speaking with them. No harm… that was what I tried to tell myself.

Being indebted to Lucrezia, to anyone, set me ill at ease.

"Lord Commander Valerie!" spoke Xavier, his arms wide in welcome. His guards allowed me to pass. "What a pleasure to see you here at court this fine evening! 'Tis rare indeed for you to attend these dinners. At last your family needn't excuse your absence."

I bowed to him. "Your Imperial Majesty." And Lucrezia—I took her hand in mine, kissing her soft, perfumed skin. "Lady Chancellor."

Lucrezia sounded amused. "Good evening to you, my lord," she said.

"You both look well," I commented, uncertain of what else to say. "I am glad."

Xavier smirked at me. "A gentleman of few words," he observed. "I do enjoy your candor, Lord Valerie. It is most refreshing. After all, I owe my recent surge in health to you."

"Please—Your Majesty, Lady Chancellor. Call me Val. We have known each other long enough, I believe."

"*Lord Val* it is," allowed Lucrezia, tasting the name. Her emphasis moved me.

"And we will know each other for a great deal longer!" espoused Xavier. "But that is a discussion for another time. Lord Val, you must be famished. The lady chancellor has beaten me to the monopoly on your time, I'm afraid. Won't the two of you dine together? I must deal with a few trivial matters."

I had to remind myself to reply with *some* grace. "I would be delighted."

"As would I," said Lucrezia, linking her arm in mine. "We shall speak anon, Xavier."

Xavier gave an exaggerated bow from the seat of his throne. "Lucrezia."

Eating dinner with Lucrezia was not awkward as I'd expected. I tended to not know what to say during gatherings such as these. I hadn't the personality to keep up with the expected manners here at court. Lucrezia appeared to enjoy my attitudes. She didn't hold me to the same standards as the nobles who stared at us together. Instead, she laughed in enjoyment over my disdain for these rules—and for everyone else's rudeness around us.

I liked that she didn't judge me for feeling the way I did.

"I must say, I find your bluntness quite charming, my lord," remarked Lucrezia, smiling.

Over time, the conversation shifted to personal details. Ones that we didn't mind others overhearing. I learned of her scholarly propensities—how she enjoyed studying the arcane, namely astronomy. I told Lucrezia of my fascination with emerging technology, namely that of guns and other ammunition. After the party at court was over that evening, Lucrezia bade me to return the next night, the night after that, and so on. I returned each time, more invigorated by her presence than the last. We kept up with one another intellectually throughout these couple of weeks. I actually looked forward to our next dinners together. Each time I left the Empyrean Palace, I wished I could return sooner—right away.

Lucrezia was far more than the indolent woman I had assumed her to be.

There were a great many people who seemed nervous about Lucrezia speaking with me like this. They knew of her renewed clout here within the palace. They knew of how I despised them for mistreating me over the years. Suffice to say, the gossip about court these past nights felt agitated, restless. The worst of them was her friend—the Lieutenant-Colonel James of Eden. He glared at me with such contempt; I feared his face would fix itself that way forever. I thought he would approach us to say something, *anything*. He did not.

After we'd had our fill that night, Lucrezia took me to a hall away from the festivities. The windows had been removed from the wide horizontal slot in the wall, opening the space up to the breeze. Lucrezia leaned on the onyx, staring out to the panorama of the cloudless night sky overlooking the capital. The uneven heights of Eden's buildings were as tightly-packed black fangs spiraling among the stars. Far beyond, the crags of Nyx Mons glowed an ethereal violet.

Lucrezia sighed in content. "I've had a wonderful time with you these past few weeks," she said. "Do you feel the same?"

"Indeed, my lady," I answered.

"I didn't mean to keep you to myself for so long tonight. I hope you don't have a curfew."

"In case you've forgotten, I'm twenty-five years old."

Lucrezia laughed softly. "Forgive me, my lord," she said. "I didn't mean to suggest a curfew as a symptom of your age. It is no secret as to what a rebel you are. Your family must worry about you, that's all."

"They know better than to expect me at home with any frequency."

"And here I hoped after your brief imprisonment that you'd learned how much some of us care for you. In case *you've* forgotten, there are many people who admire you for your work."

"It's difficult to remember that," I admitted.

"You've been fighting on your own long enough," insisted Lucrezia. "Change is on the horizon. You are at the tip of the spear, my lord. I daresay you'll have better luck achieving your goals now that we have allied together."

I recalled my father's words, his advice. "I am also in your debt."

Lucrezia noticed how unsettled I was by this truth. "Pride, thy name is Lord Val of Lysander... We shall have to do something about that." *Pride...* something we both had in spades. I saw it in her eyes—she wanted to tear mine down as much as I wanted to rip into hers. "What's on your mind, hmm?"

"You care?" I asked.

Another smile—sweeter this time as she answered, "I thought I'd made it quite clear that I do. In fact, I always have. It wasn't prudent to tell you until recently."

"You are instrumental, then."

"Yes... I enjoy the cello the most. Shaped like a woman's body—don't you think?"

I couldn't help my amusement. "And you enjoy your puns."

Lucrezia's stare roamed my face, my body, down to my boots and back up again. "It is one of the few delights I allow myself," she said. "The others being my private studies and my time spent with my associates. Life here at the palace can get predictable."

"Is the lieutenant-colonel part of that predictability? Or is he a delight?"

"Mmm, I suppose he is both. Or he was. I've not spoken to him since the night of your arrest. Why do you ask, my lord?"

She knew exactly *why*. She wanted me to say it out loud.

"I'm trying to figure this out," I admitted.

"Figure what out?"

Again.

I scowled at her transparency. "My lady, as perceptible as you are, you can't mean to tell me that you've no idea whatsoever."

Lucrezia caressed my face, down to my neck. "I enjoy your forwardness," she revealed. Her soft touch disarmed me—just as it had the first time. "As flustered as you are with my teasing, you get right to the point. So unlike others I've known. But a bit of advice, Lord Val: *don't* figure me out. That is the last thing that I want. Overanalyzing leads to the wrong conclusions. It's messy."

A few guards passing by in the hall noticed our rapport. That didn't stop me— "Then tell me what you *do* want, Lady Lucrezia."

"For now, I'd like us to speak more. To spend more time with one another. Simple."

Her vagueness left me wanting. Lucrezia noticed. I saw the warm glow in her skin.

"I don't mean to *speak* with a taken woman, my lady," I said.

"When has that stopped you before?" she asked. "I've heard the tales firsthand from a few of the married ladies at court, you know. I can't imagine why they would lie about such a thing. Besides, I am not *taken*, as you say. James is but a friend."

"It was too complicated. One of their husbands nearly caught me. I've stopped that."

"So you're more old-fashioned now?"

"If you wish to put it that way, yes," I answered. "And I have eyes for no other."

Lucrezia hummed in satisfaction. "Let's keep it that way, shall we?" She looked me over once more. "Before I allow you to have an audience with the emperor, I would like the two of us to go somewhere. It is relevant to what His Majesty wishes to discuss with you."

"What would that be?" I asked.

"The matter concerns Elysium. The scorpion's empress, more specifically. Each Sunday night, she visits one of the outdoor clubs in the Fury's Mercy."

"You want us to meet her."

"Correct," replied Lucrezia. "There is something I would ask of her. I cannot simply make this known without befriending her first. I have several tasks I must attend to during the week until then. I must postpone our dinners, unfortunately. Meet me at the Charon Bridge this next Sunday at ten o'clock sharp. You and I shall find the empress together, luck willing."

She made this sound like a business affair. I felt sour of a sudden, thinking of Lucrezia in these intimate ways over the past weeks. If she didn't feel the same for me, then I'd made myself vulnerable. Vulnerable in that I wanted her in ways that hadn't crossed her mind. If she were to find out, I would have been mortified. More so than if these budding feelings were mutual. But then I thought back to all I'd done recently, with guns in-hand... Perhaps my hands weren't pure enough to hold a woman again.

"I will meet you there, my lady," I said, bowing to her.

Distancing myself from her seemed like the logical thing to do. Yet logic had no place in this perceptiveness of my imagination. I could have sworn I saw more promise behind Lucrezia's fixed gaze. She knew what I was capable of. She hadn't flinched from me so far. Lucrezia smiled when others would have frowned and fled. Maybe she didn't need my purity after all.

Chapter Four

Elysium
(Lucrezia)

Not seeing Val for a week should have been normal. It should have been expected. After all, I'd put off much of my work in favor of having extended dinners and conversation with her. I had to catch up on my duties. As I sat at my desk in my study late that afternoon, I could barely concentrate. The prospect of seeing her again the next night lifted me with skittish nerves, with fluttering desires. Yet I couldn't stand being in this state.

I was used to making others feel this way about me. Feeling it myself for someone else, as worthy as she was of my affections, unsettled me as much as it made me smile to myself. Val was a collection of contradictions: ruthless and kind, single-minded and thoughtful. She existed in extremes at all times. Having this week to myself, hiding away, I had made up my mind that I wished to keep up with her pace. It was only a matter of letting her know. Tomorrow night. Tomorrow…

This letter from my younger brother Gustavo in Tenrose, Tibor's capital, sat upon my desk. I hadn't spoken to him properly in many years. I'd glanced at his message multiple times over the last few days, picking up a few words here and there.

There was a certain, sexist stigma in Tellus that only infertile women or sorceresses-in-hiding would choose another woman over a man, regardless of her sexuality. Sorceresses could reproduce with or without men, by the emotional bond they shared with their partner. In our adolescence, my brother had teased me over liking both men and women, claiming that I must have had dormant powers that I'd not yet realized. He and his friends would surround me at each opportunity, calling me all manner of insults and slurs.

When we were older, his friends made bets with one another to see who could bed me first—with the sole intent of fucking my powers out of me, as if their sex was a weapon that could pull off such a feat. Xavier's coronation had arrived at the best time for me. He stole me away with him here to the Empyrean Palace. Four years passed; I never looked back.

And so I wanted nothing to do with my brother. Yet his letter sat upon my desk as an annoyance, a distraction from my other tasks. I couldn't keep ignoring this.

At last I found the motivation to read it.

Lucrezia,

You haven't responded to my last few letters. I'm sending this in the hopes that you will reply this time.

Queen Beatrys has forbidden me from attending court at Castle Pandemonium. I suspect it is because you and I are family. She doesn't want me relaying her plans to you. Word has spread nonetheless. She prepares her armies to destroy your emperor and the empire both. Unless your ruler feels he can take on five thousand patriotic soldiers with his fractured units, I suggest taking drastic action. Flee the Empyrean Palace. Beseech the queen personally to reconsider this war. Just do something, will you?

I've also not forgiven you for leaving with Xavier the way you did. But you are his right hand. Whether it is his fault for this coming war, or the council's, it matters not. If our nations go to war, you or I may fall victim. When I think of it that way, I wish you would leave your old friend's side and come home to me. You've yet to meet your nephew and my wife. My wife and her friends ask about you often. You are the only part of the empire that they do not fear. Don't make them regret that.

P.S.: There is talk here across the pond that you have found yourself a new lover. Valerie of Lysander. Is she as merciless as they say? If she is, she must be as strong as you are. It's no wonder you like her.

Love,

Gustavo

I soured over my brother's nosiness. I wasn't surprised gossip about Val and I had already spread across the Eidos Sea to Tibor proper. I glanced at my arcane textbooks on the nearest bookcase. I wondered if he would continue sending me these cordial letters if he knew for certain what I was. Such a reminder of that time of my life put me in a foul mood. And *he* hadn't forgiven *me* for leaving, when I'd had every reason to leave him behind? Gustavo must have had amnesia. Either that or I really had been more skilled at hiding my pain from him than I thought. He hadn't noticed at all.

Yet the supposed *love* at the end of his letter made me scowl the most.

I set his words aside. Gustavo could wait a while for my response. Writing to him now would have only exposed my temper.

Those years I'd spent deflecting my brother and his friends had sculpted terrible deformities in me. I fought to appear perfect so as to not give anyone a reason to insult me. Never again did I wish to feel the pangs of hurt that Gustavo had caused me. That was also why I couldn't know what to do with these feelings I had for Val. I didn't want her to see me stumble. I didn't want to be vulnerable with others—and yet with her, the thought kept me up at night. The thought distracted me now, clouding my sight with the memories of her fantasy from the gallows.

Any other woman would have thrown themselves at Val, had they seen what I did. She couldn't know these things about me. I feared her eyes would stray if she discovered that I was a weak child who feared being anything less than flawless.

My dutiful servant Rosa entered my study with poor news.

"Lady Chancellor, Lieutenant-Colonel James is here to see you," she said. "He says… he says he is tired of being sent away each time he visits."

I scoffed, picking up the next letter in my neat pile. "Is he, now?"

"Shall I send him away once more?"

"No, I don't want the man complaining to you again," I answered. "Bring him in."

"Right away, my lady."

The prospect of seeing James again improved my concentration. Focusing on the tasks in front of me would help me ignore him. It had been almost a month since our last dinner together during the night of the fire. He and I had long since established that our friendship would end once we found other people, tentative or otherwise.

James' more recent demands for my time felt transparent. If it were another man I'd chosen to fool around with, he would not mind this much; this strongly. I *knew* him.

As he entered my office, closing the door behind him, I didn't pay him much mind. I read over the business letter concerning the imperial ambassador's unfortunate illness. With him bed-ridden, we had no one to send over to the Kingdom of Tibor for any possible peace talks. Not that it mattered, anyway. Xavier wished to unite his people once more with the scorpion's empress and her untold influence. Val's technologically-advanced army was to be our ace in this coming war. I was wary about setting the weight of an entire empire over Val's shoulders. Yet I trusted she was up to the task, if at least to prove her soldiers' worth in the eyes of the world.

James sighed. "Are you really doing this?" he asked.

"Doing what?" I replied, blasé as I turned to the next page.

"Ignoring me. Shoving me aside for someone else. I thought we had an agreement?"

"Indeed we did," I allowed. "The agreement was that we would have our play together so long as we had no eyes for anyone else. I am not *shoving* you anywhere, James. Not anymore."

"Lu..."

"Do not call me that. It is reserved for Xavier, not you."

James growled in annoyance. "You couldn't at least *tell me* about your new lady-friend?"

And there it was. "That term implies Val and I are merely friends who will *grow out* of these dalliances and move on to men. Had I known from the start that you were homophobic, I would have avoided you outright. I'll have to rethink the time we spent with one another."

"Has she had you?" he demanded to know.

This line of questioning felt too personal.

"Lord Val has done no more than kiss my hand," I explained. "There's no need for you to glare at her whenever the two of us dine together. It is most unreasonable of you."

There was a small part of me that enjoyed James' impatience. Old habits.

I found it difficult to quantify my growing friendship—relationship—with the lord commander. Other than the brief glimpse I'd had into her thoughts, I knew not at all how she felt for me. Without my usual forwardness, I couldn't gauge her desires. I had to stop this act.

"Is that it, then?" asked James. "Are we done?"

"I thought I'd made that abundantly clear, my good man. It appears your analytical skills have failed you yet."

Rosa entered again. "Lady Chancellor, His Imperial Majesty wishes to see you in the throne room," she announced. She noticed the sheer ire radiating from James. "Err, shall I ask the emperor to wait...?"

I waved James away. "You may go now, lieutenant-colonel." He stalked out of the room. "Rosa, please tell His Majesty that I will be there shortly. And thank you for your hard work. Tell the chamberlain that I would like to increase your pay for dealing with my near-constant emergencies."

"Yes, my lady! You are far too kind. Thank you!"

I smiled at Rosa as she gave a curtsey and left once more. I knew full-well that she and the other servants spent most of their time gossiping in the halls about my relationships. This pay raise for her was but a way to amuse myself. I liked to make them believe I had no idea. But I knew every word they whispered about me, James, Val and Xavier through the palace, and especially at court.

Despite the drama, I couldn't imagine myself anywhere but here. I was in my element, helping Xavier sort through his correspondences and advising him on how to respond appropriately. His word was law in this world. Being this close to such power would have intoxicated anyone else. I cared for Xavier too much to betray him in such a way.

The final letter on my desk surprised me. I smiled as I opened the seal from the Lysander Estate. This smell of crisp cologne mixed with the parchment reminded me so of the dinners Val and I had at court together. Seeing her professional handwriting for the first time captivated me.

Lady Lucrezia,

As you and I are both preoccupied this week, I must admit you've been on my mind more than usual. I've had to adjust to having dinner without your intelligent conversation. My sister-in-law noticed a change in me. Gabrielle is ever quick to spot when I am not myself. She thinks this has something to do with you. I've yet to confirm her suspicions. I can't. Not until this letter finds you.

When you first arrived at the palace four years ago, and my father introduced us, I recall my reticence around you. You intimidated me. I believe it was a combination of your appearance and attitude. You also had no shortage of gentlemen complimenting you. I sensed the meticulous control you maintained over yourself, how you appeared to others. I wasn't sure what to think of you. Now that I know you a bit better, I feel as if you did that on purpose.

And now that I've accepted this about you, I see you differently. The coldness in your eyes belies your compassion. The deflection in your derisive tone draws me to you. You don't exist to please anyone, unlike so many others I know. I respect that about you a great deal. Except I'm not sure what to do with this newfound respect. You are determined to keep yourself at a distance from me, from everyone.

I'm uncertain what else I should tell you. What I am allowed to tell you. You are difficult to read, my lady. I understand that it is not your wish for me to read you at all. I will have to follow my instincts tomorrow night when we meet again. This is very much out of my comfort zone. I have a feeling you enjoy that.

I wish to know what else you enjoy.
Yours truly,
Val

***

I made my way to the throne room, sorting in my mind how I would best inform Xavier of the latest news I'd pored over today. Val's letter was fresh in my mind, keeping this smile on my face. Walking through the double doors was much like entering a different world. The ceiling that once hung over the Empyrean Palace disappeared: here was the uninhibited view of Eden's horizon, accented by illusory auroras in the sky. Violet, black and silver imperial flags hung from endless masts in the air.

Each of the guards stationed around the area appeared as statues of black steel. The setting sun shone across the ethereal carpet, lighting my path to the emperor sitting upon his onyx throne across the way.

Xavier smiled warmly at me. "Lu, my dear, there you are!" he said, standing to meet me halfway.

"Your Imperial Majesty," I greeted, sweet with sarcasm. "You called?"

"Yes, I did," he replied, walking with me to one of the vantage points. "I know you will be out tomorrow evening with the lord commander. I figured I should ask this now."

That sounded ominous. "Hm? What is it?"

He lowered his voice just so, to keep the guards from overhearing. "Since you are to visit the scorpion's empress, do you think—do you think you could ask for her aid sooner? Perhaps tomorrow?"

"Tomorrow?" I echoed. "I thought we agreed that was much too soon."

Xavier winced with remembrance. "I know, I know!" he said. "But this cannot wait, Lu!"

There was no arguing with him when he was like this.

"Tell me what the problem is, dearest," I requested. "Let's go over this thoroughly."

"I don't want to go down in history as yet another emperor who waged war with the north. Or who waged war against thaumaturges, sorceresses and alchemists while the Grand Cathedral's clergy pulled the strings. Or who couldn't unite his people to engage in the war to start with! You and I agreed that we would ask the empress for her assistance in mobilizing the people of Tynan with her inspirational legacy. But what if we could avoid the war altogether?"

"I would much prefer to not see any bloodshed, yes," I allowed, frowning with skepticism. "But Lord Val is counting on this war as a way to prove her soldiers' worth. You would deny them that opportunity?"

Xavier stared off into the blood-red horizon. I had a terrible feeling of a sudden. We had decided on the course in the coming future. Val's army would be officially instated into the imperial ranks. We would then write up a draft to include women in Xavier's army, with Val and her second-in-command as high-ranking leaders for their units. The scorpion's empress would sing the empire's praises— or at least Xavier's, as a favor to me, after I'd gotten to know her.

With the advanced technology from Val's army, we would win the war, forcing Queen Beatrys to stave off her aggressions.

With morale restored, Xavier would then work to unite Tynan anew with the empress' guidance.

With the Privy Council weakened, we would finally send them on their way once Xavier had the peoples' support once more. Through all of this, Val's soldiers and women across the realm would slowly but surely have their rights restored. Thaumaturges, sorceresses and alchemists would have their retribution not long after.

I watched the perfect seams of our plan fall apart in the wake of Xavier's contemplation.

"Someone visited me in my chambers last night," he said at last.

"Someone?"

"A woman. She looked like you. In fact, I thought it *was* you. She advised me against continuing on this path. There are more important, personal matters that we must focus on instead."

With a sigh, I said, "Xavier, this is all very vague. We had a plan. Now you want to disrupt that for some— woman who you likely saw in a dream? My sweet little brother tells me Queen Beatrys will *not* back down. The only way you could possibly avoid the war is if you made endless peace talks with her, or if you stepped down and dissolved the Crown altogether to keep a successor from going to war..."

That determined look in his eyes.

"No... don't tell me," I worried. "Xavier... Xavier, don't!"

"I must."

"But—*why?* If you step down, we will have no place to go! We said—*we agreed*—that winning this war was the only way to restore your reputation! *Our* reputation, Xavier! Both of us! You cannot decide this without me!"

"Lucrezia, *please,*" he implored, gesturing for me to calm down.

"Don't *please* me, Xavier!" I hissed. "You mean to ask *me* to ask the empress to—what? Write a letter of recommendation to the people, that you might step down amicably from the throne?"

"In a word, yes... I want to end this accursed reign on a positive note. Let's enact a few more laws before I step down. Let's have the empress advocate these—notably improved rights for... for you and yours. And myself as well, I suppose. This cannot wait! The war could take years to end for all we know! If the people oppose us, Lord Val will protect us with her army. We will forge anew if need be!"

I glared at him in disbelief. "You ask too much. That sounds like a glorified fantasy out of a storybook."

"This is the only way I can find my place again."

"And what of me?" I snapped. "I've nothing without this council position. Nothing! You know better than anyone that I cannot return home to my brother! There *is* no place for us to go!"

"We will find one," insisted Xavier. "Lu, won't you trust me? This is what I want. It will work out. And if it does not, we have a backup plan. I have already stored an emergency stash of our things here, in the hatch behind the throne. Have a sense of adventure, will you? Besides, you aren't happy here, either!"

"It isn't a matter of happiness, Xavier. It is one of convenience. Of safety, security!"

"Listen to yourself, Lucrezia. You would send our people to die—Lord Val included—all for your own continued security? I have changed my mind! As should you." Xavier folded his arms, resolute, and turned away from me. "I shall write to Queen Beatrys and entreat her for peace talks. With the ambassador yet bed-ridden, I fear Her Majesty will not be amenable to me. If she chooses to be difficult, then I will dissolve the Crown as a final concession to her. That will be a last resort... for you."

How kind of him.

"I have made my decision," he went on. "This is final. You'll agree with me in due time."

Words weren't enough to express my exasperation with him. I left the throne room. As I returned to my office, I found the will to think over all that Xavier had said. Of course it was selfish to send countless soldiers to their deaths while I maintained my luxury here in the palace. Before, we hadn't considered that anyone *would* die. Val's soldiers had all manner of alchemical guns, advanced bows and arrows. I hadn't thought of risking anyone else's lives when Val's soldiers had the technological advantage, whatever they lacked in numbers.

I wanted to give Val and her soldiers the opportunity to prove themselves. To shove aside the harmful notions that women were meant to remain in the home. If I couldn't give this to them—to Val especially— what good was I for? I imagined the eventual private audience between her and Xavier as a tense one. She might have had the same initial reaction that I did.

My only hope now was that Queen Beatrys would respond favorably to Xavier's pleas for peace. Reconciling with the Kingdom of Tibor was the only way I might keep my power here in the palace.

I knew in my heart that this would not pass. Neither Xavier nor Beatrys wished to change their course. Powerless as I was, I had no choice but to accept it. I was nothing without my position here—even less without Xavier by my side.

Once I reached the solitude of my office, I stopped, looking around the room. The setting sun shining through the windows illuminated all that I'd held dear over the past four years, elevated as I'd been from my previous life in the kingdom. Part of me wished to war with them, to destroy the memories I had of my past.

If my brother was caught in the crossfire, I wouldn't have mourned his death.

But that wasn't wise of me to want.

Innocent people didn't deserve to die for my unresolved issues.

At the precipice of this edge of reason, I saw the future. I wanted to look away. It was impossible. I resigned myself to this truth, and retrieved a spare box from my storage space. I set about packing away some of my things—coveted books on astronomy, the social psychology that bred thaumaturgy in pure humans, and the magical languages from ancient times: Enochian, word of the Black Heavens, and Volenska, words to confound humans in purgatory. These I could not part with. They held within my claim to comfort, in my knowledge, in knowing that I could retreat to these pages if I needed to escape from life. I also put away most of the coin I had on hand—quite a sizable sum—and other essentials.

I decided to wait until much later to hide this with Xavier's stash in the throne room. I didn't want the guards spotting me. Waiting turned into several hours of searching through my books, full of nostalgia. I happened upon one of my astronomy tomes that mapped the constellations in the sky during each year of every day over the past century. I brought it with me to my chambers, sitting up in bed as I pored over it through the night.

A few of the pages were lost. I'd procured this tome secondhand from a peddler at the Lyceum. It had cost me thousands, despite the missing pages, but it was worth it. I once used these maps as a less superstitious form of astrology, reading divinations for the people I met. I realized then that I'd neglected to do this for Val. Her birthday this year had fallen just a few days before her audience with the Privy Council.

April 8th, 802 A.A.—After the Apocalypse.

Aries. Ambitious. Aggressive. Creative. Driven. Goal-oriented. She was meant for greater things in life.

I held a brief photogenick of her chart—a mental snapshot—and mapped it onto mine.

January 31st, 795 A.A.

Aquarius. Intelligent. Imaginative. Innovative. My quick thinking would help me solve the worst of my troubles.

Many of our personality traits overlapped, as I'd already imagined. I spent a long time matching the stars, drawing lines between the ones that were opposed; thinking about her.

I had Val's letter here. Every now and then, I smelled her cologne again, feeling my mind drift off to distant possibilities with her. I read her words over and over, noting every small detail in her handwriting. I wanted to bask in these inescapable thoughts of Val's beauty, her drive. I wanted to fantasize about how her lips might feel against mine. How she might feel underneath me—over me. This change in plans disrupted my longings. No longer did I feel I even had permission to think of her this way at all.

My heart grew heavy with anticipation over seeing her again tomorrow. If the end of this lifestyle of mine was indeed in my future, and I could do nothing to supply Val's army with the opportunities they needed, then this small pleasure was all I could have of her. I was of no use to her without my position here in the palace. Surely there was no reason for her to continue speaking to me in that case... I couldn't set aside how much that pained me.

***

Getting myself ready to see Val the next night was an unusual affair. I fussed over my hair and makeup far more than I had on any other occasion. I fumbled my clothes as I picked them out. I nearly stumbled when I put my heeled boots on. Keeping my hands still felt impossible. All I could think about was the inevitable that awaited. As sweet as Val's letter was, I imagined the words disappearing before my eyes as soon as she learned the truth about what was to come. And as I was about to leave my chambers, I nearly forgot my jacket. Even in springtime, Eden was far too cold. It was too much of a chore to maintain my heating spells all the time.

As I made my way down the halls to leave the Empyrean Palace, I passed Xavier by. I didn't, couldn't look him in the eye. He was with a group of the Privy Council, explaining half of the situation to them. Once he noticed me, he almost broke his neck to stop, turn around and catch up to me.

"Lu, I've sent the letter to Her Majesty," he said in a rush. "Express. A rush service across the Eidos Sea to Tenrose. It should reach her within the next week or so."

"Wonderful," I replied.

"I've not told the others about our last resort. This will stay between us. And Lord Val, should you choose to divulge as much to her."

"Yes, because I certainly *want* the one I adore to know that I'll soon be a vagabond."

Xavier stopped and watched me go, looking dejected as I left him behind.

"I'm sorry!" he called. "You know I care for you more than anything! This will all work out—trust me!"

Right now, I was much too pessimistic for his promises.

I took a private carriage to the area near the Charon Bridge. I used to enjoy walking about the city, taking in all the sights: the towering statues of the Holy Knights Thirteen of old who had once ruled over Eden; the sprawling series of arcades that lined our aqueducts; the sheer history behind the Grand Cathedral, the Lyceum; the Apocalypse Theater where my fellow sorceresses gathered in secret, expressing themselves through their seductive Black Waltz dance. Looking out at these locations from the window of my carriage wasn't the same. Yet as I was the emperor's adviser, and his approval levels were less than stellar these days, the people tended to also view me with disdain. I had to avoid any aggressive situations from ignorant strangers. I might have had to use my powers to defend myself. That would have been the surest way to end the life I had here.

When I arrived at the crosswalk that led to the bridge to Elysium, I stopped to stare out at the view. The bridge itself ran over the Styx River. The land underneath Eden proper should have been too weak to support an entire city of onyx and stone. Historians refused to admit that the old knights of the Excalibur used their powers as thaumaturges to secure the architecture here, given that the resources from living so close to a river were difficult to ignore. Down the incline of the bridge awaited the old city of Elysium, where Eden's homeless and outcasts lived under the empress' care.

From this angle, Elysium looked like a secondhand city deep under the earth, with a makeshift ceiling of wood. The expanse from Eden's surface was as a hole-bitten lake of wood that no one crossed for fear of drowning through the fall to the lower city. It used to be much warmer down below, almost like walking into the desert compared to the frosty weather above—and this was how we Eden citizens earned our monikers of scorpions, whenever we so decided to cross the bridge to lowtown. They were far more distrustful of us after the original imperial invasion that saw the end of Ser Videl's life. Ever since then, the empress could not leave her throne, trapped in mourning over her lover.

In the dark of night, I found Val already at the Charon Bridge. She had her back to me, staring off at the distant hinterlands over the horizon. I marveled over her uniform: military, professional and clean-cut as always. Though she was shorter than me with my heels, her fit frame, noble posture, and long hair down her back made her seem taller than she actually was. I caught myself wondering what her body looked like underneath her lord commander's garb. I didn't want her to know.

Other people milled about across the street on their way to their usual nighttime pubs—they turned to look at Val, at me approaching her. Gossip had spread outside the walls of the Empyrean Palace about us after a mere month of our time together. So long as they didn't bother us, they could stare as much as they liked.

Val heard my boots upon the pavement and turned around. "My lady," she said, bowing to me.

"Good evening, my lord," I replied. "Are you ready to set off?"

Unexpectedly, Val hesitated a moment. "I have something to give you first," she revealed. I blinked in surprise, watching as she pulled a few worn pages from her pocket. Those star charts... "A few days ago, I went to the Lyceum to read up on Elysium's history, censored as it was. I came across these. They seem to be from an astronomy book. You mentioned a few times that you enjoy astronomy... and you are a veritable scholar in your own right. I thought you'd like to have them."

This felt more romantic than if she'd given me flowers or chocolate. Especially with Val looking at me so—that concealed shyness about her. All efforts I made to hide my smile were for naught.

"I've been searching for these pages for years," I said, looking them over. "How serendipitous that you just so happened to find them now. Thank you, Val. I shall hold onto them." Still subdued, she was. It was difficult *not* to show her my gratitude in the way I wanted, deep down. "Is something else on your mind?"

Val waited until I pocketed the pages she gave me. When she held my hand in hers, I thought she might bend down to kiss me there. Instead, she pulled me toward her in the gentlest of ways. She inched her face closer to mine, to the side, with the soft swell of her lips along my jaw. I held her shoulders, the sharp smoothness of her military uniform. Val's nervous breaths lowered my guard even more. This intimacy surprised me as heat I'd never known before.

"I've missed you as well," she whispered in my ear. "I wanted to tell you in my letter. It seemed better to tell you in person. I'm glad I waited."

Ablaze in this sudden passion, my troubles lifted away. I felt her pause; felt her trying to feel me. Val's direct tenderness was as much a contradiction as her androgyny—one I couldn't resist. As soon as she sensed this through my silence, she moved just so, her lips soft against my skin; taking her time, down to my neck; I could hardly stay still.

She heard every effort I made to control myself. Somehow that spurred her more. Her grip around my waist, over the small of my back, tightened in her assurance.

"I do enjoy your company, Lucrezia," said Val. "Even if you hold back with me... I enjoy you very much."

People across the street stared with such nosiness. Only when I found my wits about me once more did I notice them.

"And I enjoy you," I replied in kind, easing her away. "But—this isn't a good time. We must… we must continue on to see the empress. She will be at her club now that she's finished her scheduled food donations. I'd like to get there before she decides to leave. Follow me."

Undeterred, Val gave me the most dashing smile. I had to walk in front of her to keep her from seeing my reaction. Down the Charon Bridge we went, with Val following close behind me. At the base of the bridge stood Elysium's guard, dressed as noble paladins—a bastion of Ser Videl's legacy. They allowed us to pass through without a word. Not until Val and I were some distance away did I hear them speak.

"More scorpions, huh," said one paladin. "Well, that's them dead if they walk down the wrong street."

"I recognize the lord commander," said another. "Seen her come through a few times. Heard the ladies she's taken in are in her army now."

"Oh, right. I remember now. My sister says she's doing great with those other soldiers of hers."

"Helps that she's the spitting image of Nyte. The lady chancellor's got Mistress Fury's same looks, too. Wonder whatever happened to those two…"

How curious. Nyte and Mistress Fury were both major players in Elysium's independence, some years before the first imperial invasion. Raj, the scorpion's empress, had been in a relationship with Nyte before meeting Ser Videl. As Mistress Fury was the original Empress of Elysium, she'd given her throne to Raj in exchange for Nyte's heart. The four of them had had their fates intertwined from the start.

Something told me it was no mere coincidence that Val and I looked like them. I made a mental note to search for visual records of them. I wanted to see the likeness for myself.

Within Elysium proper, traditional torches and fire beacons lit the streets from overhead. More paladins were stationed in the dark corners and alleyways, keeping watch over their people. This makeshift city of sprawling wooden buildings and moth-eaten curtains over windows felt more open than Eden, despite the ceiling above. Anyone could have entered anywhere, at any time. The citizens seemed to embrace this about their city. All throughout the dirty streets, I watched as people in ragged clothes walked together, from home to home, exchanging food and drink to have together as a community. They paid Val and me no mind, focused on the stories they told and the laughter they shared. Those who did notice us acknowledged Nyte and Mistress Fury in our faces; they left us alone.

I'd assumed that the citizens who lived here were miserable. Yet they all seemed much happier than Eden's people, who were all too concerned with money and religion. Our city could certainly learn something from them.

I heard the music blasting from the empress' club before I saw the building. This unusual industrial sound was unheard of in Eden—a clear sign of alchemists who had created special equipment and instruments to make such a unique sound. Slutgarden opened up to the outside without need of a formal structure. Countless dancers' tables with poles, bars, and private rooms filled the space, with a dance floor in the middle. The style of the space indeed reminded me of a garden with different places to roam freely…

The large mob of people filed into the entrance as they pleased. I thought Val and I would be able to follow suit. One of the guards at the front stopped me, leering with contempt.

"What do you scorpions want?" he asked.

"We're here to see the empress," I stated. "May we enter?"

"No. She don't wanna see no one. Get lost."

I bristled at his curtness.

Val stepped forward. "Lydia told me to pass on her regards," she said.

The guard turned his suspicions to her. "You know Lydia?"

"She is second-in-command in my family's private army. I am her commander."

"Oh... Lord Commander Val? Yeah, yeah, she mentioned you last time she was here! Head on in. Sorry!"

"Thank you, sir," replied Val. She placed her hand along the small of my back, leading me inside.

We entered through to the loud crowd of the club. "How convenient," I noted.

"Your power in Eden is useless down here," she reminded me. "Allow me to handle this, my lady."

And what a bitter reminder that was.

Val knew that something was wrong. She had enough foresight not to ask me about it. This thrumming loudness from the music and drunken people drilled at my mood, worsening it. All that helped was the feel of Val's hand on my lower back. I wished I were free to focus on her attentions. For a moment I wondered if Val really was turned off by my detachment. But she didn't mind. She stayed close to me; kept her body just behind me whenever we needed to file together to weave through the crowd. Her physical support against me quickened my heartbeat in anger and arousal both. We somehow felt like the only two in the building, just from the way Val's presence filled my senses.

One overpowered the other once I heard Val's rich voice in my ear again, "The empress should be on her throne—just over here." Val nodded toward the leftmost side of the dance area, filled with booths where couples sat together. "Lydia told me as much."

"I shall have to thank this second-in-command of yours. What is her full name?"

"Captain Lydia of Belmont, a small mining town far east from Nyx Mons. She fled her homeland to Eden after her family disowned her. Homophobes, the lot of them. She'd hoped to find a steady job at the foundry where Lee and Sebastian work, but the manager won't take women workers. She was forced to live here in Elysium instead until the two of us met. The empress got on with her quite well."

"You and your captain must also get along well, since you've entrusted her with such a high rank."

Val hummed, blunt and grumpy, leaving it at that. I smiled, finding such a small thing endearing.

There I saw the empress sitting upon her brass throne, elevated from the rest of the club. Reading so many detailed accounts of Raj's leadership and selflessness in books didn't compare to seeing her in person. She wore a dark, sleeveless shirt that showed her fit arms and her many bangles, exotic silk sarouel, and a pair of well-traveled sandals. Jaded, bored, she had her head propped along her fist, legs crossed as she stared off at the crowd with glassy eyes of emerald. Her brown skin soaked in every bit of light from the flames around the area; her dark hair running down her back shone with the same intensity.

Raj was a beautiful woman indeed who had experienced much hardship, stuck in this life after having died many years ago. As a ghost, stuck in the age she'd died she truly did appear as alive as everyone else. I sensed a foreign, dark energy around her. Raj was no thaumaturge or sorceress—that I could tell. This power came from outside of her, somewhere, surrounding her; keeping her soul and body trapped in this world. Whatever this was, it explained why she hadn't passed into the beyond after over two centuries.

She noticed us as Val and I approached. Recognition shone in her eyes, so surprised. Back and forth between Val and me she looked—in disbelief.

"Who the hell are you?" asked Raj, her loose accent very much Elysian.

Val bowed. "Valerie of Lysander, lord commander of my estate's private army," she answered. "And this is Lucrezia of Azrith, lady chancellor to His Imperial Majesty."

"We mean to speak with you, empress," I added. "If you've the time, of course."

Raj's surprise turned to curiosity. "Yeah, sure," she allowed. "I've heard of you. What d'you need?"

"It's a private matter," I stressed. "It concerns the state of the empire and the conflict it faces with the north. His Majesty would be grateful for your aid in dealing with this issue."

"Mmm, sounds important," said Raj, jumping down from her throne. "Let's head over this way."

Raj gestured for us to follow her. In the shadows of the crowd, a few paladins also stayed on our heels. We went down a set of winding wooden stairs, further underground and into a private, noise-protected den. Only the thrumming bass from the music above reached us here. Raj took her seat in a comfortable chair by the electric fireplace. She had us sit in the two similar chairs just across from her, while her paladins remained by the door.

"Want a drink?" she offered, pouring herself a glass of wine, bangles chiming.

"Please," I accepted.

"I don't drink," said Val. "Not if I can avoid it, anyway."

For some reason, Raj smiled at that. "I bet you don't," she replied, handing a glass to me. "So what brings you down here? Somethin' about His Majesty pissin' off Queen Beatrys up in the kingdom?"

"The emperor did not make the claim to Tibor's lands," I corrected. "That was the council's doing. They've since been dealt with."

"Right in their pockets, yeah."

I labored over how to word myself without giving away my unfortunate situation. "His Majesty means to apologize to his people for the misunderstanding. He has already written a letter to the queen, asking if she would be interested in peace talks. He and I would like to avoid a war with the north if possible."

"Sounds fair," agreed Raj. "So what d'you need me for?"

"His Majesty needs your help in mobilizing the people on his side. Your influence reaches far across Tynan—even those in Tibor respect you for your rule here. The emperor fears he'll not be successful if he alone were to ask the citizens to forgive him."

With a laugh, Raj said, "You really think the people'll listen to *me?*"

"The emperor is convinced they would."

"Yeah, maybe," she pondered. "What's plan B?"

"That is… still under wraps. All I can say is that Val's army would fight for us in some capacity. She has pledged her service to His Majesty and me both."

Val had her arms folded, looking skeptical. I knew I should have explained the situation to her beforehand. If I'd done that, I feared I would have told her more than I was comfortable with. She was sharp enough to read between the lines as to what I meant. If Xavier's plan failed, the people would revolt, and we would have to count on her soldiers to protect us.

Raj knew it, too. "I don't got a choice, do I?" she said. "If the queen calls for a war, everyone else 'round the empire's gonna boycott. They hate the emperor. They don't give a shit that it was the council that called for 'his land' up north and not him. If that war comes here, I'm gonna lose people. I don't need another battle here, lady chancellor."

"That's precisely why we need your help, empress. Although I'm curious as to what actually happened during the last war—the initial imperial invasion, that is."

"The fight fucked up the terrain, that's what. My people were pissed off over my scorpion gettin' killed… they didn't hold back. Then the oracles came 'round with their incantations and killed most of 'em. You know Eden used to be surrounded by a desert? Now there's a fucking mountain that's sprung outta nowhere, and it snows all the damn time up top if it ain't summer. They'll do worse than that if the kingdom comes by."

"Will you help, then?" I asked.

Raj rubbed the back of her shoulder, stressed all of a sudden. "Sure, all right," she agreed. "I'll pay your emperor a visit. When's he want me to drop by? If he even thinks about comin' down here, my people won't be happy. I've gotta figure out a way to explain this to them. Let's keep this quiet for now, yeah?"

"In all honesty, we didn't believe you'd accept so soon. I'll have to confer with His Majesty first. Will it be safe to send you a missive to your headquarters at Vassago?"

"That'll work," said Raj. She looked to Val, brow raised. "You've been real quiet, lord commander. What's eatin' you?"

"Just absorbing the implications of this plan B," replied Val. "And—the last battle you spoke of. No normal human beings could possibly pull off such a feat."

Raj nodded. "That's 'cause they weren't humans," she said. "Not really, anyway."

Val seemed to already know the answer to her question. "Then what were they?"

"Thaumaturges. Sorceresses. Down here in my city, we talk about these things. We don't whitewash history. Hell, I was there myself to see it with my own eyes. Can't argue with that."

Raj folded her arms, waiting for Val to inevitably argue with her.

Hiding this ailed me. This, about myself, what I was. For the first time, I felt dishonest for not telling Val about my identity. I hadn't felt this way with others before her. Nor had I felt this sheer dread that she would dismiss me and mine altogether. I hid my anxieties while I awaited her answer.

"I'm not a blind fool who believes what everyone else says about magic," replied Val.

Hearing her say that... it made me believe I could tell her. I could tell her, and she wouldn't run from me. Or worse.

"Good to hear," said Raj. "Looks like we'll be workin' together from here on out. At least until this problem's dealt with. Besides, you look like someone I used to know... both of you. Sittin' here's like a blast from the past."

"Nyte and Mistress Fury, you mean?"

Raj had a distant look in her eyes. "Yeah, them..." She drank the last of her wine, lips curled in distress. "Let's save that talk for another time. I've gotta head back up; make sure no one's fucking around." The three of us stood in unison, heading for the door. "You two should get outta here for now. The way you're dressed, it's obvious you're from Eden. Only reason you ain't been mugged yet is 'cause most everyone recognizes your faces. Some of my paladins'll see you back to the bridge. I'll be in touch."

Chapter Five

Stealth
(Val)

After we left Elysium, Lucrezia was in a hurry to return to the palace. I wanted to ask her out with me, as it was yet midnight and we were both wide awake. But during the carriage ride back to the palace grounds, she only spoke of this issue with Emperor Xavier and Queen Beatrys. I couldn't get a word in. I had a feeling she did this on purpose. She didn't want me to ask questions, to comment. To find out why she hadn't told me ahead of time about these plans of hers.

No. Lucrezia insisted this was a terrible time for chit-chat. She had no time for idle conversation. No time for anything other than attending to the emperor's needs.

The stress over her shoulders was obvious to me. Too obvious. That was all that kept me from pressing her about her strange behavior.

I exited the carriage first, offering my hand to her. Lucrezia stepped down to the paved walkway. I could but cherish this feeling of her hand in mine for a brief moment. During the walk to the palace, she continued on about the implications of the emperor's wishes, what still needed to be done, and so on and so forth. I didn't mind her venting at all. What unsettled me was that she clearly wished to ignore these feelings between us in favor of the crises on her desk.

Lucrezia was the emperor's top aide. She should have been used to dealing with these things.

"If the queen doesn't respond favorably," she ranted, "We'll have to think of some other way to calm her down. I may have to visit Tibor's capital as a replacement to the ambassador. He is ill with the common plague and will be bed-ridden for months…"

I tuned out once I realized she'd repeated herself for the third time.

It would have been so much simpler to get to the point with her. I glanced at Lucrezia as she spoke, to at least pretend like I heard her. I held my breath to keep this tension inside. She was so beautiful; her mind was sharp and her heart was sharper. I wanted her. I'd wanted her in *some* way for ages. I wanted to know how much she needed to be in control; if it was only in her everyday life, or if she couldn't stand to have that control wrested away from her in bed as well. Leading Lucrezia through the empress' club earlier, with my hand on the small of her back—I'd felt magnetized to her. That feeling had carried through whatever doubts I'd had about the emperor's plans for Tynan and Tibor.

My naïve disrespect for her was all that had made me resist this before. Now that that was out of the way, I thought about her like this almost all the time without stopping myself.

I could have fucked her problems away, and Lucrezia would have been better for it by the morning. Again, no—I predicted she would have stiffened at my attempts to seduce her. She'd ignored my affections thus far that night. I worried that she would have turned me down if I asked her outright.

Her clothes held her body so well. It was so easy to imagine her underneath me—

"Are you listening?" snapped Lucrezia.

"Yes," I lied.

She was too stressed even to catch such a poor lie. "Thank you," she said. "And—I'm sorry if I seem agitated. I admit I've not told anyone how I feel about all this. It's festered inside of me for the past few days. This isn't like me at all."

"I've noticed."

Lucrezia sighed as we stopped just outside the Empyrean Palace. "This will be a busy week for me," she went on. "I must prepare the emperor for Raj's visit. We'll speak again soon, my lord…"

That wasn't enough. That wasn't a proper goodbye.

This knee-jerk reaction made me follow after the sounds of her heels clicking up the palace halls.

"Lucrezia!" I called, catching up to her.

Surprised, she stopped and turned around. I grabbed her wrist, spinning her momentum; shoving her against the nearest wall of onyx. Winded and aroused, Lucrezia let out a sharp breath. She saw it in my eyes—how serious I was about her, about this. I didn't want her issues, or mine, to get in the way of our feelings. I saw all the regrets in hers, wrapped in bright hazel, bright as the sun with a verdant filter. I gripped her slender waist, holding her closer to me.

"Val," she breathed over my lips, voice trembling. "What are you doing…?"

I made my intentions known: clawing my hands up the curve of her back, disarming her more. Having her this close to me was unbearable. I tasted her lips, once, savoring the sweetness there, staring at her. Every tremor from her neck passed through to my mouth and down through me. By the stillness of Lucrezia's chest against mine, she'd stopped breathing. I breathed into her instead, my nails tangled through the silken tresses of her brown hair, natural blonde highlights shimmering.

Something in her kiss told me that she'd never allowed anything like this before. This novelty for her—for me—sharpened my senses, filling them with her. Lucrezia pulled away. I watched the heat trickle across her face, blooming as the rose she was to me.

"You're incredibly beautiful," I told her. "You know that, don't you?"

Lucrezia looked away, eyes darting all down the hall. "People are staring…"

These threads of fate stitched a novel feeling within. For the weeks I'd known Lucrezia in this way, all I could do was wonder as to this softer side of her. No matter how she dressed or held herself at court, I knew, deep down, that she wanted to relax; to take off her mask and be herself with me. She was more open now… at least in this moment. This look in her eyes; the way she held me—I was bound to her.

"I don't care."

"Val, you *must* care."

I smirked, asking, "Why, because of your reputation?"

Seeing that small smile of hers in response put the midnight sun right in my heart. "And yours," said Lucrezia, pushing me playfully. "I won't be another notch on your bedpost. I don't plan on making you one for mine, either."

"That's the last thing I want," I promised.

Lucrezia switched our places without me realizing. "Is it, now?" she wondered. "Well, either way, you must wait. Or is that too much for you to handle?"

"I've waited this long, haven't I?"

"Courting me isn't the same as waiting," she pointed out.

"Yes, but—that isn't what I meant," I explained.

Sudden aggression from Lucrezia caught me off guard—she pinned me harder against the wall, drawing out the same fear in me that I'd taken from her earlier. All those tall tales of her sadism came true in the way she regarded me. Eyes hard with want, Lucrezia studied me. She clamped my jaw in her hand, sharp nails digging into my skin. This web of skin between her thumb and index finger stitched my mouth shut.

"You will do as I say, Val," she hissed. "You will wait until a better time. Do you understand me?"

She moved her hand just enough for me to whisper, "Yes…"

"Repeat what I said."

Too many chills passed through me at once. "I'll do as you say, Lucrezia… I'll wait until a better time."

"Good," she said, removing herself from me. The look in my eyes made it plain that I didn't wish for her to go just yet—at all. "What is it?"

"May I write to you…? During these days you will be busy."

Lucrezia touched my face. "You may," she allowed. She gave me one last kiss, softness deceiving. "Good night, my lord."

I bowed to her. "Good night, my lady…"

Watching her walk away from me again, I wanted so badly to defy her. I grabbed the cuffs she'd chained to me, hidden here underneath the sleeve of my uniform. This emotion in my heart for her grew with every step she took. Not because she ignored some of my affections. Not because I believed I couldn't have her completely. Certainly not because I felt unworthy of her.

There was nothing I could do to help ease her sorrows. Nothing—except wait. Wait for this secondary plan—one that seemed inevitable, at least to Lucrezia—and pull it off as she needed me to.

***

These days passed in a blur of heated restlessness. I lay in bed for hours at a time, trapped in my thoughts, in my feelings. I had no appetite. Whatever desire I had to eat blended as a need to be between Lucrezia's legs. Mentally, I was there, far-removed from my bedroom, from the guests my family had over at our estate, from Father scolding my twin brother Yosef over skiving off his legal studies, from Gabrielle knocking on my door every so often to check on me.

Trying to sleep was pointless. I stayed wide awake during these nights, stuck in this long, drawn-out fantasy I had of Lucrezia summoning me to her chambers. This pent-up energy I had could go nowhere for as long as she made me wait. Instead of decaying, this energy only grew, and soared, warping my priorities. Some of my troops had come by, asking me to spend time with them. I was in no state to go anywhere; I ignored their calls.

On the third day, I sat at my desk, resting my head upon the surface. This unfinished letter to Lucrezia was right under my face, filling my nose with the brittle smell of parchment. Several discarded letters filled the space over the surface. I couldn't decide how to begin.

I want you.

Lucrezia, I think I'm falling for you. I have been for a while. I wasn't sure how to tell you.

I'm not used to relationships. But I want one with you. Only with you. Would you say yes if I asked?

I still find you impeccable, no matter your imperfections. As odd as this sounds… I would follow you to the ends of Tellus and back, even if your cause was in vain. The last time I managed to sleep, I had a dream about following you through the Empyrean Palace during a ball. I assume the emperor will continue the tradition of his annual birthday party at court this June. It is only two weeks away… Will you be my date that evening?

I decided on a variant of the last one, writing more from there. I also asked Lucrezia to join me for a night out tomorrow—if she was available. My soldiers had again asked me to spend time with them. I figured this was a good time to introduce Lucrezia to them. Yet by the time I finished the letter, I couldn't find the will to send it off. This one was far more personal than the last. I feared my sentiments would have been lost upon Lucrezia, as preoccupied as she was with political matters at the palace.

All I could do was resume resting my head upon the desk, stricken by my uncharacteristic indecisiveness.

A gentle knock sounded at my door. "Val?" called Gabrielle from the other side. "Val, you've not eaten since yesterday. Unlock the door, please." It was already unlocked, as she soon discovered. She entered, closing the door behind her. Not a moment later, I felt her long nails running softly through my hair. "Sweetheart, what's wrong? What's the matter?"

"I'm not sure where to begin," I explained, my voice muffled against the desk.

Gabrielle picked up on it right away. "Oh!" she said, sitting upon the bed. "It's the lady chancellor, isn't it? I asked you weeks ago and you ignored me. I was right, wasn't I?"

"Possibly, maybe…"

She laughed. "This is new for you."

"I know," I agreed. "I'd rather not discuss it. Not until I have a better idea of what's going on."

"Mmm, if you insist."

I regarded her thoughtfully. "Gabby, I've been meaning to ask you something."

With a bright smile, she asked, "What is it?"

"Are you happy with my brother?"

That brightness dimmed. Gabrielle paused, thinking over her answer. "I'm not."

"Then why do you stay with him? You could leave; return home to Eidos, to your father there. Living in a baron's castle on a luxurious island must be more bearable than dealing with my brother's skittishness."

"I'd never leave you, Val," she said, averting her eyes.

"Gabby, I'm not your husband," I insisted. "Yosef is. If he's too busy messing about instead of giving you what you need, then he doesn't deserve you as his wife."

"And the simple fact is that you need me more than he does," she replied with finality. Gabrielle stood anew, holding her hand out. "Come along. I've made dinner for us. I can have your letter sent off while you wash up."

I handed the sealed envelope to her. "Thank you—for everything."

Gabrielle kissed my forehead. "You don't have to thank me. This is what I'm here for."

As luck would have it, we passed Yosef by in the hall. "Good evening!" he greeted loudly. Gabrielle ignored him. Yosef stopped, watching her go with a frown. "Well hello to you, too, beloved!"

"Yosef," I warned.

"What?" he asked, clueless.

"You have no idea?"

"No," he said. "What's her problem?! She never fucking talks to me unless it's about *you*."

"If you don't ask her yourself, you won't ever find out."

Yosef laughed it off. "Yeah, yeah, you say that. What the hell's it mean?"

"You've grown complacent, that's what it means."

"If she's got a problem, she can tell me herself! Gabrielle's a grown woman. This damn silent treatment, passive-aggressive nonsense, is for children. I won't confront her if *she's* the one with the issue!"

"Then she might disappear one day," I said, leaving him behind. "If she does that, I'll not forgive you."

He had nothing to say. Regardless of Gabrielle's promise to me, I would have urged her to return home in the worst-case scenario. Though my father cared for me more than anything, he was often gone because of his work. We didn't have a close relationship. Gabrielle remained my one support system I could count on. I believed that I could rely on Lucrezia, one day, for more than the time we spent with one another. Only if she trusted me as well.

***

I wished I'd told my troops that I wanted them to meet Lucrezia someplace else. It had slipped my mind.

This version of Nirvana here in Eden was a continuation of the famous brothel that had kept Elysium rich in coin for decades. I'd heard that much of these new funds still tunneled down to the empress, supporting her people. The entire west wing was devoted to working women who preferred other women or passing men as their clients. It was much more civilized compared to the east wing—even maintained better by the owners, enough to pass as a regular place to have a night out. The building of warm mahogany remained hidden in the Maleficus district, not too far from our usual drinking hall. Lights throughout the area burned crimson, shrouding the polished walls and exotic furniture with a distinct, erotic glow.

On the lower level, the workers ran the bar and restaurant that stayed open until two in the morning. All of their activities with clients stayed behind closed doors, upstairs. Despite how nice the place was, I wondered if Lucrezia took offense to meeting at a brothel of all places. She hadn't expressed as much in her return letter to me. That didn't stop me from considering the idea.

As we were to meet at the bar, I stood near the packed area with Sebastian and Lee, keeping an eye out for her arrival. A few women had caught their attention; Sebastian flirted openly with them, while Lee was subtler with his conversation. My second-in-command was also due to arrive at any moment... I pulled out the letter Lucrezia had sent to me in reply earlier that day, reading it over.

Val,

Yes, I would love to meet you tomorrow evening. I would also enjoy meeting a few of your comrades. Though this Nirvana location sounds foreign to me. I don't frequent the Maleficus area in the city. As you've assured me the brothel has a selection of drinks, I shall treat it as a normal setting. I will need a glass of wine or two after these past few days I've had. Let us meet at the bar at nine o'clock.

As for the emperor's birthday at the start of June, he does indeed plan to hold his annual ball here at court. I hope you know what this means, asking me to be your date. I've never taken a formal date with me for this occasion. We will be the talk of all of Tynan if we do this. Not that we aren't already. If you are serious with your request, then ask me again when I see you. I will have my answer ready.

Thinking of you, always,

Lucrezia

No matter how many times I read this over, it left me wanting. The smell of Lucrezia's perfume across the page was stuck in my senses. It so reminded me of kissing her the other day, being that close to her. Since I met her, I'd never dreamed of feeling this way for her. It was far beyond mere physical attraction. My hands felt empty without hers in mine. My presence in this building, at home, out on the field with my troops—anywhere—felt incomplete without her next to me. I wanted to be her gentleman; to treat Lucrezia with the respect she deserved.

I grit my teeth and held my breath. This sexual tension inside of me had nowhere to go. Pacing around did no good. I kept looking to the bar, hoping to see Lucrezia there already.

"Lord Commander Valerie!"

That brazen, feminine voice. I saw dirty blonde hair in my periphery, light blue eyes and tan skin—

She shoved Lee aside. "Hey!" he blurted. "Could you say *excuse me?!*"

"I'm excused now, aren't I?" said Lydia with a scoff.

Sebastian laughed. "Such a lady, this one," he teased.

"That's enough, lieutenant," ordered Lydia. "Val, where have you been? I've not seen you in ages! Then all of a sudden I get word that we're to meet your lover, and that's the only reason you've come out?!"

I sighed. "Hello to you, too, captain."

"Yes, yes, hello! That's something I've not said to you in over two weeks!"

"It isn't my fault you've missed training all this time," I insisted. "You complain to me that I've not gone out for drinks at your beck and call, yet you ignored my orders to meet in the field. Such a hypocrite."

"As are you for only having a night with us when your dear lady chancellor wishes it!"

Brash wasn't enough to begin to describe my second-in-command. Lydia and I had known one another for almost a decade now. I met her not long after she'd escaped her small hometown of Belmont, back when she relied on the empress' charity services in Elysium to get by, along with countless other women and young girls. That was what originally gave me the idea to unite us under my family's banner. Because Lydia had been with me from the beginning—and our soldiers respected her during training—it made sense to entrust her with such a rank.

Despite our frequent personality clashes, I also respected her steadfast resolve. And it was *because* of those disagreements that I preferred not to see her around in these more casual settings. She was the only one in this world who riled me up without trying.

Lydia's favorite way of annoying me involved debating with me about thaumaturges and sorceresses. I would tell her that they were no different than the rest of us, and that they deserved kindness. Each time, she would call me a witch sympathizer, a heretic—as if she truly meant it. Her religious fervor caused this. Something about how God had saved her from her fate before meeting me. I had no need for God, as She had done nothing for me that I could not have accomplished on my own. Lydia debated me on that, too. Yet she didn't mind at all that we employed alchemists—actual heretics—in our army.

Hypocrite.

Lydia placed her hands upon her hips, vindicated by my silence. "Conceded to me now, have you?" she guessed. "Well, since you're here, why don't we have a drink? I'll pay."

"Really?" asked Sebastian. "You'd do that for us?"

"Not you! Val!"

Lee rolled his eyes. "Should've known."

"I'm touched, really," I said. "But you know I don't drink, Lydia."

Sebastian and Lee both grinned. They knew I only drank with them whenever they begged me to.

Lydia groaned. "Then *why* are we near the bar?!" she asked.

"This is where Lucrezia wishes to meet. She enjoys her share of fine wine. Nirvana has plenty of it."

"Gods, she must be something else. If she can get *you* away from your usual affairs, then I must meet this Lucrezia of Azrith. I should like to hear that uppity northern accent of hers myself. Curious how she's got one of those, though. I could've sworn Azrith was a poor farmer's town miles from Tenrose."

A farmer's town? My knowledge of the kingdom's geography failed me. Lydia was more traveled than I, having spent a great deal of time on the road after leaving her hometown. I'd hardly left the city, if only to travel with Gabrielle across the main continent to visit her hometown of Eidos along the archipelago to the northwest. Indeed, by Lucrezia's 'uppity' northern accent, I'd assumed that Azrith was a highborn city like Eden was.

Such a small detail reminded me that I hadn't had the chance to ask Lucrezia much about her childhood, her family. She was cagey about her past. Likely for good reason. Any attempt I'd made to discuss it resulted in her changing the subject. Maybe tonight would be different.

"Mind you, my usual affairs brought us together to begin with," I said to Lydia. "You and I, that is."

She gave me a sweet smile. "As if I could ever forget that."

"Makin' eyes at the commander, now, are you?" noticed Lee, brow raised.

"*Please*," said Lydia, pushing him lightly. "She's made it clear that there's no fraternization allowed. Not with us officers, anyway. Besides, I wouldn't want the lady chancellor after me. Word is she's a sorceress-in-hiding. A sorceress! Don't you care, Val? What if I look at you the wrong way while she's around? Will she flay me alive?"

"You ask too many useless questions," I told her, searching about.

Was Lucrezia a sorceress, really? Her interests in books and the arcane were coincidental in this case. I recalled her muted anticipation the other night while Raj had discussed the thaumaturges in Elysium. If such a rumor was true, that might have explained Lucrezia's perfectionist personality... she didn't want anyone to perceive her as suspicious, as less-than.

Her occasional detachment with me was also cause for concern. At times—like now—I thought that I felt too much for her. That my affections for her far outweighed hers for me, and that I should curb these, lest I turned her off. This bile of guilt in me was almost as strong as how much I wanted her. Anyone else would have been too intimidated by this and run off by now.

When I saw Lucrezia on the other side of the bar, sitting upon a stool, surrounded by drunken people too oblivious to her beauty, I felt my concerns lifted from me. Lydia again courted my attention; I moved her aside and went to Lucrezia, ignoring the complaints my captain hurled in my wake.

Lucrezia's mood hadn't improved from the last time we saw one another. She argued with the hostess as to the specific year of wine she wanted. I smiled. She was never one to hold back her anger, no matter how 'unladylike' someone else may have found her. It only made me that more determined not to incite her ire; to please her. An accomplishment—one to be proud of.

"I don't *care* how expensive it is!" chided Lucrezia. "I want the bottle of 683 Valdivia. *If* you wouldn't mind. I have the means to pay for it."

"Yeah?" said the hostess. "Well I ain't never seen you in here before. Who's to say your coin's real?"

I leaned over the bar, right next to Lucrezia's shoulder. I found her body heat intoxicating as always. "Here," I told the hostess, handing her the coin. "I assure you, this isn't counterfeit. It is Lysander money, tested and true. You'll have to forgive my charming lady for her mood. She's had a rough week."

"Mmm, sure thing, lord commander," replied the hostess, pouring Lucrezia's glass at last.

Lucrezia turned to me with an amused smile. "*Your* charming lady?" she echoed.

"Yes," I answered, whispering the tail-end of the word along her lips. "I've missed you, Lucrezia."

Her sharp nails clinked against the wine glass as she reached up to hold my neck. "Thank you for handling that," she said, just over my mouth. "Such a smart look you pull off, my lord. I appreciate how immaculately you dress for me. You smell wonderful. I've missed you as well." Lucrezia pushed me away by my jaw in good-humor. "Now what's this about me being yours, hm?"

"But a minor slip of the tongue, darling," I evaded.

"Hmm, was it, really?"

This sheepishness about me gave away my plans. "I suppose not," I allowed. Lucrezia smiled, rich with delight. "As much as I want you as my date to the emperor's ball…

I need you by my side. In more ways than one. These days without you were more difficult than the last."

"How unexpected…"

"Did you think that all I wanted was sex?"

Lucrezia laughed softly. "Perhaps I did," she revealed. "Your reputation precedes you, as we discussed."

"You are not like the others," I assured her.

"Oh? How am I not?"

Lucrezia was determined to make this as challenging as possible for me. She *knew* my soldiers stared.

I clenched my jaw in embarrassment, searching for the right words. "You are far more to me than anyone I've known like this… I don't wish to lose you to my pride, Lucrezia. I want you—exclusively."

Thoughtful, Lucrezia hummed, thinking her answer over. "We will see how things go over the next few weeks," she allowed. "If this time goes well, then I will certainly consider your offer. Although I'm curious as to what it is about me that's inspired this sincerity in you."

"You should very well know already," I said. "Fishing for compliments again?"

"I'm quite the angler," responded Lucrezia.

I laughed at the pun. "Are you, now?"

"Indeed. Back in Tenrose, the emperor and I enjoyed ice fishing in the winter. Those were simpler days."

"You can't be serious."

Lucrezia smiled anew. "Oh, I am. It was dreadfully boring, but his company made it entertaining."

"Then tell me more about your childhood in the kingdom," I requested. "I've noticed that you tend to avoid that subject for the most part. At least until now."

"Mmm, yes, I *have* avoided it," was all she said.

I was about to pry again until Lydia came barging through, with Lee and Sebastian in tow. "Lady chancellor, how good to meet you!" she greeted. "Val's only had the greatest things to say about you. Then again, I've had to hear all this second-hand. She's not been around to tell me herself!"

Lucrezia took cruel enjoyment out of my annoyance. "And you are…?" she asked, polite as ever.

"Lydia of Belmont, my lady. I'm the lord commander's second-in-command and captain of our fair Lysander army. This here's Lieutenant Sebastian of Svärd and Lieutenant Lee of Valdivia."

Lee bowed his head. "Lady chancellor," he said.

Sebastian gave her a hearty salute. "Pleasure to meet you!"

"The pleasure is all mine," replied Lucrezia, smiling in kind. "Val has also mentioned the three of you."

Lee narrowed his eyes, wary. "How *much* did she mention?"

I knew why he asked that. Lydia and Sebastian seemed baffled by the question.

"Cursory details, old friend," I assured him.

"Fair enough."

"If I remember correctly, captain," continued Lucrezia, "Your name saved us quite a bit of trouble in Elysium. I must thank you for your many connections."

"No need to thank me," replied Lydia, modest for once. "I just thank God that I'm out of that hell-hole. Loved living under the empress' care and all, but she's got too many to look after. Felt like a burden."

"You're religious?"

"I am! I make sure to pray to God every day for my blessings. Why's that surprising?"

Lucrezia gestured to the three of them at once, saying, "Your band of soldiers is nothing but the norm."

"Borderline heretical," noted Lee.

"Pretty sure it *is*," said Sebastian.

Curious, Lucrezia asked, "In what ways?"

Lydia was about to say the words. She paused and frowned, almost as if questioning her own hypocrisy. "... I've no idea," she lied. "No idea what you two are on about." She locked eyes with a working woman on the other side of the room. "If you'll excuse me..." I kept my eye on her speaking with the woman, watching them head upstairs together.

Lucrezia stared after them as they went. "Did I miss something?"

"Don't worry about her," said Lee. "The captain's a fucking nutcase sometimes."

"Your comradery cannot be denied in any case."

"Sure can't. All the troops respect Lydia as much as Val. Those two built our army from the ground up."

By her easy smile, Lucrezia took a liking to Lee's level-headedness. "How exactly do you procure your weapons for training?" she asked. Such an innocent question made Sebastian frown, wrought with nerves. "The emperor and I are aware that your regiment is highly advanced—but that is all we know. We've no details. If you'd rather not share, I understand."

"We have our arms crafted individually," replied Lee. "Some of our troops have got disabilities. Visual impairments from old diseases. Physical injuries that ain't healed from abuse they suffered from their families. Makin' each gun for each soldier gives her a specialty."

Lucrezia looked me over. "And does your commander have a special weapon?"

"Yeah, Sebastian and me made one of Val's guns. She's got asthma. Whenever we see a real battle, Val can't be on the frontlines runnin' about, even though she's our leader. Decided to make her a glass cannon, which specializes in stealth instead. She can spot trouble from a mile away."

"How fascinating," said Lucrezia. "I wonder—how did you go about making this weapon for her?"

Sebastian pulled Lee along, cutting off his response. "We'll follow the captain's cue and leave you two alone now," he offered. "Have a great night!"

Lucrezia watched them go, confused. "What an odd fellow, that Lieutenant Sebastian," she noticed. "Does he normally interrupt conversations in such a way?"

"Not really," I answered. He wasn't sure how Lucrezia would respond to their identities as alchemists...

"Your captain is also rather strange. Friendly, sociable. But strange."

"Lydia is as much a mystery to me as she is an annoyance," I said, hoping she would drop the subject.

"Val."

Lucrezia wasn't pleased. Her disapproval made my stomach drop.

"Yes...?"

"Honestly," she soured. "If there is anything I ought to know, I wish you would just tell me."

I thought it over for a moment. If I wanted Lucrezia to be more open with me, then I had to do the same with her. "Some of my soldiers are alchemists. They have the power to imbue our weapons with technological magicks that are unheard of outside of our group."

"I figured that out already," replied Lucrezia.

"How?"

"Your sniper rifle is one of unique make. I've never seen anything like it. No normal person made that."

"And when did you see my rifle up close?" I asked, suspicious. "Have you read my mind or something?"

Lucrezia opened her mouth to speak, only to close it again. She hummed to herself and went back to her wine. *Had* she read my mind? I recalled the night of the fire, when Lucrezia was in my cell with me in the gallows. I'd felt a strange sensation—as if she'd been in my mind with me, observing my thoughts...

I looked down at my cuffs again. Her name was there...

I sat down next to Lucrezia, watching her drink without a word. She wouldn't make eye contact with me. I considered asking her outright if she was a sorceress. That seemed tactless. If she hadn't told me by now, then she was determined to keep it a secret. Yet she had to have known that I would have understood, that I wouldn't judge her.

I had to think of a way to broach the subject with care.

"Lucrezia, what *was* your childhood like?" I asked. "Back in Tenrose, in Tibor's capital. Everyone in the palace knows of my background... Yours is more of a mystery. I imagine you had many enjoyable years growing up with the emperor. What about your family?"

"I am an orphan. I only have a younger brother. Gustavo of Azrith. My parents abandoned us when I was nine years old. I had to care for Gustavo on my own. Homeless and starving, we stumbled upon a kind woman's home. She was the emperor's mother. That was how he and I came to be childhood friends..."

Try as she might to conceal her pain, I heard it in her voice. This was a difficult subject for her.

"How much younger is your brother?"

"Five years," she answered.

"Did the two of you get along well?"

Lucrezia moved her wine glass to me. The bottle was closest to my side. I poured her another serving.

"We did not," she said, and drank more. "Our relationship was fine when he was a child. After that..." She glanced at me, noticing my quieted respect for her space; my interest in her past. Lucrezia ran her hand down my face, my neck. "You're not to tell this to anyone. Only Emperor Xavier knows. And my brother, of course." She had my silent swear. "Gustavo was very cruel to me. As with my interest in women, so went the superstitious belief that I was infertile—or a sorceress. He and his friends teased me relentlessly because of it. I've not spoken to him properly since I left the kingdom for Eden."

"How did they tease you?"

"His friends made aggressive passes at me, all the while betting to see who could rape me first. Those memories have kept me from letting go in my relationships. Other than with you... I don't remember the last time anyone made me feel vulnerable. Or if they did, I didn't allow it to continue." She was thirty-two years old. She had never been married. Her age and experience spoke to the lengths she'd gone to keep her pride. "And now I must ask something of you."

"All right," I agreed.

"Are you a pervert?"

Her matter-of-fact tone and the sharpness in her eyes gave away her meaning.

I had no need to think it over. "Yes."

Lucrezia smiled, satisfied. "We shall see about that."

This seemed like the perfect time to ask. The only time to ask.

I couldn't do it. If I was right, and she grew defensive and didn't want to tell me, Lucrezia might have stormed off in a rage. If I was wrong, the same thing might have happened anyway. Too distracted by her drink to notice my indecision, Lucrezia stared at the many alcohol bottles lining the wall nearby. I wanted to do something to lift her spirits—not tear them down with more prying.

I had my answer at any rate. After this whole time, during her conversation with my troops, with me, and now our silence, Lucrezia had drank the entire bottle of wine. She wasn't as tipsy as she should have been.

Perhaps she'd be open to doing something different tonight.

"Why don't we go upstairs?" I suggested.

"Upstairs? What for?"

"There's fun to be had. I know which room Lydia's gone to. We can spy on her."

With a laugh, Lucrezia said, "You are a pervert, indeed."

I smiled and held her hand. "Come on."

But minor protests from her, and she soon followed after me. I guided Lucrezia through the drunken crowd. We weren't allowed upstairs without an escort or an appointment. I had to get us over to the winding stairwell while the other working women were yet preoccupied.

Here some of Lucrezia's tipsiness showed, with her occasional giggles and the slight sway in her steps. She almost stumbled over me when I stopped near the stairs. Lucrezia stayed just behind me, her front pressed against my back as she laughed once more, freer this time. I pursed my lips to keep from catching her infectious amusement, lest we attracted too much attention.

"We must be silent," I whispered to her, glancing up the stairs. "Can you handle that?"

Lucrezia wrapped her arms about my shoulders. "Mmm, yes," she said. "I'll need you to support me... My heels may be a problem on these wooden steps."

I held her waist close, almost carrying her weight up the stairs. Lucrezia muffled her girlish glee against me, doing her best to stay quiet. It took everything in me not to laugh any louder than this. I suspected if she weren't drunk, she wouldn't have agreed to this little excursion.

By the time we reached the second landing, we heard loud and clear the sounds of creaking beds, moaning, and whipping coming from the rooms. Varied sexual conversation filtered through the walls, through the peepholes visible only to those who knew where to look. Lucrezia let a laugh slip, just in my ear. I worked harder not to make a sound as I led the way down the hall to Lydia's usual room. When we arrived, I smoothed my fingertips over the wood to find the peepholes. I found them with ease. Holding Lucrezia up for her to look through hers— while I looked through mine—was the difficult part.

It was worth it.

Lydia was there in my view, obscured through this narrow looking-glass of wood. She'd stripped down to her trousers, kissing the long-haired, dark-skinned woman in her arms. In a swift motion, Lydia lifted her woman in her arms and threw her down to the bed. She took off her trousers then, giving us a full view of everything from this angle.

"Do you see them?" I whispered.

"Oh yes," said Lucrezia, riveted. "I must say, Captain Lydia is quite practiced. Have you any first-hand experience with her?"

"What? No... She's not my type."

Lucrezia laughed quietly as Lydia moved down between the woman's legs. "There's no need to be defensive," she cautioned. "That makes me wonder what your type really is. And don't say *me*. I've heard that line one time too many."

"I enjoy women who don't seek to push my buttons with everything they do."

"Hmm, and which buttons are those?" she asked, drumming her long nails along my shoulder.

"My religious beliefs... or lack thereof."

Lucrezia noted the irony there. "And here is your captain, an unmarried woman, pleasuring another before marriage. I certainly see why you have grown bored of her duplicity."

The words came out without my say-so— "Not to mention she desperately despises thaumaturges and sorceresses for no good reason... other than because the *Hallows* tells her to. Whenever she argues with me about them, I tell her that they deserve to be treated just like anyone else. That is what we fight for as an army, as women and passing men. I won't exclude anyone from their due rights. We have *alchemists* in our group, for God's sake…"

Lucrezia pulled away from the wall, looking up at me in sincere surprise. I vaguely kept my eyes to the goings-on inside. I couldn't look at Lucrezia just yet. If I did, I would've asked her outright. Or I would have given away that I knew. Still, it didn't feel right. As long as she knew how I felt… that was enough for now. She would tell me on her own if—when—she was ready.

"Hey! You there! Are you spying?!"

The brothel's madam spotted us from down the hall. She stormed toward us.

"Shit," I muttered.

Lucrezia groaned. "Oh… Oh, God, not this. Not now."

I grabbed her hand, taking off in the opposite direction. "Come along!"

"Val! Val, wait! You're too fast!"

I could only move in quick bursts due to my asthma. I put this burst to use. We hurried around the corner and into an unused room. Lucrezia's heels across the wood and the madam's shouting alerted everyone on the landing as to what went on. I slammed the door shut while Lucrezia caught her breath. I heard doors opening all across the way: concerned voices and annoyed conversation. The window was open—it led to the alleyway just one floor down.

"What are you doing?!" cried Lucrezia as I went to the window. "Val, no! I refuse!"

"This is the only way!" I said, backtracking to hold her hand once more. "We'll be fine—trust me."

"It isn't *you* I don't trust… It's *this!*"

I stared at her as we waited just by the window, asking, "What's gotten into you? What do you mean?"

She wouldn't say. I rolled my eyes at her strangeness before jumping out the window. Lucrezia almost screamed as I landed. Then I heard the door burst open behind her.

"Lucrezia!" I shouted, holding my arms out. "Lucrezia, come on! I'll catch you!"

Lucrezia looked over her shoulder, and then to me, fearful, and held her breath, as if diving underwater. She shut her eyes as she jumped. I caught her with ease. I ran down the alleyway with Lucrezia gripping her arms about my neck. As we heard the madam shouting at us from the window, we broke down laughing. I had to set her down; I couldn't keep this up, for it pained my breathing. Lucrezia leaned against the back of the nearest building, holding me as we laughed together.

Even through the pain in my chest, I adored this moment with her. I'd never heard her this carefree before. I didn't remember the last time I felt this way, either.

"That was too close!" said Lucrezia, still laughing.

"Much too close," I agreed. As we calmed down at last, I had to ask, "Are you afraid of heights?"

"Embarrassingly so…"

"And yet you enjoy the view of Eden and the hinterlands from the Empyrean Palace?"

Lucrezia held me closer, rubbing the back of my head. "I've grown used to those heights," she countered. "It took me quite a while. The emperor enjoyed teasing me over it." That made more sense. "Despite almost getting caught… I enjoyed that. You've made me feel ten years younger again."

"And you've made me finally feel like my age," I said. "I tend to be too caught up in serious matters. I'd forgotten what it feels like to laugh that way."

"I have a feeling that won't be the last time."

***

Before the madam sent her girls to find us in the alley, Lucrezia and I returned to the palace, hands interlaced. At last the alcohol had taken its toll on Lucrezia, exhausting her. She needed to rest. It would have been selfish of me to ask for more of her time that night. And yet as we stood in this same spot where we'd departed before, the look we gave one another spoke volumes. I kissed her, letting Lucrezia know through my affections what I wanted. She turned her head away but a breath's length after, overwhelmed.

"Lucrezia," I said, tasting her neck instead. "You make me feel too much. I can't keep holding this inside. I need to give it to you."

"And you will… when I say so."

Pain of disappointment rushed through me. "Why are you doing this to me…?"

"Because, Val… I don't only want *one thing* with you. I'm not used to this. In such a short time, you've made me question my character, my truest desires. I need more than a month to undo this—this hesitation I have to let go."

I stepped back, respectful. Her confession was as earnest as it was aggrieved. I wanted to ask if I could at least go to her room with her. To sleep in her bed with her, to hold her, to comfort her… anything.

The words wouldn't come. I was too afraid she would tell me no.

Lucrezia moved her lips just over mine. One lick from her tongue softly asked this last of me. I savored this closeness with her as much as I feared it. This pounding in my chest dipped down to my stomach. I wanted to take her there and now. I couldn't. I couldn't do more than this. She had the power to lift me up, to break me down and piece me back together again, all by a single snap of her fingers. Her fingertips kneaded my shoulders beneath my uniform, relaxing this brief aggression she'd sprung in me.

"Val," she breathed, pulling away. "Come see me tomorrow. I will have some time while the emperor waits for the queen's response to his letter. Or—will you be busy?"

"I'll make time for you," I promised.

"Thank you, love," said Lucrezia, kissing me one last time. I could have fallen to my knees before her—just from her using such a name with me. "Good night."

"… good night," I replied, dazed.

Again, I wanted to run after her. That wouldn't have worked. It hadn't last time and it wouldn't this time. I heard the far-off sounds of Eden's clock tower striking midnight. It was tomorrow. By Lucrezia's puns and loquacious loopholes, I had permission to see her now.

I followed her—up the staircases lit by torches along the walls, past the stoic guards of black steel, down the shadowed halls of onyx with paintings that seemed to follow us with their eyes, all the way to the landing where her chambers awaited. I stayed in the shadows as I went, keeping my footsteps quiet. The sounds of her heels clicking along the marble floors masked whatever mistakes I might have made.

I made it all the way to the hall that led right to her room. Here at the intersection, the guards were plentiful. The throne room was not too far away. As Lucrezia neared her bedroom door, Emperor Xavier intercepted her. I stayed hidden behind the nearest corner, watching them speak in low voices, both of their silhouettes lit by the moonlight.

"Lu, there you are—"

"Not now, Xavier," said Lucrezia, rubbing her forehead. "I am drunk. I've no time for your apologies…"

"Please, my friend, this is important," beseeched Xavier. "You may sleep in late afterward."

"Fine. What is it?"

"It's about the lord commander. Are you certain we can trust her with our—with *my* plans?"

Lucrezia leaned on her door, arms folded as she stared out the window across the way. "We can trust her with far more than that," she replied, gentler this time. "If I were you, I'd be more worried about the scorpion's empress. Raj lost the love of her life to the first imperial invasion. It's also no secret that she detests what's become of Tynan. Find some way to appease her and the queen both. We will need them as our allies moving forward."

"Yes, of course. There is the play—the selfsame one written by Ser Videl, chronicling how she and the empress gained Elysium's independence. It is their love story, is it not? I shall commission the Apocalypse Theater to prepare an adaptation that will please the empress first and foremost. I assume it will take them some months ahead of time to prepare."

Lucrezia stifled a yawn. "Very well, dear. I'm glad I could help. Is that all?"

"Well… no, but you are clearly in need of sleep. The rest can wait until the morrow."

"It already is the morrow."

Xavier chuckled. "I knew you would say that."

"Mmm. Good night, dearest."

With a bow, Xavier said, "Good night, Lu."

I hid behind the corner as he turned my way. The nearest gargoyle statue provided extra shadows to hide behind—I moved there just as Xavier turned to walk down this way. He took a few steps past me before stopping. I glared right at him, at his military-short hair, at his strong build beneath his regal robes, at the paranoia there in his tense neck. After how much his decisions had upset Lucrezia, I didn't trust the man. He was the one in power. He could have assured Lucrezia's power here in the palace alongside him. But—perhaps that was my idealism speaking. If I were in his position, I would have sacrificed anything and anyone to keep Lucrezia happy here. Tyrannical, indeed.

Fortune kept Xavier from turning and spotting me here against the wall. He shuddered and continued on down the hall, muttering about wraiths and demons haunting the palace.

I went to Lucrezia's bedroom door. I thought it would be locked; that I would have to knock. As I turned the doorknob, fortune worked in my favor once more.

Chapter Six

Unity

(Val)

Entering through to Lucrezia's room, I held my breath, intent on staying as silent as possible. I locked the door behind me, greeted by the scents of fresh water and lavender soap. Lucrezia's chambers surprised me not at all. Spacious, lavish, decorative: she lived as a near-empress in the palace here at Emperor Xavier's side, reaping the benefits of the crown without the shackles of marriage. I noticed the many bookcases lining the walls, the actual books absent, as if packed away elsewhere. Numerous surfaces about the room spoke of the same tale. Did she mean to leave any time soon?

She hadn't communicated any such thing to me. Then again, that was typical with her. It had to end.

I felt my eyes drawn to the other side of the room. There I saw Lucrezia walking toward a wooden basin full of bathwater, her back to me. She shed her nightgown. Black silk slipped to the floor, pooling along her bare feet over the carpet: soft and red as velvet. Fairness of her skin glowed in the warm candlelight in the room. I stared in wonder as she stepped into the water, submerging her body from my view. She leaned back against the basin. Her stress left as she sighed in relaxation.

Soon Lucrezia's body coiled anew. She shifted and turned, water parting for her movements. When she eased her head back, I feared she would spot me here, upside-down in her view. Yet her eyes were closed in a beautiful, frustrated bliss. When I heard her whisper my name, I knew where her hand was.

My breath taken from me, I was light-headed enough, free enough to think *without* my head. Emotions crept up to fill this space that I'd reserved for my pride and stubbornness. I removed my boots, balance fumbling as I kept my eyes to the back of Lucrezia's head. Her hair cascaded down the side of the basin: brown-blonde shimmering in the light of the candles. I set my boots next to hers by the door: organized, careful. I removed my military jacket, and folded it over the chair where Lucrezia had tossed her usual jacket aside. Cuffs around my wrists exposed, I went to her, opening more with each step.

I had to broach the subject—of her blood, her sorcery, and her possible fears of discovery. If Lucrezia could not confide as much in me, I feared we would never grow as close as I needed us to be.

And *I needed her*—so much closer than this.

With Lucrezia's eyes yet closed, sharpness of her lashes edging her pulsing temples, I knelt behind her. I wrapped my arms around her neck, her shoulders, holding her close. Lucrezia gave a start. She calmed down once she saw her handiwork along my left wrist; she knew it was only me. Feeling her like this tamed me. I breathed in her every move, her sighs, her disbelief and settling comfort. She smelled wonderful: soft skin soaking in the lavender of the soap that pooled around her.

"Val," she said softly, placing her damp hands along my forearm. "How did you get in here...?"

I nestled the bridge of my nose along her neck, kissing the slope of her shoulder. "Your door was unlocked," I replied. She shuddered against me, surprised by my softness. "It's tomorrow."

Lucrezia laughed. "So it is," she allowed. "Now tell me why you couldn't *wait* properly, hm?"

"Because... I'm tired of sleeping alone, without you."

She didn't expect such sincerity from me.

"Lucrezia, you've no idea," I went on, tracing the chills up her neck with my lips. "I've done terrible, terrible things in my life… The most terrible thing I did was ignoring you for four years. I won't allow myself to suffer anymore. I must give you my honesty… even if you won't give me yours."

I bit back my weak sounds of protest when Lucrezia moved from my hold. She turned to look at me, disbelieving. The foam-white suds of her soap mostly hid her breasts from my view. Only her generous cleavage could I see—and that was enough to intoxicate me, the rest of my words spilling from me: "It's true. I hate being alone. Yet at the same time, I fear getting close enough for someone else to hurt me. I'm used to strangers *trying* to hurt me. It's always worse when I know the person. When I trusted them. When I believed in them. Lee—he almost did it to me in his apathy a few weeks ago. I didn't let him go through with it."

"What do you mean…?"

"Perhaps you know already. Do you recall me holding a revolver in my hand?"

Lucrezia's eyes trailed down to my cuffs. "No, but I sensed something similar some weeks ago. What happened?"

"Lee wanted to die. He was sick of having to hide as a man in a woman's body. He went up to some close-minded man who came close to granting him that fool's wish. I took the stranger's gun… I made him shoot himself instead. He begged me not to. He said he had a wife; children. I didn't care. All I wanted was to make him pay for his sickening beliefs… and to protect my best friend."

By the hardness in Lucrezia's gaze, she wasn't surprised at all.

"Do you usually kill for your loved ones?" she asked me.

"I will if I must. That wasn't the first time. I acted similarly in the past for my sister-in-law. Some man tried to corner her in an alleyway. I killed him before he could violate her."

"So you didn't hesitate."

"I did not."

For some reason, Lucrezia found solace in my ruthlessness. Her stare calmed down once more.

"And I will sacrifice anything for my soldiers," I explained. "I've cared for them for years. They are loyal to me, and to my dear Captain Lydia as well. Ever do I go out of my way to secure their needs. And yet... in these weeks that you and I have grown closer, I haven't done the same for you. I *want* to."

Lucrezia looked away. "Why would you do such a thing for me? I've done nothing but keep my heart just out of your reach... Surely you would want to save those sentiments for someone more expressive than I."

I couldn't answer her with my words. I leaned in, speaking in silence over her lips, licking, gently; breathing these sentiments into her mouth; down her neck, across the soft strength of her proud shoulders. Sensing Lucrezia's understanding through her soft response pacified me to no end. This carelessness in my limbs subsided: the one that made me hate, kill and destroy. I was focused on her, devoted to her. This comfort she gave me soon grew into a rush deep within. Molten fire, soaring—*burning*—and only her pleasure could subside this, for a time, before it returned once more.

When Lucrezia eased me away, both her hands along my jaw, I thought about *asking* her. Yet I was too afraid that she would send me away if I didn't choose the right words.

She saw this fear in my eyes. It pooled together with how terrified I was of my feelings for her. Terrified, yet here I was regardless. I couldn't escape her. I would be a fool to not show her how I felt.

Lucrezia licked her lips, languid. "What's this, I wonder?" she asked, brow raised. "Your expression. It's new. I don't believe I've seen you wear it—not even with others."

"It's for you," I said.

"I quite like it," she replied, about to exit her bath. "You must tell me more about this change." Lucrezia looked me up and down. "Turn around."

I abided her order. "Am I not allowed to see you?"

"Not yet."

I gripped my trousers as I knelt, only able to listen as she dried her body. Draped anew in her black silk nightgown, Lucrezia went to her bed and sat there. She beckoned me to her—on my knees. I crawled over to her as she wished. Pleased, she gave me a small smile. Such a small thing indeed roused me.

I had to be honest. I had to ask her…

Just as Lucrezia made to cross her legs, I held onto one of them in both of my arms. She sighed, content, as she rested her other leg down my shoulder, locking me in place. Her skin was so smooth. Her shin was narrow beneath the gloss of her lavender-scented skin, still a little damp from the bath. She had her graceful foot pointed between me, raising it on occasion to tease my keen throbbing. I could have stayed here for hours like this… if it would please her. Lucrezia felt it in my hold. *She was here.* Her full presence filled me with purpose.

When she reached down to free the tail of my hair, I shivered, exposed of a sudden. Lucrezia fanned my hair down my back, running her long nails along my scalp. She relaxed me as much as she aroused me.

"There is something else on your mind," she observed. I clung to her tighter. "As endearing as you are like this… you must tell me. I don't wish for us to keep secrets from one another."

"Neither do I."

I crawled up to the bed with her. Lucrezia meant to remain upright. I moved her down over her back, her head resting along her pillow. Surprised, she stared up at me on top of her. Lucrezia combed my hair from my face, holding my head just so. She controlled me, holding me here. My heart picked up—too fast, abnormal. I felt that familiar sensation of her here in my mind with me. Telepathy. That had to be it. This was the same feeling from that night in the gallows.

She couldn't sort through the myriad of thoughts running through my head. Lucrezia could only guess. By the rage that flashed through her eyes, she assumed the worst. She gripped my head tighter, as if she wished to force the truth out of me.

All I had to do was say the words. Ask the question. No more, no less.

That didn't make this any easier to bear.

"*Speak*, Val," demanded Lucrezia, her voice blowing just against my face. "What is it?"

"Lucrezia... are you a sorceress?"

I expected her to throw me from her, from her bed. I expected her to yell at me to get out and never speak of this again. And yet... she did not. With fervor, Lucrezia searched through my thoughts. She wanted to find even a spec of doubt—any reason that I might turn her in, or otherwise betray her if she relayed the truth to me.

Instead, she saw how loyal I was to her.

Lucrezia softened her hold over me, yet she did not leave my mind. Instead she pulled the most primal thoughts from me; made me act them out. Sudden fire took over my spirit: the same sexual awakening she'd instilled in me when I first laid eyes on her four years ago. Then, and now, I wanted to tear at her, to rip away her control. That fire manifested itself as a literal one over my hands, horrifying me.

"Don't resist me," warned Lucrezia. Her control over me tightened—I gripped her nightgown, willing myself to stop. "You are powerless. Accept it. Act out your desires. *Overwhelm me.*"

Overwhelming her was the only way to make her let go. An antithesis of the highest order—

Yet I couldn't resist her any longer.

With strength beyond me, I tore her nightgown in half, down the middle. That satisfying rip sounded just as Lucrezia cried out, voice bent by the arch of her back. She pulled my shirt from me, tossing it aside. I hurried out of my trousers and smallclothes, kicking them off somewhere near the foot of the bed. Nothing existed between us except time. I kissed her, deep; deeper when I felt her open her legs for me. I spread them wider, inching my knees underneath her thighs. Lucrezia held me around my neck just so. Begging with her touch. The slant of her soft hands along my spine kept me attached to her. When I felt her tongue along mine, lightly penetrating, my mind went right there.

I made to move my hand between her legs. Lucrezia grabbed my wrist, stopping me. I locked my arms about her torso instead, down to the small of her back. She arched again for me. I had no say—she kept my head in place, over her breasts, one at a time: full, *everything.* Feeling her like this drugged me. I looked up at her, pressing my tongue over how hard she was for me. Face reddened, Lucrezia averted her eyes, body arching anew.

She couldn't stand this intensity in my gaze. I couldn't look away from the struggling in her expression.

"Stop it, Val," she panted. "Stop it, I said..." Lucrezia clawed through my hair, settling her palm right between my eyes. Breathless, she pushed my head away from her breasts.

I kissed the bend of her ribs, content with this partial view of her behind her wrist. "Am I too much?"

"*No,* I just—I can't deal with this novelty… I've never… felt this before."

Further down her stomach, undefined muscles tensed, trembling with her nerves. Lucrezia's control left me bit by bit as she let go. The fire she'd conjured in my hands dissipated.

I was so close. I could almost taste her. I smelled her: thick, natural sweetness, dripping to the sheets; slicking along her smooth thighs. I only moved to lick her legs clean. Lucrezia dug her nails into my scalp, her hold unsteady. Her tremors grew worse once I finally had a taste of her—just here. I took my time. I kissed up her thighs, one at a time, higher than the last, drawn to the scent of her, how soaked she was for me already. The taste of her skin mixed with my breath, leaving a trail.

At the thickest base of her thighs—supple, succulent—I breathed against her, waiting.

Lucrezia shook so terribly. I feared she would push me away.

I wanted to say something, anything, to calm her down. A sick part of me enjoyed her fear. This was nothing like the woman I once knew at court from a distance. I'd sensed—hoped—that her core was much softer than her façade… and now that I knew I was right, I could never leave her side.

Everything I felt for her, I gave to her through my mouth. I latched onto her—lips testing, tongue tasting. Lucrezia's sharp breaths goaded me, hard. I should have been softer for her, slower. More deliberate. She was afraid. I lapped at Lucrezia's fear, faster and faster. Every taste, every texture of her, I memorized with my taste. I found what she liked best and did it—over and over. Tongue flat against her folds, I pressed my head into her, hard enough to inch her closer to the headboard.

When she let go of my hand, I slipped my touch inside of her. One, two together, and then three, going at a maddening pace; matching the speed of my mouth. I groaned at her tightness: soaking wet; pulling me in more and more. Lucrezia clamped her thighs around my head, forcing me in place; almost suffocating me, but I loved it.

Listening to Lucrezia's moans for me was all the air I needed. Filling my senses with her made up for every moment I'd gone without her over the years. Soon this physicality from me grew emotional. She sensed it. Her quavering body settled; her sounds deepened. As she cried my name, louder, louder, my heart felt fit to burst. I poured this energy into her, pleasing her more.

When Lucrezia lost all control at last, shaking down to her core, I knew what I'd given her. The *way* she said my name spoke of her release. I stopped; stopped breathing.

After a time, I heard the wetness in her sniffling. I was about to move up, to go to her. Lucrezia wouldn't let me. She kept my head here. She made me keep going, again and again and again. Each time I *heard* her, I fell for her more. By the third hour, I had fallen into her completely. I couldn't escape. Here I saw the beauty of Lucrezia's heart: how closely she had guarded it after so many years. I came closer to holding it each time she came—so much closer.

Once Lucrezia beckoned me to stop, to hold her in my arms, I grasped it. As dangerous as this was, I couldn't let her heart go—not for anything. She trusted me with it. I had to protect it. Burrowed in the comfort of her sheets, her duvet, her pillows, Lucrezia rested her head over my chest, holding me tight, as if freezing. She didn't want to speak. I stayed awake for some time, listening to her deepening breaths as she fell asleep. I licked her taste from my lips, sucking on it in silence for ages even after it had gone.

The one thing I feared was how willing I was to sacrifice anything for her. I worried over my capabilities. My callousness in the face of my goals. Lucrezia deserved this of me. I wondered just how far I would go for her in the coming days or weeks, depending on how these politics with Tynan and Tibor played out.

When I felt Lucrezia move into me more in her sleep, I felt my answer by this passion in me—

All the way. No exceptions.

***

Fierce knocking at the door awoke me from my brief sleep. Vague dreams of seeing Lucrezia smile as I gifted her a bouquet of roses dissolved into the chill of the morning. Insulated in the heat of Lucrezia's skin and her bedding that had absorbed our warmth, I didn't want to move. She was still fast asleep. I wanted to be here whenever Lucrezia awoke, to kiss her good morning—or afternoon. I wondered if there was some way I might cook a meal for her. I fantasized about it, how I might set it up with those flowers I'd dreamed of. I ignored whoever was at the door, hoping they would take the hint and leave.

They did not. They knocked harder this time, more urgent. Annoyed, I untangled myself from Lucrezia's hold, moving as slowly as possible so as to not wake her. I had a feeling I couldn't disturb her if I tried. She had passed out after last night. That helped to curb my irritation with her visitor, somewhat. After kissing her once, twice, thrice, I reached for my smallclothes on the other end of the bed. I stopped, feeling dirty already. I couldn't wear these again.

I searched through Lucrezia's drawers for the most masculine articles I could find. I put them on amid that person's feverish knocking. I donned an overlong shirt that covered my thighs. These had to have belonged to some man she'd had in her bed before me. Hopefully not Lieutenant-Colonel James. As I opened the door, I kept myself mostly hidden behind the wood, peeking my head out.

"Yes?" I answered, tired.

Lucrezia's servant Rosa didn't appear surprised to see me. "Lord commander, is the lady chancellor awake?" she asked in a rush.

I glanced at Lucrezia sleeping away in her bed. "Err, no. And she won't wake any time soon."

Rosa sighed, exasperated. "His Imperial Majesty requires her presence in the throne room—immediately! There's an emergency, my lord. I cannot say more!"

"I'm afraid that's not possible. Lucrezia will wake on her own time. She needs this."

"Then I beseech you to go in her place!" urged Rosa. "Please, Lord Valerie. It is important!"

"Very well. Tell His Majesty that I will be there in a moment."

Rosa hurried off to deliver the news. In Lucrezia's armoire, I found an imperial officer's uniform: a sharp leather doublet lined with violet, with Emperor Xavier's coat of arms on the back in silver, and tailored dark trousers with heavy knee-high leather boots to match, along with a silver chain of service. The imperial obsession with leather, black and purple, still struck me as strange after all these years. Overall this was more severe than my uniforms that Gabrielle had made for me herself. I found that it fit me well—too well, in fact. There was even a holster for a sniper rifle for me to wear along my back.

Just in front of the boots, I found a note bearing my name. This was for me.

Once I was dressed, I went to Lucrezia. I whispered my thanks for the uniform.

I knew what this meant.

"Hopefully you are still asleep by the time I return," I said, brushing the stray locks of hair from her face. I looked her over, how peaceful she was. "You are so beautiful…"

I made sure she was tucked in properly, and kissed her lips again. I could have fallen into her once more, but now wasn't the time. I hated that I had to leave her.

I found her keys over her desk and took them with me. After locking her bedroom door behind me, I made my way down the palace halls to the throne room. Panic set about the space, with the usual stoic guards pacing around, whispering to one another over the latest crisis. Other lords and ladies who lived in the palace at the emperor's behest wandered about in confusion, wondering what was wrong.

I picked up my pace, worried now. The chain around my neck chimed in time with my hurried footsteps. When I arrived to the throne room, the doors were already open. The dark clouds of the morning washed over the enchanted sky and walls of the room, opening the space up to the horizon. Scores of guards lined the perimeter around me: agitated, unprepared. The Privy Council shouted and argued with one another. They stopped once they saw me.

In the far distance, I saw an organized group marching toward Eden, as but mere specs from this far away. Like toy soldiers coming right to us. Imperial soldiers mobilized along the palace grounds, readying their advance north.

Unexpected, Lee walked over to me, also in an imperial officer's uniform. "Lord commander," he said.

"What are you doing here?"

Sebastian and Lydia approached as well. They, too, donned similar uniforms to Lee's.

"What's going on?" I asked. "Why are you dressed like that?"

Lydia shrugged. "Same reason as you," she noted.

"I put this on because there was nothing else to wear after—"

"After what?"

When I didn't answer, Sebastian burst out laughing. "I *knew* it!" he cheered.

Lee hit him upside the head. "This ain't the time, for fuck's sake," he scolded.

Lydia was oddly muted this morning. "As much as I'd love to tease you, Val, this is serious," she said. "Guards woke us up not half an hour ago and told us to put these on. Soon as we got here, the emperor didn't even say hello before telling us what the problem was." She pointed to him sitting at his throne, arguing with Lieutenant-Colonel James. "You'd better go talk to him yourself."

I approached Xavier and James, listening to their quarrel.

"You are too rash!" insisted Xavier. "If the queen means to speak to me, we'll not hear a word of it if we attack her now!"

"And you're too passive, *Your Imperial Majesty*," said James, sneering. "Why let her get any closer? You *do know* what she's capable of, don't you? Send the girl's troops in. They'll take care of the threat. Meanwhile, my men will secure the palace grounds. We need to keep the nobles calm."

Xavier scoffed at him. "*The girl's troops?*" he repeated. "She is no mere girl! If you allow your envy and hatred to continue speaking for you—"

"Then what? You'll dismiss me? I'm the highest-ranking officer you have left. *I'm* your general now. Get rid of me and you won't have anyone gunning for you in this army. No one with experience, anyway."

James glared at me. He knew I'd never seen a day on a real battlefield. Only because I wasn't *allowed.*

"Lord Val," said Xavier, sour. "Thank you for arriving with such haste. Where is the lady chancellor?"

I glanced at the lieutenant-colonel as I replied, "She is fast asleep."

Xavier bit back his laughter. "… I see." He knew what I meant—as did James, frowning now. "Well, I did give her leave to sleep the day away. No matter. We shall have to do this without her." Xavier waved his hand over his shoulder, gesturing to the threat across the way. "As you've no doubt noticed, Queen Beatrys of Tenrose advances with her army as we speak. They number five thousand, officially. We've no idea if she increased her ranks. They do not appear to be hostile, but we cannot take any risks. There are but fifteen hundred loyal to us. Two thousand if we include your Lysander numbers, as of now."

I needed him to say the words. I couldn't get ahead of myself with this budding relief.

But a brief smile Xavier gave me. "You found the uniform I intended to have Lucrezia gift you," he noticed. "Due to your theoretical tactical experience as an officer, I hereby instate you as the unique lord commander of our imperial ranks. We are in need of your soldiers and their technological expertise. Will you add them to our numbers to protect our great Empire of Tynan?"

I felt Sebastian, Lydia and Lee just behind me, the three of them swelling with pride. All around us, the Privy Council held their collective tongue. James was downright livid, but he could not protest. I had fought for this with my troops for almost a decade. I smiled despite the dissent in the room. Only Xavier's permission mattered: his knowing smile, his sympathy and understanding.

I wished Lucrezia were here to share this moment with me.

With a bow, I said, "Of course, Your Imperial Majesty. My soldiers are yours. Thank you..."

Xavier smiled wider, clapping with fervor—forcing everyone else to clap for us, however bitter they were over the news. I looked to my three officers, finding their grins infectious. This felt like a new beginning for us. At last, some of the hatred I'd held for the establishment and status quo left me. I trusted that the rest would leave in due time. There was still more that needed to be done.

"Congratulations, lord commander," grunted James.

"And congratulations to you on your unofficial promotion," I allowed. "*Acting* General James of Eden."

"I look forward to having you and your troops under my command. Their guns will do us well. I can't have them missing training for any reason. Not even for… personal days. I expect they'll try it."

"Well, hopefully you won't be too emotional over Lucrezia to lead as you must."

Xavier laughed freely this time. James walked away in frustration.

"All right, all right," said Xavier. "Now, for your first mission! Lord commander, I would have you scope out the scene with your rifle. Determine if Queen Beatrys means us harm: if she is armed with sword in hand upon her horse, if she has her general by her side—anything. Assign a scout to relay the news to me. Your other two officers will inform the remainder of your soldiers of the situation."

Lee was the fastest runner out of all of us. I trusted him to be factual and precise as well.

"You're with me," I told him.

Lee gave an imperial salute: legs together, arms firmly crossed as an X across his chest—right over left.

"Understood."

"Sebastian, Lydia—go to the safehouse. Tell them what's happened. Don't mobilize just yet. Wait."

They, too, gave imperial salutes in unison. "Lord commander," they said together, and left.

Xavier nodded to me, encouraging, and sent me on my way. Lee and I left the palace for the Lysander estate across the grounds. It was strange to see so many of my neighbors out and about this early in the morning. Imperial guards maintained order in the residential area. Because the queen's troops were so far away, the other nobles had yet to make out what the issue was.

Thankfully, Father, Yosef and Gabrielle had yet to wake from the commotion. Lee and I snuck inside my home and went to my room. I took my rifle from my hiding spot, holstering it over my back. With no time to linger, we left back outside. We took two horses from the stables and rode out to the city.

I led the way to the top of the clock tower. From this vantage point, I could watch the queen from a distance, uninterrupted by the commotion going on near the palace. At the very top, I unfolded my rifle. I looked through the high-powered scope in the queen's general direction. Lee made a few adjustments as I peered through the scope, sharpening my view for me. Right away I noticed the royal soldiers were without swords and shields.

"See anything?" asked Lee.

"Yes, but... it's unusual," I responded, checking more closely. "They don't have any weapons."

"Maybe the emperor was right."

"Possibly," I agreed, zooming in a bit more. I spotted Queen Beatrys on her horse in the center. She wasn't as regal as I expected her to be. Her beauty was plain, normal: tan skin, dark hair, and a long face similar to any other woman one might meet on the street. Only the hushed anger in her stare set her apart from most women I'd seen—and her regal robes. "Her Majesty is at the fore. She doesn't look to have any officers around her. No one in armor. She's wearing... oracle's robes."

Lee sounded as surprised as I was. "Had no idea she was an oracle... I thought Tibor wasn't religious?"

"They don't follow the Anathema doctrine, no... But they still despise heretics. That is one of the few things Tynan and Tibor have in common, it seems. Royal oracles focus more on witch hunts... eradicating anyone who might *appear* to be a thaumaturge or a sorceress. They don't have a single woman in their army."

"Think she'll have a problem with us in the imperial ranks now?"

"Alchemists are the exception to the rule whenever it benefits those in power. I'm sure she'll understand now that the emperor's allowed it…"

I trailed off once I had a better look at the man who rode beside the queen. He was the very image of Lucrezia: hazel eyes, slicked-back brown hair with visible blond streaks, and his stern face sculpted as a handsome mirror of his older sister's.

That had to be Gustavo of Azrith. He wore a gentleman's outfit of pale red, emerald and white— Tenrose's colors—riding his horse with distinction and honor. He didn't appear at all as a man riding off to war. By his lean features, I imagined he hadn't seen a single battle in his life. He held in his hand a letter bearing the Imperial Crown's seal.

"They're not hostile," I decided, setting my rifle down. "They mean to speak with Emperor Xavier."

Lee needed confirmation— "You're sure?"

And I needed Lee to go tell the emperor before I sniped Gustavo's head clear from his neck. Lucrezia's brother had caused her no small amount of pain before. It took everything in me to not make him pay. I teased the trigger of my gun, but refused to pull it all the way.

"I'm sure."

With trained speed, Lee took off down the clock tower. He rode back to the Empyrean Palace to tell Xavier the news. I took my time in following after him. By the time I arrived to the palace grounds, I found Emperor Xavier on his horse surrounded by his personal guard. James tarried along just behind them. Lee's work was done—he opted to return to the safe house to tell everyone else what went on. Xavier gestured for me to follow, and together we all rode north to speak with the queen.

Across the plains that stretched out to the Eidos Sea beyond, the royal soldiers grew closer—larger in size than mere toy soldiers in the distance. Once we were close enough, Queen Beatrys raised her arm, gesturing for her men to stop. She rode forward with Gustavo at her side. From the way he looked at me—curious, eyes full of questions—he knew who I was and who his sister was to me.

"Lord Val, this way!" called Xavier, going ahead without his guards.

"Your Majesty."

"That is far enough!" announced Beatrys. Xavier and I came to a stop within speaking distance. "I wonder— how did you know we mean you no harm? I would have called you foolish indeed for approaching five thousand men with your dozen or so imperials." She noticed the rifle along my back. "Ah, so I see. An alchemist, are you?"

"She is no alchemist, Queen Beatrys," spoke Xavier for me.

"*She?*"

The queen recoiled, taking another look at me. Beneath my chain of service she spotted the swell of my chest, camouflaged by the black of my uniform in this dark morning. I felt her eyes scanning me overmuch. Beatrys took offense to the old scars along my face—unladylike as they were. That I did not smile at her annoyed her more.

"Lord Commander Valerie," spoke Gustavo, stoic. "A pleasure to meet you at long last. I am certain you know who I am."

"I do," was all I said, leering at him for but a moment.

I didn't expect Gustavo to frown sadly at me.

"The exception," noted Beatrys. "Yes, the exceptional one. I understand. Forgive me, lord commander. Women in the kingdom do not act beyond their stature as you do."

"Nor do the women here in the empire," I supplied. "You said I am the exception, after all."

Beatrys soured at me once more. "It appears you have ears. How wonderful."

And how predictable that she disliked me already.

Xavier changed the subject. "Your Majesty, what is the meaning of all this?"

"Your fortuitous timing changed the course of history, Emperor Xavier! I meant to march on Eden with my men and decimate your dear city, your Empyrean Palace. Alas, during the voyage here across the Eidos Sea, I received a letter in which you all but bent over for me. I could not ignore such graciousness from His Imperial Majesty himself. Thus we left our arms aboard our ships. I am here as a friend to the empire."

Gustavo held up the letter Xavier had penned some days ago.

"You're lucky," he said. "During the first half of our trip here, I attempted to convince Her Majesty to stand down. She would not listen to me, convinced I was too soft in my concern for my older sister."

"*Concern*," spat Xavier. "What concern could you possibly have for her?!"

"I am her brother. I always will be, no matter my mistakes with her in the past."

Xavier laughed to the skies. "Mistakes, he says!" he mocked. "Did you come to make up for the past, sweet Gustavo? To apologize to your sister? The one who sacrificed for you, endlessly in your youth, only for you to betray her in your cruelty? You know she'll not give you the time of day. Not even if it had been your voice alone that stayed the queen's hand. *You should have stayed in the kingdom!*"

Gustavo lowered his head in shame. As protective as Xavier was of Lucrezia, it was unwise of him to air her business with her brother to the soldiers nearby. Still, he was riled up in his emotions. No one could deny the red in his eyes—how he wanted to hurt Gustavo for his sins. If I had known Lucrezia for over twenty years as Xavier had, I likely would have felt the same anger.

The protectiveness I felt was fresh, different. I could have killed her brother and gotten it over with.

Approaching sounds of a running horse stopped these thoughts. I turned and found Lucrezia on her steed, racing toward us, fully dressed. I noticed how warm my cuffs were. Lucrezia had used them to track where I was.

"There you are!" she said, relieved.

She stopped her horse between Xavier and me. I basked in her morning glow as much as I could, knowing it would end soon. Lucrezia held my hand, smiling. I tried my best to return her smile. I couldn't. She looked to Xavier, expecting him to make a childish joke about her sleeping in. He did not.

"Hello, sister."

The inevitable sinking feeling in Lucrezia's stomach—I felt it with her as she stared at Gustavo, caught off guard. Worse was Lucrezia's stony reaction when she saw the oracle's rod tucked away over Queen Beatrys' horse. The witch burnings here were only for show. Oracles had originally had the power to dispatch thaumaturges and sorceresses by their incantations, with the help of their staves. As Tynan's oracles had rejected their own possible magical roots, they chose to burn sorceresses instead. Royal oracles were different, it seemed. If the legends were true, then I suspected the queen's staff spoke to her own magical aptitude—and how she might have used those magicks to control others.

Practiced in the art of masking her emotions, she soon found her poise once more. From night to day, it was as if she expected her brother's company.

"Gustavo," greeted Lucrezia, cordial. She acknowledged the queen. "Your Majesty. To what do we owe the pleasure?"

By the scrutiny in Beatrys' stare, she despised Lucrezia already as well.

"Lady chancellor," she said. "How good of you to join us this morning. I believe your dear partner would be more than happy to provide a summary for you. I should like to continue on to the palace now—if you wouldn't mind. It's been a terribly long journey."

"And what of your men?" asked Xavier. "I apologize, Your Majesty, but we do not have... room for thousands of soldiers in our barracks."

"Oh? Your deserters didn't number enough to provide a roof for my army?"

Lucrezia was in no mood for Beatrys' thinly-veiled insults. "I'm afraid you must send some of your people back," she said, giving Gustavo a pointed look. "We do not have *room,* as the emperor stated."

"Of course. As Lord Gustavo is my acting adviser, he shall have to remain with me."

Xavier didn't have a choice but to concede. "So be it."

As much of an expert as Lucrezia was at hiding her feelings, I knew better. I learned to look deeper and found the one sign she couldn't hide. The color from her eyes was gone. That sharpness, that brilliance I saw when Lucrezia was in her element—it was nowhere to be seen as we rode back to the palace.

Chapter Seven

His Friends
(Lucrezia)

Accessorizing gave me comfort. At my vanity, dressed for Xavier's ball for his thirtieth birthday, I chose which tone of silver I wanted to adorn my wrists with. I had this choice left. With the freedom that had been taken from me with Queen Beatrys in the palace, I needed this choice. A few rings: the ostentatious ring that each member of the Privy Council wore, one of diamonds that Xavier had given me—our friendship ring—and a much older one, a ruby ring, that had belonged to my mother.

This was all I had left of her. In honor of dear Gustavo attending the ball tonight, I decided to wear it. If it would spite my brother to see this reminder of our mother who abandoned us, then I could be happy with that much.

I couldn't stand dresses. They were too complicated to put on, to walk in for hours while the men had the comfort of their suits; to take off again and stow away. I had already told Val to expect me in something similar to what I always wore. I wasn't one for variety in my wardrobe—not even for special occasions such as these. As it was the first day of June, the poor excuse for summer had heated Eden somewhat. I didn't want to wear anything out of my comfort zone in this weather.

Any other time, I would have taken the risk, if only to please Val, to surprise her. I couldn't maintain my temperature spells anymore. Not with a royal oracle in the palace. Queen Beatrys had a keen nose for magic. I recalled last week, during a dinner party at court, I was about to remove a sudden urge I had to sneeze impolitely. Right as I'd meant to activate the spell, Beatrys had stopped eating. Had I been careless enough to use such a small, personal spell, she would have sensed its origins and obliterated me then and there.

I couldn't *stand* having to hide any more than I already did.

My only solace was getting to express these issues to Val now. Now that she knew.

I needed her to fuck me tonight—someplace where we might get caught, for the thrill of it all. This was beyond me, and yet I couldn't care anymore.

I was mad about her. *Absolutely* mad. The way she touched me every night made me thank every god imaginable that I hadn't let anyone have me before. To finally feel the way I'd made others feel... I was embarrassed to need more of it from her, as emotional as it was. Emotional, because Val gave me all of her, every time.

She wouldn't say the words. I knew how she felt about me. Opening myself to her was all I could do to tell her that I felt the same.

When I heard a knock at the door, I smiled to myself, assuming it was Val. I thought she might have wanted to skip the festivities and spend time in my bed instead. I went to answer the call with my remarks ready, only for them to die in my throat.

As I opened the door, I stared back at my own reflection. Some differences: her olive skin, her bone-straight raven hair held up in a long tail, and her red-russet eyes, yet her gaze held the same force as my own. In structure, in shape and in spirit, she was a striking image of me. I thought back to the strange woman who had visited Xavier some months ago—the same woman who had advised him to seek peace with Queen Beatrys. The stranger carried an oracle's staff in her hand, her shapely figure adorned in regal robes befitting a monarch. By her posture and the strength in her eyes, she was as proud as I was—if not more.

"Lady Lucrezia," said the oracle, her sultry voice deepened by a relaxed, yet dignified accent I didn't recognize. "How wonderful to meet you at long last."

"Who are you?" I asked.

"My name is Elysia Azrith." *Azrith?* "Indeed. We are related—distantly. As you may have guessed, I am an oracle. I am not an imperial oracle with the cathedrals in your time, however. I'm what they call a temple oracle. Different denominations, you see."

"In—in *my* time?"

"Yes," replied Elysia. "I have crossed the boundaries of time and space to find you. There is an important matter we must discuss. It concerns Elysium and the scorpion's empress. I'm aware you mean to speak with the empress again soon." She glanced behind me to my chambers. "May I come in?"

I stepped aside. Elysia entered my bedroom, looking around as she went. I locked the door behind her. I'd read about certain people of great power finding ways to travel the Waves of Death to reach different timelines. Actually seeing the product of that theory unsettled me.

I sensed a strange air about her. Something unnatural.

Elysia cast me a knowing glance over her shoulder. "There's no need to pry," she chided. "If there is aught you wish to know, ask me."

"How exactly are we related? I assume I am your ancestor."

"Your younger brother Gustavo is my great-grandfather. Your nephew, his son, is my grandfather. My mother was an only-child… I maintained your surname due to shifts in society: from patriarchal to matriarchal. I should not say anything more than that. These issues with time are ever so finicky."

I observed her foreign, elegant garb. "And you've arrived from another timeline?"

"I've the freedom to travel as I please, now that I am dead. A terrible tragedy befell my village... I died protecting my husband and daughter from a group of maddened Anathema missionaries. No ordinary person would be able to come and go as I do. The skills you passed onto me through our bloodline helped a great deal. I'm here because I need your help."

"If you are as clairvoyant as I think you are, surely you must know what a terrible time this is."

Elysia took a seat in the velvet reclining chair nearby as if she were right at home. As if she were me. She only gave me a look: she would not accept no for an answer, and that she would do whatever it took for me to agree to her wishes. It was strange indeed to see a mirror of myself in make and mannerisms. Never had I met this great niece of mine in my life, and yet she and I were so similar. Perhaps whatever enabled her to travel across time through death was what also linked us this way.

"I had hoped," continued Elysia, "that you would at least hear me out. We are family, after all. His Imperial Majesty assured me that you would do that much for me. After all, it was my counsel that saved your empire. Were it not for the letter he penned, the royal army might have decimated you."

I had some time yet before Val was due to meet me in the hall. And Elysia certainly had a point as to her worth. Needless to say, I was curious now.

"I'm listening," I said.

"Which tale of the scorpion's empress have you heard? The historically correct one or the censored one meant to protect our delicate sensibilities?"

"I tracked down the correct one. I would be a terrible scholar if I hadn't."

"Then you know what befell Archangel Vespair," noted Elysia.

I took a seat across from her, thinking back to Raj's despair. "Yes… Ser Videl did what she needed to do in order to protect her empress from the archangel's ire. Her comrade Nyte then donned Vespair's dark knight armor and assumed her persona from then on."

"Mmm, indeed. Ser Videl was a valiant, protective paladin to the last. Unfortunately, her actions came back to haunt her some years later. The first imperial invasion was no accident."

"How not?"

"In the Golden Era of Elysium's history—the fifteen years after its independence—thaumaturges and sorceresses roamed freely. They were not termed as such. They were merely paladins, dark knights, clerics, or the odd men and women who had unusual talents such as shifting shadows or manipulating dreams. Vespair may have been gone, but her rage grew within her armor. It eventually overtook Nyte, spreading to the rest of the world as an indiscernible fog of close-mindedness."

Such implications were not lost upon me. "Do you mean to say that Vespair's rage was what caused the sudden, negative shift in perception toward magic-users? Her angry spirit?"

"I believe so, yes," replied Elysia. "Vespair was a terribly sadistic woman in her living years. She was patient and calculating, able to take out any corrupt nobles who crossed her, all the while ignoring any who filled her coffers with enough coin. She decided that Videl could no longer enjoy her freedom as a thaumaturge—as a knight who wielded protective magicks; that Nyte could not do the same with the manipulative magicks she had inherited from her armor. Like a phantom, she haunted history's first Holy Oracle into changing the early *Anathema* texts into the Anathema religion as you know it."

"As I recall, there *was* a sudden shift in rhetoric around the year 590. People cared overmuch about the purported apocalypse the sorceresses brought about centuries ago. They feared it would happen again if they allowed magic-users to live as they pleased. Their paranoia seemed to come out of nowhere."

"That *nowhere* was Vespair's doing. If you ever come across Holy Oracle Jyrn's journal, you'll note how he describes his own paranoia as a demon in his mind. He spread the new teachings, converted the old churches into cathedrals, and wrote the *Hallows* as the new scriptures to follow. Emperor Xavier's ancestors then took advantage of the people's fear, eradicating most of Elysium's thaumaturges and sorceresses. Ser Videl perished in the war in a failed attempt to protect her empress. From there, the remaining thaumaturges retaliated. The first imperial emperor then established Tynan as you know it today."

I looked to my door, wondering where Queen Beatrys was at this very moment. The powers in her staff that could have annihilated me at any moment were born of the selfsame close-mindedness that Vespair had inflicted upon the world. All for revenge—all to get back at Raj, Videl, Nyte and Mistress Fury for intervening in her affairs two hundred and fifty years ago. And now we all had to suffer for it.

I could only imagine how different my life would be if I didn't have to hide. These stricter laws against thaumaturges and sorceresses had also unfairly affected women. Men were just as likely to be sorcerers, and yet they were excused from the witch hunts. They scapegoated us as women to maintain power over us. I had never seen a supposed male sorcerer burned at the stake. Only women.

"Do you intend to stop this madness, Lady Elysia?" I asked. "Stop Vespair's wrath from spreading more?"

"I do," she responded. "Will you help me?"

"Of course. Explain what you have in mind so far."

"We have a few points in our favor. As I mentioned, Vespair is patient. Sadistic. She will wait and allow us to mobilize against her, only to find some way to thwart us in the end. We must adapt to her tactics each time we take a step forward, no matter how long it takes. She also cannot reach us physically in this world. We must go to her when we are ready."

"Where is she? In some other dimension?"

"In the Beyond, past the underworld where the dead reside. There lies immortality for the living who breach the barriers to that land. We will have untold time to perfect our plan against our enemy."

"You mean for me to leave?" I said. "Leave the palace, leave Xavier behind? And—and Val?"

Elysia gave me a knowing smile. "I will take care of that small detail," she informed me. "For now, I need you to convince the scorpion's empress to leave first. Ser Videl awaits her in Valdivia, the land closest to the underworld. She will tell you that she needs time to gather her people and ready them for the journey. I have a feeling that time will coincide with the play that the Emperor Xavier commissioned for her and for Queen Beatrys. That is when I will orchestrate events in our favor."

"Our favor?" I echoed, watching Elysia stand, as if readying to leave.

"Yes. I require the four of you for our plans—Lord Valerie, Raj, Ser Videl, and you, of course. Once you are together, I will create our means of breaching the barrier to the Beyond. From there we will craft our strategy to defeat Vespair. She will wait, and sabotage us in small doses, but we must persevere."

Elysia noticed my distance. I could not imagine leaving my place here behind. Not even with a royal oracle about the halls. I had come close to believing that my time here was limited—when Xavier had first introduced this plan for peace to me, back when I hadn't believed the queen would be amenable to us. Now that that threat had passed, here Elysia told me that, again, I had to expect to leave.

I didn't *want* to leave. This was where I belonged. I knew nothing else except for these palace walls of onyx and the gossip hidden within; these backhanded politics and the finesse required to navigate them. I would be useless outside of my position as chancellor. Completely useless...

"Come now, Lucrezia," warned Elysia. "There are larger matters at stake than your velvet seats and feather pillows here in your chambers. Our whole family has been marked by our enemy. You will suffer, as will your brother Gustavo, and his son, and his children, and so forth. Lord Valerie's family is also affected, as she and Nyte are directly related. Had Raj and Ser Videl found a way to have children, their offspring would have also been haunted as we are. If we do not stop Vespair, this cycle will never end."

She was right.

"Convince Raj to leave to Valdivia," she recited. "Do not mention Ser Videl. Simply remind her of the dangers of remaining in Elysium with her magical citizens while a royal oracle is but a few miles away. I will handle the rest."

"Yes... very well," I allowed.

Elysia gave me a curt nod. A vortex of violet and gold appeared behind her—she walked through the chasm in time, leaving me here. I caught a glimpse of the area she left for: a lush, tropical area with a clear blue sea and pearl-white sands. The heat from that place blew through just as the vortex dissolved.

I sat in place for a while, thinking. I had no idea where my backbone had gone just now. This invisible threat shouldn't have been more important than my position here in the palace. Elysia had gone so far as to mock my obsession with appearances and comfort. For roughly the first ten years of my life, all I'd had were tattered rags to wear. My childhood room had been filled with persistent dust and grime that no amount of scrubbing could wipe clean. The rest of the house spoke of the same tale.

My father had forced me to help him in the fields with our crops—in the hot sun, in the rain, in sleet and snow. He would have made Gustavo help, until I used my magic one day to speed up the process. I was smart enough to know to keep this hidden from them, yet still oblivious enough to not know *why*.

Our parents caught me eventually. I found out why I'd had to stay hidden—they yelled at me, beat me, called me names. Gustavo tried to stop them. He was only four years old at the time. I took him up to the roof of our home to escape our parents. He clung to me as we sat there all day and night. All the while I stared at the high drop from the tall roof, knowing I could not save my brother or myself with my powers if we fell. If anyone else saw me use my spells, they would harass me more. I didn't want them to. I associated that height with the hatred I had for my own blood.

I believed our parents had calmed down after a while. As soon as I thought to climb back down, they escaped into the night with their things, leaving us there. I couldn't find my voice to cry out to them.

My fear of heights, of my powers, and of the ones I loved abandoning me were one and the same.

I associated that abandonment with living below-standard. As I knew I would if I followed Elysia's plans.

I trembled in my seat.

When I heard another knock at the door, I knew it was Val this time. I sensed the cuffs I'd placed over her wrists, just outside my door. This was the only way I could communicate with her magically without Queen Beatrys knowing. When I opened the door, far-off conversation from the ballroom punctured the silence in my room. Val had her back to me, waiting for me to exit my chambers. I had a feeling she was tempted to skive off the ball and spend time with me in my bed instead.

Once I locked my door, she turned around. I was surprised to find her in an all-white suit, the sides lined with black and silver stylized decorations. I had expected her to be in her new imperial uniform that she'd found weeks ago. Val seemed to have something in her hands—behind her back now. She looked up at me with a rather self-conscious expression. I adored this look on her.

Val's eyes lit up with my smile. "You're as beautiful as ever, Lucrezia."

"And you are handsome as always," I replied, running my hands down her shoulders. "I thought you might be a man of the empire tonight for the ball. Why did you choose to wear this instead?"

Embarrassed once more, Val struggled to keep her eyes to mine. "Because I wish to be your man—if... you would have me." This fluttering in my chest was as sweet as it was foreign. Only she had ever made me feel this way. "I know you said to wait to see how things went over these past weeks. I remember."

She had to know I'd only said that to maintain my aloofness—*before* she had made me feel all the ways she had in bed.

Val winced when I didn't say anything. "I could not possibly ask you to be mine," she said. "I'm asking to be yours. You are a woman of power, Lucrezia. You command respect all throughout the empire. You have the world at your fingertips with Emperor Xavier at your side. Where anyone else would condemn you in their misogyny and double-standards, instead I admire you... I'm in awe of you."

I loved her sincerity.

I loved her uncharacteristic posture—shoulders slumped forward, head down as her eyes roamed. Val shifted her stance every now and then in her nerves.

I loved everything about her. Even how she could not find the words to continue speaking.

Anyone else would have grown flustered with me for not replying in kind. Val didn't mind at all.

"Is this why you chose to wear white?" I wondered. "As a concession to me?"

"Yes, as it symbolizes purity," said Val, handing me the white rose she'd hid behind her back. "As I do so enjoy the purity in your heart. It's what keeps me falling for you more and more each day. I know you only reserve it for me. If you accept this rose, then you would have mine."

"Your purity?" I asked, smiling wider; holding her hand with the rose.

"My heart."

I wished I were more eloquent with sweet nothings and romantic gratitude. Taking this flower in my hands wasn't enough. I nestled the stem inside my jacket, admiring the fresh scent. I held Val's face in my hands, shyness in her skin and all, and kissed her as fully as I could. When I felt her touch along my waist, hesitant as it was, I fell into her more. I was hers just as much as she belonged to me.

As much as this growing zeal for her in my chest frightened me, I needed it. On this precipice of great change, Val was my only constant. Xavier had proven himself easily swayed by someone as persuasive as Elysia—though I did not blame him. That incident had still put a damper over our friendship. It was worse, still, that Queen Beatrys now took up most of his time. He knew I could not go anywhere near her save for mealtimes. He knew I was afraid of her, though I was too proud to admit it.

There was something about Val that made me feel safe for the first time in years.

We went to join the festivities in the ballroom. The opal chandeliers hung freely along the ceiling, enchanted to show heavenly skies with the same set of stars as the night outside. The marble floor reflected that art, making it look as if everyone stood along glittering clouds. Xavier had yet to arrive with the queen. As we waited for them, a cello quartet played music as divine as the sky overhead. The cellists belonged to the underground group of Black Waltzes in the city. The secret assembly of sorceresses expressed their frustration with having to hide through dance. Xavier had reached out to them in private, promising to help restore their standing in the empire. As a show of this new bond, the Black Waltzes had sent their personal quartet. Even if I had to leave without Xavier, I hoped he would fulfill his promise to them.

It wasn't until then that I noticed how anxious Val was in large crowds. Or perhaps it was only here in the palace amid everyone's judging stares. She was stiff, leading me by my arm with an unnatural strength. By our closeness, and by the rampant gossip that the servants had spread, they all knew as to our intimacy.

By the time I sat down, everyone seemed to have forgotten how to lower their voices beneath the music. With no available chairs nearby, Val knelt at my feet, gazing up at me as I drank a glass of champagne. We heard a few people wondering as to how Val had gotten me *under control* to bed me. I was reminded of my brother and his friends—how they had played their adolescent games, betting with one another to see who could have me first…

"What is it?" asked Val. "What's wrong?"

How did she notice right away?

I spotted Gustavo standing on the opposite wall with a few new nobleman friends he'd made here in the palace. He stared at me from behind his drink, muttering to his friends—about me, most likely. Val turned and matched my line of sight. She turned right back around, scowling.

She hadn't judged me when I'd told her of my shameful past.

Perhaps now was the time to tell her about what loomed over the near-future.

"Back when I had plans for you to meet with Xavier," I began, "I did not change my mind of my own volition. The situation changed. He would not tell me all the details before."

"And now you know?"

I explained everything to her: why Xavier had initially changed his mind about our plans for the empire and the war, and the conversation I'd had with Elysia in my chambers. I had to lean down to whisper in her ear, lest anyone overheard. With my hands along her slender shoulders, I heated my gaze and licked my lips, making it look as though our conversation was sexual in nature. Val's mind spun these factual details and my tone into suggestiveness. She fought hard to stay still.

When I was finished, I rested my head along Val's warm one, still holding her about her shoulders. The warm roots of her silken hair soothed me. It was as if I could hear her racing thoughts without using telepathy at all. Her thoughts raced for me. She worried for me. She wanted to do all she could—for me.

"Lucrezia, I know you are unhappy," noticed Val. "This unseen threat might chase you from the life you're comfortable with. It frustrates me that I cannot stop Vespair on my own."

"Believe it or not, your human rights efforts *do* combat the close-mindedness her spirit perpetuates."

"It isn't enough…"

"That is why Lady Elysia wishes to carry out her plans. With or without our approval."

Val growled, asking, "But what *can* I do that will be enough? I feel useless!"

"We will have to improvise, love," I explained. Val calmed down by this pet name I saved for her. "I shall tell you once I figure out what I need. I'm certain you will do everything in your power to provide for me. That gives me comfort—for now."

"If you do need my army to protect you, then I will make it so."

On cue, Captain Lydia, Lieutenant Lee and Lieutenant Sebastian found us with a dozen or more of their comrades, all in imperial uniforms. Val stood to meet them, grinning. I hadn't exchanged many words with her top officers that night in Nirvana some weeks ago. I expected them to only smile and greet Val. Instead, they seemed just as happy to see me—to see me with her.

"Lady Lucrezia!" said Lydia, waving to me. "How great to see you again. You're positively glowing!"

"Good evening, Captain Lydia," I replied warmly. "Lieutenant Lee, Lieutenant Sebastian. You both look well tonight. I'm glad you could make it."

Lee cracked a smile for me. "Likewise, my lady."

On the other hand, Sebastian looked a bit frazzled. Frustrated.

He did his best to cover it up, smirking at me instead. "Couldn't miss this for the world," he responded. "Training with that prick James has been a damn nightmare. I swear he looks down on us just because of what we are. He refuses to believe our artillery strikes are more efficient than a band of regular archers."

Val spotted James mingling with her father, Magister Pathos—of all people—across the way. "Sexist, he is," she said.

Lydia laughed. "We'll see just how sexist he is when we show up his prized soldiers again," she quipped. "But we didn't come here to speak about work... Val, come here! I must solicit your advice!"

"Yeah, me too," added Lee, smiling anew.

"About what?" protested Val, as Lydia and Lee dragged her away. "Hold on! I'm here with Lucrezia!"

Lydia smiled at me from over her shoulder. "The dear lady can wait, can't she?"

I laughed, waving goodbye to them.

Sebastian accepted a glass of champagne from the roaming servant. "Weird," he muttered. "They didn't tell *me* what that's all about."

"A shame," I noted. "I was about to ask if you had any idea."

"I don't."

From what I remembered, Sebastian was one of Val's more jovial friends. It was strange to see him in such a mood. I was about to take it personally. But he and I had hardly exchanged more than a few words with one another. Making irrelevant small talk now didn't seem like the best of ideas.

Sebastian had his eyes fixed on Lee and Lydia, on how Val smiled with ease with them.

"Is something troubling you, lieutenant?" I asked.

"Somewhat," he said, before drinking to buy time. "How'd you notice? No one asked me before now."

"Why, your furrowed brow, your scowl and your mood might have pointed me in the right direction."

Sebastian scoffed. "So you've got no idea, huh?"

I sensed some hostility from him. Even *some* was too much. "Speak your mind," I said.

"Everyone's figured out that most of us in Val's regiment are alchemists. No one bats an eye because we're with the imperial army. But before? *You* were the one who signed that damned bill to throw us out of our homes. Heretics and traitors, you called us! Now you love us! Now you need us."

"You mean the Relocation Bill from four years ago," I recalled.

"More like the fucking Homelessness Bill."

"I did not sign that document, lieutenant," I explained, uncaring of whether he believed me or not. "I was overruled. The rest of the Privy Council voted in favor of the decree. In fact, the oracles in the Grand Cathedral lobbied for its passage by bribing most of my associates. Not that they needed the coin in order to sway their views. They threatened the emperor and me when we fought in your favor."

Through Sebastian's disbelief, he was reasonable enough to hear me out. "How did they threaten you?"

"They warned they would expose us as sympathizers. Or as sorcerers. We would have been sentenced to death. We had no choice but to keep quiet. That is the manner of corrupt politics your lord commander ended when she stripped the council of their power nearly two months ago. Nevertheless, I apologize for what you suffered. You didn't deserve that. Their hypocrisy now is telling, indeed."

Once Sebastian had nothing to say, I finished my champagne in peace. I heard the cogs of his mind working. He had to know that I wouldn't lie about this. Perhaps he would find it in him to forgive me, even though I'd done nothing wrong. Nothing—but I might not have fought hard enough, smart enough for him and the other alchemists in the city. That was the first battle Xavier and I had fought—and lost—not long after our arrival here in Eden.

There was no point in dwelling on the past.

I spotted Raj alone out on the balcony. She smoked something—billowing out glittering clouds of silver. I excused myself from Sebastian's lovely company to go speak with the empress. I had last seen her the other week when she came to the palace to speak with Xavier. Raj had agreed that seeking peace with Queen Beatrys was best. I could tell that there had been something else on her mind—much like now.

"Lady chancellor," said Raj, leaning on the balcony rails. She stared out at the expansive garden beyond. I wasn't surprised to find her wearing her usual attire— nothing formal for the ball. She was the only one who could get away with such a thing.

"Good evening, empress."

"Thought I told you to call me Raj?"

"And did I not request that you call *me* by my name?"

Raj chuckled. "Guess you did," she remembered. "All right, then. Lucrezia it is. Nice to see you again. I needed to see a friendly face tonight. All these snakes out here, trying to talk to me about my city. I ain't lettin' no scorpions have land down there again. They're nothin' but trouble."

"As I recall, the Garden of Eden was once rife with corruption. It's no wonder you'd rather keep us out."

"Yeah, no offense."

"But of course," I replied. Raj smoked again, looking forlorn. "Forgive me. The last time we saw one another, I wished to ask you something. Seeing you like this now... I regret holding my tongue before."

"What's up?"

"Do you miss her? Tonight most of all. I read that the two of you attended a number of parties here together after Elysium's independence."

Raj knew who I spoke of.

"I do... I *really* do. After over two hundred and some dozen years, you'd think I'd have moved on by now. I couldn't. *I can't.* Women stay away from me 'cause they know where my heart is. All I wanna do is go to Videl— look for her—but I can't leave my people behind. They'd be lost without me..."

I took this opportunity to tell her about my meeting with Elysia. I left out the information about Ser Videl's whereabouts in Valdivia. If I'd told Raj now, it was possible she might have changed her mind about her people and left right away. Elysia had stressed the importance of waiting for *The Scorpion's Empress* play first. I hated not knowing all the details. This had to do for the time being.

"Fucking Vespair," hissed Raj, scowling. "Makes sense that *she* was the one who messed everything up. Didn't have no problems with the clerics before. They stayed in their lane and the rest of us did whatever the hell we wanted. Now you can't go nowhere outside of Elysium and talk about magic. Someone'll call you a witch and burn you at the stake. I didn't get what the big deal was... I see now."

"Whatever happened to Nyte?" I asked. "She was the one who wore Vespair's armor after the fact."

"Some darkness tore at her the night before the war, sent her away... Stella—err, Mistress Fury—said somethin' about different timelines and went after her. Opened up a portal with her magic to somewhere. It was a lot like that one her mother left through in your room."

"Her mother?"

"Yeah, Elysia was Stella's mother. The one you talked to probably wasn't from this timeline. Wouldn't be surprised if Elysia and her husband were reincarnated years down the line. Same with Nyte and her parents. That's probably *when* and where Stella and Nyte went off to."

"That's likely what happened as a result of the spell you mentioned."

Raj shrugged. "Who knows? But anyway, Elysia wants me to get my people ready and just—leave?"

"To Valdivia, yes..."

"And this is supposed to happen on the night of the play? When's it gonna be ready?"

"Not until the first day of autumn," I replied. "You'll have all of summer to prepare. The theater will begin advertising two weeks before the production date."

"Well, hopefully the queen don't come waltzin' down to my place before then. If she smells my thaumaturges in Elysium, she'll burn my city down with her troops. That's the *only* reason I'm agreein' to this, by the way. Never been to Valdivia. Heard it's a different kinda place. Unsafe, what with it so close to the underworld."

"You may find yet another reason to leave the city," I hinted.

Raj raised her brow at me. "What about you?" she asked.

"What about me?"

"Elysia said you've gotta leave, too. I'll be there to look out for you, sure, but there's some things I can't make up for. Think you can survive out there without a real place to stay?"

From inside the ballroom, we heard the round of applause—no doubt from Xavier's entrance with Queen Beatrys. Raj's question burned a hole within me. Val had promised she would also be by my side. I had no idea how I would react once the time came to leave. I was put-together now. I was prepared, knowing that this was for the greater good, for my family. And Val's. And yet...

"No... I don't think I can," I said, keeping my voice from breaking. I returned inside with everyone else. I felt Raj's sympathetic eyes on my back as I left.

This cacophony of clapping made me feel small, weak. Everyone around me was glad to see the emperor in high spirits with the queen. Deep in my heart, I hated Beatrys for all that her presence had wrought. Seeing her smile with my best friend, knowing how she, too, manipulated him with empty talks of peace... I couldn't stand it. Grandstanding politics aside, I didn't forget how her thousands of soldiers waited aboard a few vessels along our shore of the Eidos Sea, waiting for the opportunity to burn Eden to the ground.

But one misstep from me, from Xavier, and Beatrys would no doubt pull that trigger. I knew she would.

Xavier went to the middle of the dance floor, arms spread wide in welcome.

"Thank you all for attending this evening!" he announced. "I must apologize for keeping you waiting. Now that I am here, the festivities can truly begin!" Xavier grinned when he found me in the crowd. "Lucrezia, my long-time friend! Won't you share this first waltz with me for my thirtieth celebration?"

That slighted look on Beatrys' face made me smile more than Xavier's proposal. The nobles around me parted for my path; Xavier held his hand out to me.

"I would be honored, my dear," I accepted, taking his hand. Everyone clapped anew.

The quartet began the song, and I led our dance together. Xavier was all too happy to follow. I smiled at him, genuinely glad to see him wearing the crown I gifted him for his birthday today. We could not speak as we needed—not with so many eyes on us. Not with Queen Beatrys watching. All around the ballroom, I noticed the gossip, the pointed staring. Sebastian may have accepted my apology, yet he continued to scowl at me nonetheless as he stood alone where I'd left him. Lydia and Lee looked glad to see me once more, nodding as I made eye contact with them. Gustavo wouldn't look away from me, almost as if he had tracked me all night.

I thought Val might have at least smiled at me. She had her attention fixed on the other end of the room. I noticed Gabrielle arguing with Yosef. Their bickering seemed quite heated. It wasn't enough to disperse the crowd around them, but Val worried anyway.

"Will we be silent this year?" asked Xavier, doing his best to hide his disappointment.

"Much has changed within these halls," I replied. "You know that."

"Are you still angry with me?"

I could not be—not with Xavier looking at me like a lost pup.

"No, darling. It is not *you* I am angry with. I am… uncomfortable having to hide. Having to hide more. Whatever legislation we intended to pass for me and my own will not bode well with *her*. Not to mention the promises we made to the Black Waltzes underground."

"I suppose not. I know not what else to do, Lucrezia. I'm sorry. All I wish to do tonight is forget…"

When the song was over, Xavier bowed to me and kissed my hand. In between the renewed applause, more people joined us on the dance floor. All around us, they danced to the new tune that played. I sighed in relief when I felt Val's hand along the small of my back: romantic, possessive.

"Lord Val!" greeted Xavier. "How wonderful to see you again!"

"Your Imperial Majesty," said Val, bowing. "May I steal Lucrezia away from you?"

"Be my guest! The both of you must promise to meet me and a few friends in the throne room in one hour. It is meant to be a bachelor party of sorts to poke fun at my celibacy. My birthday gift from the empress will provide much entertainment for us all! Won't you join us?"

The clock tower in the city chimed ten times.

"Yes, all right, dear," I allowed. "We shall see you in one hour."

"One hour!" called Xavier as he left the dance floor.

Val stood before me, her front against mine. She held my waist just as I reached to hold hers. We stared at one another, perplexed. We both laughed once we realized neither of us knew how to follow. Following another in a public dance had seemed too submissive for my tastes, thus I'd ignored those lessons in my youth. Val *was* legally male, thus she'd had no reason to learn how to follow.

I draped my arms about her shoulders, saying, "Well, I suppose we could simply stand here..."

"... and enjoy the music," finished Val.

She held me close, resting her head along my neck. I thought this might be a relaxed moment for us. As soon as I felt the evidence of what she wore for me—against my navel—I breathed slower. All day I'd looked forward to this. To running off somewhere with Val. Giving into her all the way. Much like Xavier, I wanted to forget about the politics and the threats that awaited our inevitable mistakes. I wanted to stop thinking about Elysia's plans and how they would uproot me.

At least for this night.

Just this one night, and then I could go back to my persona, to my duties, energy restored.

"Lucrezia," sounded Val's voice—rich and deep. "I want you..."

She pressed her waist against mine, making her point loud and clear within me. We were secluded within this crowd. Everyone danced around us, oblivious to us. Val pulled me closer, gripping my waist. Slowly, with controlled rhythm, she moved her hips into me.

Val whispered in my ear, "I want to be inside of you."

I held her tighter, trusting her to keep me upright in this crowd. Yet her tone—sexual, sinister—and the way she touched me over my clothes sparked my madness for her. It was so steep, sudden. I couldn't see. *Literally.*

The ballroom grew dim, as if someone had placed a dark filter over my eyes. The goings-on continued; the people danced, ignorant to this change. When Val continued whispering in my ear, I knew it was only me.

Only my perception had changed.

A foreign, female voice shadowed through my head... as sinister as Val's did.

You who shares blood with the night's North Star: you will suffer for as long as I see fit.

A shadowed spirit loomed right behind Val, immaterial at first. The spirit shifted into something I recognized. Clad in dark knight armor, the woman stood within Val's body. Without possessing her, without acting as a ventriloquist, Vespair spoke to me through my love's lips, seeking to haunt me: *"I know your deepest fears. Your lowest sorrows. Your basest desires. Why don't we pick one tonight and act it out? I wonder how loud you will scream once you realize which one I chose…"*

I felt Vespair picking at my memories. Picking at the skin over my forehead, probing inside my mind. When my sight cut to Gustavo, watching me still with his new friends, I bit my lip to keep from screaming. He had a curious look in his hazel eyes, *seeing* all the ways Val touched me just by gauging my reactions, however small. I looked away from him.

My periphery refused to cut him out of my view.

As the minutes passed, with Val teasing me with her touch, I tracked my brother as he left the ballroom. That particular door he went through… he left for the throne room. To mock me, to build this bubbling fear in my chest, Val had us follow them: Gustavo and his friends. I wanted to make her stop. I couldn't get my voice to work. Only to moan for her, to whine her name whenever she touched me again in the palace halls.

Vespair choked me without choking at all. She railroaded me on this path.

We had promised to meet Xavier in the throne room in one hour.

As the clock tower sounded eleven times, the guards opened the double doors for us. Val led me through to the thunderous laughter inside. With the clear night sky overhead, Xavier's male friends joked loudly over their alcohol, crowding the throne room with their lewd conversation. Along the perimeter, I saw men flirting with the few other women they'd invited to the party. I clutched onto Val's arm intertwined with mine, feeling like a lost, scared child wandering across a strange area. The clouds of smoke that we walked through smelled just like Raj's black velvet from earlier. Her drug of choice.

"The throne is yours!" said Xavier, holding his arm out toward the onyx in the fore of the room. His laughter was affected by the black velvet bobbing from his lips. He smelled of sweet smoke.

"Are you smoking, Xavier?!" I asked, bewildered. "Is *that* what the empress gave you?"

"Indeed! It is the perfect gift to forget all our troubles! I know how you are about these things, thus I'll not offer you any! I hope you will change your mind, however. If you do, I will have plenty to share!"

Raj must have gifted quite the stash to Xavier for his birthday...

Xavier held Val about her shoulders, walking with us. "Now I know just what the two of you need," he spoke in a low voice. "It should remove the stress from your shoulders. The rest of us will be high as the stars above in about ten minutes. I suggest you take full advantage of it. A little exhibitionism is in order, don't you think?"

"For your entertainment!?"

"For *yours,* my sweet Lucrezia! My friends shan't notice your cries and fucking once they are long-gone!"

With Xavier's express permission, Val sat down over the onyx throne. Back straight, legs wide, she placed her hand along the inside of her thigh. She gazed at me with such intensity, I had to look away. Xavier joined his friends near the center of the room, leaving us here. He truly meant for us to do this.

Val held my hand, bringing me to her. "Come here, Lucrezia," she said. I almost stumbled in my reluctance. I straddled her waist, facing her. "You're nervous. Don't be."

In this dark of night, I couldn't tell if Vespair was still in my head, in my throat, in my limbs. And yet she was. *She was.* "I want to enjoy you. Do you want the same?"

Another corrupt noble who allowed supposed heretics to suffer while she enjoyed her comforts in the palace. You are the worst of your kind, Lucrezia of Azrith. The pinnacle of self-interest and cowardice.

And sweet Valerie—she shares blood with the one who stole my armor, my identity. It is only right that I should act through her tonight.

"Val—Val, please," I begged, breaths scattered as she kissed my neck.

"Please what…?"

"Listen to me—"

Val wedged her hand in between my thighs, feeling how wet I was beneath my clothes. "I hear your body loud and clear," she murmured. She held my legs, firmer than I was used to from her. "I can almost feel the chills over your skin. All I need is to feel you wrap your long legs around my hips while I drive into you—deep, deeper… hard, harder." She pushed the tips of her fingers into me—as far as this barrier of fabric allowed. I sucked in my breath. "Mmm… I have to have more of you. *All of you.*"

Of a sudden, Val stood up. She kept my legs wrapped around her. I held her around her neck for dear life. She knelt to the velvet carpet on the floor and set me down over my back. Uncaring, unfeeling, Val thrust her hips against me. Friction from our clothes frustrated me in the worst of ways. I wanted her inside—but not like this. *Not like this.* She sensed my growing panic by the way I held onto her. She heard it in my voice, in my whines. I couldn't find the words to make her listen to my fears.

Just in my view, I saw Gustavo again. His friends. They weren't the same ones from his adolescence, back in the kingdom. And yet—I remembered. I remembered anyway how they would all conspire to take me against my will. They wanted to make me cry and beg and scream. They wanted to take my dignity from me—all because they believed I was a sorceress. Because they knew I enjoyed women as I cared for men, and they wished to convert me, to change my mind, to *straighten me* with their sex as their weapons.

Seeing this reminder of them boiled too many feelings inside of me. I wanted Val to fuck me in front of my brother, if only to show him I'd risen above those memories. But—this wasn't her. *It was Vespair.*

"Val, wait!" I cried in her ear. She moved faster against me, harder, hiking me up. "Please no—Val, stop! This isn't you! Gods, *listen to me!* Stop!*"*

She came to a grinding halt. Val grunted next to my neck, into the carpet, her body shaking. I felt her protruding veins over her neck. She looked around, as if waking in a foreign place with no recollection of where she'd been before passing out. When Val saw and felt me underneath her, she calmed down.

I shouldn't have been able to reach her through Vespair's manipulations. And yet I had, somehow.

"Fuck... how did we get here?" asked Val, dazed and out of breath.

"I'll explain later, love," I said to her. "For now... I need you to hold me. Don't ask any more questions. I won't have answers for you. Not yet..."

Val set her confusion aside. She set her full weight over me, holding me as I needed. With my eyesight sheared by the dark silk of her hair, I stared up at the night sky above. There within the brightest band of light in the sky did I see the North Star. I imagined the anathema that was Vespair's spirit as the same darkness there above. If it was as inevitable as the night, how could we hope to defeat her? Elysia's vagueness irritated me. I needed more answers before throwing this life away—the life I'd worked too hard to forge and keep.

The way Val held me made up for these questions left unanswered. Her touch breached the chasm underneath me, filling the space with certainty instead of fear. Certainty, at least, that she would always be by my side. No matter what.

Chapter Eight

The Scorpion's Empress
(Val)

I marveled over Lucrezia's bare legs in my hands, glowing in the golden light pouring through the Grand Cathedral's lancet windows. I knelt between her along the bench in the front row. With dozens of rows of empty benches behind us, Lucrezia's soft laughter echoed through the grandiose space of the cathedral: hanging chandeliers overhead, imperial flags along the perimeter of the ceiling, the whole building awash in the warm glow shining in from the autumn sunset outside. Caressing, kissing her thighs, the bends of her knees, her shins and her ankles—no further than that, as she detested it—I watched as Lucrezia relaxed after the time I gave her with my mouth, right here on the bench. Right here in the most hallowed of places in all of Tynan.

Lucrezia wished to escape those memories of Vespair taking my mind from me back in June, inundating herself in oral sex instead. Night after night, near-constant; testing my prowess. On this night, but an hour before *The Scorpion's Empress* play was due to start, Lucrezia had reserved the area for us. A borderline abuse of her power as chancellor to the emperor, she had sent all the oracles, clerics, nurses, students and visitors away for a time, giving us free reign of the Grand Cathedral.

We had no idea what would happen tonight. Our fates were in Elysia's hands.

Lucrezia didn't want to think about it. The sex we had helped her to forget. Whenever she did think about it, she overstressed herself to the point where I could not get through to her. This was better.

Drinking from the champagne she brought, Lucrezia covered herself with my military jacket. "We should have thought of this sooner," she said with a sigh, leaning back more along the bench. "These things are far better when they're not allowed."

I procured a charity copy of the *Hallows* from behind the bench. "There must be a passage in here about our actions sending us straight to hell."

"I've no idea. There might be."

"You've never read the veritable tome of our salvation?" I asked, sarcastic.

Lucrezia plucked the book from my hands, smiling wide. "Once, but it gave me nightmares, actually," she told me, flipping through the pages. "The scriptures about burning my kind... about how we're not to be trusted..." She found the lines. "Hmm, reading them now, the sexist overtones are plain. These witch hunts are nothing more than a concerted effort to control women—sorceresses or not. Any wife who dares not to be a dutiful slave to her husband must clearly possess magical powers." Lips curled in a sneer, she burned the book in her hands, ashes disintegrating before my eyes. "What a waste of trees."

I thought back to our first night in her chambers together. "Lucrezia, how did you set my hands on fire that time...? It didn't hurt at all."

She held my hands in hers, both of her legs bent over my shoulders. "There's a particularly long-winded, scholarly explanation about thaumaturges and sociology that's certain to bore you. The short of it is that you are an Aries, and Aries is a fire sign. If you were a Libra, it would have been wind instead. And so forth."

"What about you? You are an Aquarius, so does that mean you're best with wind?"

"Mmm, yes, I am aspected to wind. Sorceresses are able to control each of the elements, though we tend to be more natural with our astrological alignment. Because I am forced to hide my powers, the wind specialization I once had ended up shifting to shadows."

"Could you show me?" I asked with interest.

Lucrezia pulled me toward her, kissing me; testing her flexibility. "I will later, love," she promised. "In all honesty, I fear what's to happen tonight. Never have I... leaned on another for support in the way I do with you. Xavier always needed me to be *his* rock, *his* certainty. The only time he ever protected me was with my brother."

"I'm full glad you choose to lean on me... Will Lord Gustavo attend the play tonight?"

"With Queen Beatrys at his side, yes. I'm waiting for the news that they're to be wed. I shall be ecstatic."

I gave her a worried look and said, "Please tell me that was sarcasm."

Lucrezia kissed my forehead this time. "Of course it was," she assured me.

The stone double doors of the Grand Cathedral opened wide. Only a few people entered before the doors closed once more. Lucrezia and I hastened to clothe ourselves. We bumped heads and limbs as we bickered over the mess of clothes and champagne glasses we'd caused. We stopped, however, once we heard who it was that had interrupted our private time together.

Lydia's bellowing echoed up to the elevated altar. "Lord commander, lady chancellor!" she called in a sing-song voice. "Emperor Xavier gave us permission to enter! We've to come collect you now!" She stopped in the middle of the aisle once she saw us. With a gasp, she yelled, *"Blasphemers!"*

Lee chuckled. "I told you, didn't I?"

"Gods! Val, what is this?! Lady Lucrezia!?"

Lucrezia laughed in delight. "It is so terribly easy to offend you, captain," she remarked.

"What did you think we were here for?" I asked. "To pray to the Twin Goddesses?"

"Nah, *I* knew," said Lee. "This one here shot me down, said I was wrong."

"I thought you *were* here to pray!" argued Lydia. "This was where Ser Videl practiced her piety. You mentioned some time ago that you look up to her as a hero. What was it you called her? *A paragon of excellence.* Whereas you believed yourself a selfish renegade. Perhaps you still do."

I rolled my eyes. "I can't believe you remember that."

Fully clothed, Lucrezia went to the large, shallow fountain at the base of the altar. "How touching," she noted, pouring the leftover champagne into the water. "I must find some way to dispose of these bottles and glasses outside. Leaving them here isn't wise. It is a shame that we have to waste this."

"Lucrezia," I said, watching as the alcohol tainted the crystal-clear water there. "Darling…"

"Hmm?"

"That is where the young oracle children drink from during their morning sermons… The water."

As the last dregs of champagne dripped into the fountain, Lucrezia gave me a horrified look. I had never seen such an expression of fear *and* accountability on her face before. Even Lydia could not contain her entertainment, laughing loudly.

"That's brilliant," said Lee, smirking.

"Gods, take me now," groused Lucrezia.

Lydia kept laughing. "Those poor children! They shall be drunk before midday tomorrow."

"The adults can blame the holy spirit for passing through their acolytes," said Lucrezia, full of spite. She held my hand and had us leave down the aisle. Lydia and Lee stayed at our heels. "Let us be off."

***

As we made our way to the Apocalypse Theater that evening, the crowd ahead of us yelled and shouted in excitement. This showing of *The Scorpion's Empress* fell on the two hundred and fiftieth anniversary of Elysium's independence from Eden—the political move that eventually set the stage for the Empire of Tynan's inception.

Rising above the masses of playgoers, the high Epitaph Archway of the Apocalypse Theater stood as a monument to Tellus' destructive history. Past the welcome way awaited the perfect acoustic setting—the amphitheater within the earth's embrace spanned for an audience of thousands. As sorceresses were to blame for the fabled apocalypse that had destroyed civilization, the theater's plays maintained the witch hunt status quo. The Black Waltzes who snuck into the theater to practice their magical dances did so out of spite.

Yet tonight, Archangel Vespair—Ser Videl's former mentor and dark knight—would finally be portrayed true to history instead of watered down as a common knight. I thought the actors would have kept this detail quiet. They had advertised it instead. I knew they weren't ignorant to the dangers. Drawing a crowd of this scale, with the imperial guard on high alert.

Someone must have done this on purpose. I suspected it was part of Elysia's plans.

I looked around as we neared the Epitaph. "Lydia, Lee," I said. "Where is Sebastian?"

"Said he'll meet us there," responded Lee.

Lydia scoffed. "He was incredibly rude about it, too," she recalled. "I've no idea why he couldn't walk with us. It's as if he's avoiding you for some reason. He's been like this since the emperor's ball way back when!"

"He dislikes me," said Lucrezia, matter-of-fact.

Hearing that made my blood boil. I had suspected as much; having confirmation was another matter.

"If he does, then I will have words with him," I told her.

"There's no need, love. The lieutenant requires an outlet for his anger over the city's policies against alchemists. If he wishes to hate me, then so be it."

"He's cherry-pickin'," explained Lee. "Sebastian had no problem with you before when he thought you and Val were only fucking around. Now that he sees you're serious, he's jealous of all the time you spend together. Whatever bullshit he told you about that Relocation Bill is just that—bullshit."

Lydia noticed how angry I was. She frowned in concern. "Will you demote him?" she wondered.

"This has nothing to do with work," I replied, in more of an effort to convince myself so.

"And if *I* told you to demote him, for no reason other than my own vanity," said Lucrezia, "would you?"

"Yes," I answered, feeling my convictions burning in my heart. "I would do anything for you…"

Lucrezia smiled at me. Her beauty heated my neck, my face.

Lee nodded. "And that's why he's jealous."

"I was for a while, too," admitted Lydia. "But not like this. Definitely not like this…"

We passed through the Epitaph, meeting up with Xavier and his personal guard. Through the archway was the decorated indoor mezzanine that led out to the amphitheater. Religious masonry of the Anathema religion stood tall among the mythical paintings of eld over the stone walls. Nyx Vevina, our one true God, appeared as a shadowy statue of onyx holding a dark scepter: an attractive outline of a powerful woman, yet Her face was unfinished. Her twin sister Venus was next to Her, ivory white, as the standard of beauty throughout Tynan's lands.

Nyx Vevina and Venus were our Twin Goddesses, feared and revered, respectively. The people feared Nyx

Vevina because of Her mutability, Her darkness. She was not easy to understand. Passages in the *Hallows* described Her as a wicked woman who despised the light. Whereas Her twin sister Venus was relatable by the trials she faced at the hands of the other gods, thus more human, despite her inhuman beauty. She was demure, polite, unassuming—everything women in Tellus were expected to be.

Yet they worked in harmony for the sake of the world, and because they loved one another as sisters, despite their differences. Venus was the morning, the evening, as her single star represented, and everything in between on Tellus' surface; Nyx Vevina was the night, the darkness, the space, and the unknown of the universe, as our God. They tolerated one another at dusk and dawn as the only two times they were required to interact. Just like bickering sisters.

I looked at the inscription on the high wall above them, telling of how our world Tellus earned its name: *'Tell us, Nyx Vevina. Tell us what is beautiful. Tell us what is right. Tell us what is wrong. Tell us what is just. Tell us what is fair. Tell us what to love. Tell us who to marry. Tell us how they die. Tell us why we cannot follow. Tell us why we cry. Tell us why we scream. Tell us why we curse you for picking and choosing what to give us and what to withhold from us.'*

I heard Raj's voice not far behind me. "What a load of shit. Why can't they figure it out on their own?"

She stared up at the inscription with a scowl. While Lucrezia spoke with Xavier about security during the play, I went over to Raj. I darted my eyes to the long, curved two-handed sword sheathed at her hip. The hilt alone was too decorative to be of this time.

"That sword," I said. "Doesn't it belong to Ser Videl? Her *Mutsunokami?*"

"Yeah, it's hers," replied Raj, thumbing the hilt. "I want it with me once it's time to go. Used to wear it all the time. Stopped after a while 'cause it just depressed me more." I was still annoyed over Sebastian's attitude toward Lucrezia. Raj noticed. "What's botherin' you? Worried about the plans tonight?"

"That seems like a world away for some reason," I said.

By the sympathetic look on her face, Raj wanted to ask more, yet she chose not to. "After the play, we'll find you in the underground passage beneath the Lyceum. There's a good couple hundred of my people left with me. The ones that'll be with us are special cases."

"Special?"

"You'll see," was all Raj said. I spotted Gabrielle on the other end of the mezzanine. She looked upset. "Val, listen. I know Vespair might seem like a joke to you. She ain't done nothin' to make you *really*... hate her the way I do. She's gonna fuck things up tonight. I can feel it in my bones. There's nothin' I can do except let it happen. It seriously pisses me off."

Raj couldn't know that I was terribly afraid of Vespair taking me over again. Taking me—forcing me to force myself onto Lucrezia again... I could never forget how I had blacked out for several minutes at a time.

"Something's gonna go down," she went on. "Make sure you've got everything sorted."

"You should stay with the emperor," I requested, pointing him out in the crowd. "We'll all sit together during the play. For now, I need to go speak with my sister-in-law. I trust your judgment. If this is a bad time to be in Eden, I must make sure she gets to safety."

Raj hummed in agreement. "I'll let Lucrezia know where you're at."

I pushed through the crowd, over to Gabrielle standing by herself. She had her arms folded close to her chest, tapping her foot beneath her long gown. Agitated as the rest of the crowd, Gabrielle didn't notice me as I approached her.

"Gabby?" I said.

Gabrielle lit up once she saw me. "Val, there you are!" she cried, embracing me. "Please tell me Yosef isn't here yet. *Please!*"

"I've not seen him," I assured her. She sighed, sounding stressed. "What is it? What's wrong?"

"You've not been around as much... Not that I blame you, but—your brother is different when you are not at home. He complains and yells and says things he would not dare utter if you were under the same roof. I don't mean to whine about him—I'm sorry—"

I held her shoulders, trying to calm her down. "Gabrielle, you needn't apologize for how you feel."

She took a few deep breaths, saying, "I know I shouldn't. I don't wish to ruin your evening..."

I glanced at Lucrezia in the crowd. She matched my gaze, noticing the energy about Gabrielle and me.

"Oh... she's coming over here," worried Gabrielle.

I noticed Gabrielle's wedding ring in her hand—not over her ring finger. "Do you want to leave him?"

"Yosef...?"

"Yes! Do you want to leave my brother? If he treats you terribly, then you've no obligation to stay."

"I want to... He says he wants children. Yet he expects *me* to care for them alone while he runs the streets with his friends. I couldn't find a way to tell you. I didn't want to worry you, to upset you, or to go back on my promise that I would always be here for you..."

Lucrezia stopped just next to me. "Is something the matter?" she asked. "Lady Gabrielle, you look positively fraught."

"My brother is an idiot," I explained. "Gabrielle, give me your ring. Go back to the house while he is yet on his way. Pack your things, take a carriage and return home to your father. Return to Eidos and don't look back. As a matter of fact, I'd appreciate it if you took whatever is left in my room with you. I don't need those things anymore. I want you to keep them."

"But what about my promise…?"

I wasn't sure what to say to that. I appreciated her support… yet her safety was more important. Eidos was a whole continent away from this city. She should have been there instead.

"Allow me to take over, my lady," offered Lucrezia, surprising me. "I noticed the two of you arguing in the palace. If you are unhappy with Val's brother, you must place yourself first. I don't plan on leaving Val's side any time soon. Trust me to look after her."

Gabrielle smiled—somewhat. "You have kept my dear Val out of trouble," she said. "Far more than I ever could… And you keep her happy, focused. That is rare indeed." She handed me her wedding ring, holding my clasped hand in both of hers. "Val, promise you will write to me. I cannot send anything to you for fear that *he* will read it first."

"I promise to visit," I said instead. "We both will—Lucrezia and I. Eidos is a journey away, but it should do us some good to see the sun along the archipelago with you. I will write when I can, of course."

Gabrielle held me again, tighter this time. I couldn't possibly tell her of what might happen that night during the play. I couldn't find the words to tell her about Vespair, about Elysia; about Raj's plans to leave with Lucrezia and me. For these long years that I had known Gabrielle, she had always been my confidant… and yet I kept this from her, to keep her from worrying about me. She had enough on her mind as it was. Asking her to take what was left in my room was practical—for my sake. I had already left a number of my articles in Lucrezia's secret stash that she'd shrunk on her person.

With my sniper rifle holstered over my back and Lucrezia alongside me, I was ready for anything tonight.

I was surprised once more when Gabrielle embraced Lucrezia, whispering words to her that I could not hear. Lucrezia gave her response in a similarly low voice, prolonging their hold. Seeing the two people I cared most for in this world share such a moment... it made me miss Gabrielle more; made me fall for Lucrezia faster than I had over these months combined.

As I watched Gabrielle hurry out of the mezzanine, I felt a stinging ache in my chest. I didn't want her to leave... But this was for the best.

Once it was almost time for *The Scorpion's Empress* to begin, Lucrezia guided me to our seats in Xavier's private balcony. Raised above the ground along the outdoor amphitheater, we had the perfect view of the large stage lit up at night. Raj sat on the rightmost side, next to Xavier. Lucrezia sat next to him, with me on her left. She looked away from the long distance to the ground. I recalled her fear of heights; I admired the way she steeled herself, setting that fear aside as much as she could. Across the way, I spotted Queen Beatrys sitting with only Gustavo in their balcony. Lucrezia seemed not to notice either of them, pulling me closer. She focused on me to keep from looking down below. I relaxed over her body... for now.

Xavier smiled at us. "Lu, I swear you baby her too much," he teased. I noticed he, too, had a sword sheathed at his hip—one similar in size and scope to Ser Videl's.

"Val is mine to pamper as I please," she said, running her nails through the tail of my hair.

"Real cute," commented Raj, glaring at Beatrys on the other side. "You've even got an audience."

"I would much rather pretend that my little brother doesn't exist."

"Bad blood, I take it."

"More than you can imagine," spoke Xavier. The lights along the stage dimmed. "Ah, it's starting at last! Let us see how the actors chose to reinvent this story of an age."

Raj looked apprehensive, folding her arms and legs as the play began. I could only imagine how she felt. I would have been just as awkward if I had to watch a play of how Lucrezia and I had met. The first person to take the stage wore modern clothing. He was present to offer the overture speech to set the tone for the rest of the production. As he stood before the hundreds present in the audience, I grew nervous of a sudden. *When* would this scheduled trouble happen? Now? Ten minutes from now? Thirty?

Worse, I hadn't told my soldiers of what was to come. I had promised that I would have them protect Lucrezia if necessary. She took solace in that fact. I had only assumed that they would be on board for this— whatever it was. They had no reason to deny my request, and yet Sebastian's behavior made me question that. I spotted him sitting in the front row with Lydia and Lee. He looked downright irritated.

Sebastian and I had been best friends for a handful of years. Was our friendship destined to end all because he couldn't stand Lucrezia and how much she meant to me?

"Good people of Eden," spoke the actor, natural acoustics amplifying his voice. "We all know the story of how Elysium earned its independence from our city, branching off as an asylum for those we reject. But what of that rejection? What of that ignorance that causes us to close our doors to the needy, to the poor? We who take pride in our possessions will never know the hardships we ignore."

Mild rumblings in the audience told of the controversy he had sparked already. I quite enjoyed this.

"We are all guilty of selfishness—even the scorpion's empress, who chose love above all else. Yes, we know of the selfless woman who provides for any who seek shelter in Elysium. But what of the fearful details? What of the orphan who escaped her negligent parents to pull herself up by her bootstraps, seeking opportunities here in a city that denied her everything? What of the woman who suffered such crippling loneliness, that she resented her need to maintain order and remain the same? And the paladin who fell into her life... she was not as pure as we would all believe."

More conversation sparked from but a single word. *Paladin.* Each rendition of this play before had noted Ser Videl as a knight and nothing more. I noticed Raj growing emotional already. She hid it well. Xavier appeared pensive, fully absorbed in the goings-on so far. Lucrezia was... unreadable as she held me.

"This is a story of sacrifice, of devotion. Of piety, of steadfast beliefs. Of paranoia, of shadows. Ser Videl sacrificed endlessly for her empress, as her slave—by choice. And the empress, as we all know, set aside her demons to be with her scorpion. Would that we could all learn to set aside our own differences with our loved ones... to have the unbreakable bond that these two women shared..."

In a show of awkwardness, the actor retreated off the stage. I was certain he had meant to say *paladin* once more toward the end there. By the death glares he'd received from most of the audience, he had decided against it.

Once the curtains reopened, the stage showed a view of Raj's office at her headquarters, Vassago. Within the warm wood of her surroundings, the actress playing Raj looked eerily like the one sitting up here with me. She practiced the empress' iconic kindness, giving out food and drink to her citizens. The events quickly spun toward the machinations against her from Lord Kurtz of Eden and Mistress Fury.

I was impressed by the sheer vigor the actors displayed, playing their parts with passion and conviction. The set pieces gave the illusion that these events truly took place in the single city of Tynan in the year 577. The stone architecture in Eden was downright archaic compared to the towering spires we had now. The only building that remained the same was the Grand Cathedral, if only for tradition's sake.

Once the play shifted to the cathedral, I felt a surge of pride, seeing Ser Videl there. Though it wasn't her—it was only an actress—I was glad to see her likeness. Lydia remembered that I looked up to Ser Videl as a hero. I was no paragon at all. I caused destruction wherever I went so long as it matched my goals. Watching her now, I was glad that I had calmed down.

I would have self-destructed if I hadn't had Gabrielle—and now Lucrezia—to keep an eye on me.

At the scene where Zephyr Seraphim Rin punished Ser Videl with the lashes upon her back, I noticed my mind wandering away. Lucrezia nudged me, noticing my thoughts.

"This doesn't make you uncomfortable, does it?" she murmured in my ear.

"Why don't we do those things?" I asked her. "I thought you were into the more physical aspects…"

"I was—with men. With you, I find that the bond we share challenges me emotionally. That is worth more to me than whatever whipping I might deal out to you. Even holding you like this in front of Xavier is different for me… It is difficult to explain."

"Letting your guard down is more meaningful," I filled in for her. "Since you've never done it with anyone before. If it matters at all, I've not been like this with others before you, either."

Lucrezia wrapped her arms tighter around me. "It *does* matter, love," she spoke. "And it means the world to me. Remember that."

***

Throughout the play, the crowd grew more and more disturbed over the continued references to thaumaturges in the script. By the halfway mark, I feared they would break out in protest. Once Raj cornered Lord Kurtz in the alley, I had the worst feeling. I knew what was to come.

Vespair appeared in her dark knight armor as black as night, with a visor over her face and a great-sword over her back. She threatened Raj to stay away from Ser Videl.

And then, once the conversation was over, it happened.

By special effects, Vespair disappeared through a vortex of red and black magic in the ground.

The crowd rose to their feet, shouting over the sheer heresy on display. Raj's actress tried to go on. She stopped where she meant to spy on Nyte and Mistress Fury together. The three of them stared with wide eyes at the open crowd, fearing for their lives. The guards on watch should have intervened. They should have protected the actors, yet they did nothing. As the playgoers screamed as to the blasphemy, I looked across the way to the balcony opposite us. Queen Beatrys glared at the actors, scandalized over what she'd witnessed. As for Gustavo—I didn't expect to find such a thoughtful look on his face. He didn't seem offended at all...

"Oh, hell," cursed Xavier. "Where are the guards?! The crowd's about to mobilize on the stage!"

Raj had half her face covered with her hand. "The guards ain't gonna help," she muttered. "You know that. They step in now, and they're dead. Those swords and shields they've got'll only do so much."

"I must do something! If they won't protect the actors, then I will! I won't let anyone die over this!"

I thought Lucrezia might have said something. Stood up to stop him as Xavier took off downstairs for the stage. She sat still, statuesque. She was pale. Far too pale. These events had paralyzed her. I looked into her eyes, trying to *see* what exactly had happened to her. Lucrezia wasn't focused on the stage, on the crowd. She stared off at… the space, the height, the fall from here to the crowd below. Her eyes were not blank at all. It was as if she watched something play out before her—something I could not see.

Whatever it was, it haunted her.

Lucrezia trembled in her seat, fixated on this invisible apocalypse happening across these heights she so feared.

"Lucrezia!" I shouted, shaking her. Xavier was on the stage now, trying to calm everyone down. "Damnit, Lucrezia, wake up! The emperor needs you!"

Raj moved to her feet. "This is it, Val," she said, prepared in her cynicism. "Handle this how you need to. Once this is over, remember the plans. The Lyceum. The underground passage that leads outta the city—"

"I can't remember a fucking thing with Lucrezia like this!"

Taken aback, Raj finally noticed what the issue was. She moved her face in front of Lucrezia's, observing.

"Looks like her past demons came back…"

I paced about, panicking. Raj didn't know what to do. *I* didn't know what to do. The crowd and the guards heckled Xavier, calling him a heretic, a sympathizer. The guards surrounded the stage, blocking the three actors from leaving. The actors on the stage cowered behind Xavier instead. Try as he might, Xavier's diplomacy was useless. Things were bound to get worse—worse—far worse, and I had no idea what to do—

"Val," said Raj, far too calm. "Keep your head on. Let this play out as it will. I can't do shit, so I'm outta here.

I need to make sure my people are safe. We'll wait for you to join us, all right? No matter what, I won't leave without you. Not unless I know for damn sure you were killed. Stay alive."

Raj clapped my shoulder and took off. It took me a moment to remember I couldn't be angry at her. She was right. She was sensible. I needed to *find* my head before I could keep it on, as she'd advised.

I was about to call out to Lucrezia again. An otherworldly sound from the stage chimed across the amphitheater. Iridescent light formed a protective barrier above and around the stage. Holding his sword close to his chest, Xavier stood strong as he maintained the protective barrier. Shining blue light spiraled around his sword, his magic source, his catalyst.

All this time, the magic-fearing people of Tynan had a paladin for an emperor, and they had no idea.

Lucrezia stirred from her waking nightmare. "Xavier!" she yelled over the crowd, bolting to her feet. "Gods, what have you done?! Why this? Why now? Damnit! Damn you!"

I watched her grip her face, trying not to cry in her sudden helplessness. An antithesis.

She knew exactly what she needed to do.

"Lucrezia...?" I tried. "Whatever it is you're holding back... you might as well do it."

We both watched Queen Beatrys cross the aisle on the ground, approaching Xavier with her staff.

Lucrezia trembled anew. But one incantation from the queen, and Xavier would die.

"I'm here," I promised, holding her hand. "If you would risk your life for his, then take me with you."

I stared into Lucrezia's eyes, watching the photographs fly by—the years she had spent with Xavier, the good times she'd had with him, and how she could not stand to throw those away. She closed her eyes tight shut, gripped my hand and made her decision—

—seconds later, she'd teleported us to the stage at Xavier's side.

"Lu!" cried Xavier. "What are you doing here? This is *my* battle, not yours!"

Exhausted from the teleportation, Lucrezia leaned on me, unable to speak. I felt her effort—how she tried to take Xavier with us for a second teleportation. She couldn't. She was too weak. Untrained from the strain she'd placed over herself, having to hide her powers.

"As I suspected," said Beatrys, just beyond the barrier. "A thaumaturge and his witch, ruling over half the world together. You thought I didn't smell the tainted blood in your veins. I gave you the benefit of the doubt only because Lord Gustavo asked me to. Now I must wonder if he knew that his sister was a heretic."

"This isn't heresy!" yelled Xavier. "Magic is no more impure than the rampant political corruption and bribery that plagues Tynan and Tibor both! I sanctioned this version of the play to spread awareness, not hatred! It is time to shed the fear of magic! Whether it caused the first apocalypse or not, we must move forward!"

"Your idealism would be admirable were it not for such a horrendous cause… You are a fool, Xavier."

Beatrys raised her staff to the audience's applause. She smashed the heavy tip to the ground, shattering Xavier's barrier of light with shadows. I gripped Lucrezia's hand in mine, willing her to do *something*. She was frozen in her fear again. Xavier backed away, shaking as he held his sword in front of him. For as powerful as Xavier and Lucrezia were in their own rights, they were inexperienced with the *real thing*. They knew not what to do. And I was just as powerless. I could not ready my sniper rifle in time—not with Beatrys just seconds away from killing us.

Right as she was about to use her incantation to burn the very magic in Lucrezia and Xavier's veins, I watched as someone snatched the staff from her hold. Gustavo tossed the catalyst clear across the amphitheater. He matched Beatrys' outrage head-on.

"I won't let you murder my sister in cold blood!" he declared.

"Have you gone mad?" accused Beatrys. "Your *sister* is a witch! Are you to allow her to kill us all so that she might get away?"

"I don't care *what* she is... I am her brother, and I will protect her from anyone!"

"Then protect her from yourself!"

Beatrys grabbed Gustavo by his head, channeling her skills through him. She raised him above ground by her powers alone. He cried out in pain as shadowed bolts of lightning consumed him. His body was no longer under his control. In need of another catalyst without her staff, Beatrys used him instead to send a shockwave toward the stage, toward us. The playgoers near the front dispersed, freeing the space.

Lucrezia awoke again—right on time.

"Let go of my brother!"

She raised every shadow from each person in the theater, joining them as a mass of power. Lucrezia sent that immense force toward the shockwave. The shadows absorbed the lightning and exploded over Beatrys, knocking her back. Lucrezia stepped off the stage and went toward the queen along the aisle. Writhing in pain, Beatrys held her hand out, beseeching Lucrezia to stop her advances. With Gustavo hovering overhead, his cries of pain echoing across the amphitheater, nothing would stop Lucrezia from freeing him.

Lucrezia stomped the heel of her boot next to Beatrys' face, holding her up by the collar. "I will only say this once more!" she avowed. "Let go of him! *Now!*"

Xavier pulled me along. "Lord Val, we must hurry!" he said.

Confused, I followed Xavier's lead, leaving the stage with him. He put up another barrier, shielding us from those in the crowd who had yet to flee. When Beatrys did not comply right away, Lucrezia scathed the very veins in her limbs. Beatrys screamed, and screamed, so loudly that her throat bled, forcing her to choke. She coughed and sputtered, defenseless.

That choking continued. It persisted. It killed her.

Only after Beatrys breathed her last breath did the magic holding Gustavo in place disappear. As he fell from the sky, I barely caught him in time, winded from his weight. Xavier pulled Lucrezia up as the spectators howled and screamed. *Regicide.* The magic, the murder; they could never go back from this. *We* could never go back from this.

Circling, spiraling, the hundreds around us called for our heads. They shouted to remove Xavier from the throne. They yelled at the guard to burn Lucrezia at the stake. Panic, screaming, overwhelming: I couldn't see anything, I couldn't think, I couldn't plan or focus. Demonized and targeted, we had no time anymore. Vespair's doing, or Elysia's, or fate's—it mattered not. This building, rising cloud of chaos, was inescapable, yet Lucrezia saved us. She teleported the four of us away to safety amid the screeching of their shrillness, climbing higher, higher, higher, endless, still going.

Everything was done, over.

Chapter Nine

The Unseen
(Lucrezia)

We reappeared within the depths of the Lyceum in the heart of Eden. Surrounded by dusty tomes stacked high along bookcases, the screams and shouting from the city were but an echo from here. Exhausted, I leaned against Val, breathing hard as I at last woke up to the reality of the situation. What we'd done. What *I* had done.

Lost in my rage, I'd killed Queen Beatrys as the audience looked on. The people of Tellus would never, *never* accept my kind. I hated knowing that my actions would be held up as a standard—as something to fear. That burden was now on my shoulders. All for my brother who had protected me... And now Gustavo lay crippled in Val's arms, his body twitching, convulsing as he struggled to breathe. Xavier took my brother from her hold, rushing to meet Raj at the end of the corridor. When he noticed that Val and I had yet to move, he stopped.

"We must leave!" urged Xavier. I watched Val stare off at nothing. "What is it?"

"My family," she said, hollow. "My soldiers... I can't leave without them."

Raj chimed in with the hard truth. "Your family's likely not gonna be happy with you. As for your troops, maybe they'll be different. Can't say for sure. Depends on how much they trust you."

"I took them in when they had nothing," explained Val. "Ten years ago... I gave them shelter, gave them work, gave them a purpose in life... Surely they will look past everything else and come with us. To protect us." She looked to me, her eyes mixed with uncertainty and resolve. "I promised you they would. I must keep my word."

"You sure?" asked Raj, pointing behind her. "'Cause my people are more than willin' to look out for us on this trip."

Val turned to leave. "They are your family, not mine. I need my soldiers."

"Val, wait!" I said, grabbing her hand. "You aren't going anywhere without me." She didn't have it in her to argue. "Where are they?"

"I assume they ran off to the safehouse not far from here. Do you need directions, or…?"

"No, I don't. Xavier, Raj—wait for us."

Xavier nodded. "Of course, Lu," he promised. "We will look after Gustavo in the meantime."

Raj leaned against the wall, sighing. She didn't like this idea. It wasn't up to her. Val had already decided. She gave us her word that they would wait, and sent for a healer to see to Gustavo's pains.

By a flash of shadows, I disappeared with Val into the night. As two smoke-like serpents intertwined, we crossed through the riotous streets as wisps of black mist in the wind. I followed Val's heart for directions to her soldiers' safehouse. All throughout Eden, the people called for my head, for Xavier's. Filled with rage, seeing blood, they screamed in their fear, their hatred of what we were; of what I'd done.

Because it was so easy to condemn us as magic-users, as outsiders. Whenever we did something terrible, then *all* of us were to suffer the consequences. If I were a mere human who had killed Beatrys with my bare hands, it wouldn't have mattered like this. Somehow, because I had sinned, every thaumaturge and sorceress couldn't be trusted. As if we were a monolith: a single unit, a hive mind.

But, really… if they'd had my powers, and it had been *their* brother and *their* oldest friend in danger, what would they have done?

I feared that saving Xavier and Gustavo might have cost me more than my home in this city.

Behind the safehouse, I spotted a large gathering of imperial soldiers. Val's soldiers. All five hundred of them, in the wide-open space of the back garden. Lydia, Lee and Sebastian were at the fore. They all appeared angry. Terribly angry. They shouted at one another, rows of rage in the garden, saying words I could not hear. I materialized with Val around the corner of the house, just out of their view. I sensed a cloud of despair—*Vespair*—hanging over the troops, twisting their thoughts and speech.

Confident and undeterred, Val walked over to them. She made the mistake of holding my hand, of having me walk by her side.

Or perhaps it wasn't a mistake.

Their minds were already made up. It was only a matter of facing the inevitable now.

Her heelless boots and my heeled ones flattened the grass beneath our feet, in sync. Val's troops noticed us. They glared, voices lowered, muttering to one another instead.

Lydia whipped around. "You!" she hissed. "How *dare* you show up here with—with *her*!"

Val expected her resistance. "Lydia, please," she said, her calm rather charming to behold. "It was a bad situation. Lucrezia made a judgment call in order to save Emperor Xavier and her brother. If it were you in her place, wouldn't you have done the same for me?"

"No!" shrieked Lydia. "I would have killed myself the moment I found out I was one of those things!"

Arms folded, Val stated, "They are no viler than women who are not beholden to their husbands, brothers or fathers in this day and age. Your beliefs are grossly limited and hypocritical."

"And you think arguing with me about them now will change things?! You knew all this time what she was, and you stayed with her! What did you expect to have happen, *lord commander?* That you would come here, tell us we must leave the city to protect your *woman,* and that we would go—just like that?"

By Val's hesitation, it hadn't occurred to her that anyone other than Lydia would have resisted. Scores of the other women and passing men behind her three officers shook their heads, glaring at the both of us with clear contempt. And those advanced weapons they held: plasma cannons and shotguns; rapid-fire rifles and halberds loaded with artillery. They worried me a great deal.

Sebastian looked me up and down with a sneer. "She sent most of us out on the street," he spat. "Now look at her! She's got no place to go, and she needs our protection from the empire and the kingdom who want her dead. I won't be your puppet, Val. Drop her, and maybe we can talk about all this… I refuse to go anywhere with you if she's there."

"Yes, *maybe,*" emphasized Lydia, leering. "If she's poisoned your mind—brainwashed you—"

"—Lucrezia's done no such thing!" argued Val, gripping my hand. She spoke with such enraged passion. "For God's sake, there's nothing wrong with her! She is a sorceress—so what? If she had used a gun or a sword instead of magic, the outcome would have been the same! And you wouldn't be furious with her right now! Or me!"

No one had anything to say to that. They knew she was right.

"I've cared for you all for *years!* Most of you for five years—some of you for over a decade. You are more than friends to me. I love you all as if you were my real family… Please, come with us."

Sebastian and Lydia were both torn in their silence. They looked away from us. The others didn't react.

Only Lee. He holstered his high-powered rifle over his back and crossed over to our side of the garden.

"She's right," he said, facing the others. "For what it's worth, I already knew I was gonna do this. Val's the only one in this city who gave a fuck about us! And now that we found out Lady Lucrezia's a sorceress, you wanna turn on her? She's still the same person! She's still our lord commander!"

Val stared at him in awe. If we weren't surrounded, she might have let her emotions overwhelm her.

"Lee..."

"You helped me. I've got your back. That's how this goes. I don't give a damn about witches or none."

Lydia stared at us, pained. "We don't have a choice," she said, aiming her weapon at us. "The lieutenant-colonel... he gave us orders to kill you on sight." Sebastian and the others followed suit, their weapons raising, level with their waists, or shoulders, pointing right at us, some shaking in fear, hesitation... "Or you can surrender now—make this easier on all of us." Val's eyes hardened; reddened by this betrayal. "Don't make us do this."

Lee and Val both stood their ground. They trusted me; I knew what I had to do. Lydia took one look at me, contemptuous once more, and gave the order to Val's troops to fire. As the barrels of their guns lit up with charging force as bright lights in the night, I teleported us to safety.

***

Beneath the Lyceum, we all followed Raj as she led us through the underground passageway. Xavier carried my brother along; a few hundred of Raj's people from Elysium followed behind us, silent after the events above ground. As we descended further beneath Eden's surface, the walls of stone around us changed gradually from an unremarkable gray to a vibrant blue filled with magical energy. Dankness and echoes shifted to a vibrating hum of power around us.

As Lee was from Valdivia, he spoke of the dangers to expect past the sealed barrier. I had never been to these lands, as dangerous as they were. The city, so close to the underworld, was once a passage for the dead to return as ghosts. Most did not make it past the barriers that had sealed the city off from the rest of the world. Their hopes and dreams had died within the space, emotional energies coalescing into an illusory land. One could have easily been tempted to stay within Valdivia, lost in the mirages instead of facing reality. Time moved much faster there compared to the surface.

Lee's parents had had him before the seals were put in place almost thirty years ago. Back then, the city was a hermits' and wine connoisseurs' haven, with houses scattered across the many vineyards of the land, far away from one another. The living had communed with the ghosts who passed through, penning their stories, their biographies, and then travelling to the surface to sell the books in order to make a living. Those less skilled with pen and paper had found their fortunes in the wine business, taking advantage of the city's hastened time to breed the best bottles.

The imperial oracles had then discovered the breadth of magical energy within the city and sealed Valdivia shut. I anticipated my powers would be enough to open our way. If not, then I had a feeling Elysia would make her return. She would not send us down here without a means to see us pass.

And as fascinated as I was to hear of Lee's escape during the imperial intervention, I could not focus on his story for long. Val did not walk with me. She trailed behind our main group. Any attempt I made to walk with her was for naught. She would slow down or veer off to the side, avoiding me.

I had prepared myself for this journey, but not Val's resolve wavering.

Her soldiers meant the world to her. It was my fault they followed her no more. Mine—and Xavier's. As he carried my brother, I noticed the guilt clear in his face. I couldn't face either of them right now. Not with Val refusing to speak to me. My own guilt crept through my stomach, up to my chest, and up to my throat like a sick bile.

All of this happened because of what I was. It reminded me so of my parents abandoning me over two decades ago. Val was not my parent. I was more dependent on her than I had been with them. I needed her care and attention far more than I'd needed anything from anyone before. I knew she saw it in my eyes; felt it in my aura. She ignored me anyway. Not that I blamed her, and yet...

Did she know that I loved her already? She couldn't have known. I was terrible at expressing even a hint of these feelings. Val didn't judge me for my aloofness. She seemed to enjoy that part of my personality. Where anyone else would have scorned me, Val instead held me close to her heart.

I could only hope she would do this once more. After this ordeal passed... I hoped she would forgive me.

When we arrived to the sealed entrance to Valdivia, everyone looked to me to open it. I surveyed the area. The high ceiling looked like the inside of a tree, opening up to shining pale blue crystal beyond: an open tree trunk, an open window letting in beautiful glimmers of light. The barrier over Valdivia's entryway rose up as a stained-glass window of the same color of crystal. I placed my hands just over the light, sensing something strange.

Raj waited behind me, containing her anxiety. "What's goin' on?" she asked. "Can you open it?"

"Yes, but it appears there's someone waiting on the other side," I explained. "These magicks are powerful. They will only allow me to let one person pass at a time. Whoever's on the other end will serve as a test. If I can get them through, then perhaps I can find a way around these limitations..."

Even as I said the words, I doubted myself. These attempts I made to breach the barrier were useless. I was far too weak from living my life as a normal human. I should have kept up my training. I should have put my magic to better use. I was so afraid that someone would discover what I was. Now that everyone knew, I was no better than a child performing her first spells.

This magic was beyond my capabilities.

Murmurs from the crowd alerted me to someone's presence. Elysia made her way down the path, over to me. She wore a different set of oracle's robes—just as elegant as the last—with her staff at hand.

"Hello again, dear," she greeted. "You did not think I would send you here without a means to proceed, did you? Allow me to help."

Elysia and I both stripped away the seals over the entrance. These wards were also too powerful for her: she winced as she forced her staff toward the window-like blockade. Violet lightning surged forth from her catalyst, joined by the tangible shadows passing through my bare hands—a spectacle of light and dark tearing away at the decades-old magic in place. All we could do was breach the seal temporarily, allowing whoever was on the other side to pass through.

It didn't cross my mind to think if this person was dangerous or not. Elysia had proven herself capable; loyal to us. Whatever the technical age difference between us, I trusted her as my equal.

The way I saw it, Vespair would have found a way to disrupt my life here in Eden somehow, someway. At least with Elysia's aid, we controlled that chaos a little bit at a time. This was far better than having no control at all.

I didn't recognize the person's silhouette on the other side. Long, armored robes and long hair, possibly a woman—in my periphery, I caught Raj treading toward us, her steps careful, uncertain. When the woman forced herself through the opening, her outline emitted a bright magical light. She protected herself from the last few safeguards that would have burned her alive. That light reminded me so of Xavier's magicks as a paladin.

When the light receded, I recognized her blonde hair, her green eyes, and her violet and white robes as a seraphim from the Excalibur of old. It was Ser Videl, Raj's lover who perished in the imperial invasion nearly two hundred and fifty years ago. Raj, too, had died, but Vespair's rage lingered in her soul, keeping her here in this life. They had been separated by death—by Vespair—all this time, until now.

Raj couldn't breathe. "Videl...?" she asked softly. Her eyes glinted with hints of tears. "Is... is that you?"

Videl smiled, radiant. She nodded to Elysia and me, walking toward Raj, her empress. As a loyal knight, she knelt at Raj's feet, head bowed.

"It's me," she replied. "I've been trying for so long to get back home to you... I'm glad you're all right." Videl looked up, smiling brighter. Raj was too choked up to say anything more. "I missed you."

When Raj still could not speak, Videl stood and embraced her. As the moment sunk in, Raj held Videl tighter. Much tighter—harder to keep from breaking down and slinking to the ground. Videl kept Raj upright, holding her—steadfast. Such a reunion pulled at my own heart. I couldn't imagine being separated from Val for over two centuries... nor could I picture how I would feel once I saw her again.

I caught Val looking my way. She sat against the wall with Lee, her gaze fixed on me. Raj and Videl's moment had affected her, too. I saw our shared thoughts pull away the natural steel in her eyes. There, I knew for certain: she didn't resent me for what I was, or for what happened. She cared for me still. I smiled at her, knowing she couldn't return the gesture yet.

Elysia's smile was warmer than I expected. "Let us give them a moment," she suggested. "I will need the four of you to help with our way forward." She looked to Raj and Videl—to Val and me, one at a time. "This is the same key I spoke of earlier: the one that will grant you passage to the new world. There's no rush just yet."

Val spoke with Lee, staring at the ground, at the wall, at Elysium's citizens—everywhere but at me. I sensed that she, too, needed time first. I went over to Xavier kneeling at Gustavo's side as he lay upon the ground. My brother's convulsions had stopped. I didn't recognize him as he spoke with Xavier. Throat swollen and stuck to the top of his mouth, his voice sounded thick with struggle.

"Lu!" said Xavier, standing to meet me. "Gods, are you angry with me? This is all my fault…"

"It *is* your fault," I agreed. "But no, I'm not angry with you. Beatrys already knew what we were, apparently. She only stayed her hand because of Gustavo's pleas…"

I knelt down with my brother. Gustavo looked at me with the utmost apologies. After these years I spent being angry with him, I didn't have the energy to maintain those grudges. Not after all he had done. Not after he had changed his mind about me of his own accord, and risked his life to save me.

"Lucrezia," he struggled to say. "I'm sorry… for everything. I was a fool."

I hesitated before running my hand over his forehead, down to his toned jaw. I recalled the last letter he sent me. Gustavo had asked me in the most roundabout way to come back home. He hadn't exactly said that he worried over the upcoming war. He hadn't apologized for his actions in the past. Now I understood that that was what he'd meant to do before. I couldn't fault him for his pride.

Discovering the truth about me hadn't diminished his protectiveness for me.

I bent down, holding his head in my arms. I still hated what he and his friends had done to my spirit. They had made me fear my own blood; they had made me close myself off, all for Val to find me and bring me back to how I once was. Considering all that had changed in a matter of hours, I couldn't hold onto the past anymore. I wanted our relationship to heal. I wanted to enjoy having a brother again. I forgot the last time Gustavo and I had smiled together. Feeling his weak grin just against my face brought a much-needed calm to my spirit.

"Thank you, brother," I said, pulling away. "This was all I wanted. I wish it didn't have to happen after the devastation I caused in the city... I've no idea if your body will recover from the ordeal."

Gustavo shook his head, replying, "The healer said... not for a long time..." I didn't enjoy the sound of that. "You should be happy... I heard how—sadistic—you are."

I pushed at his shoulder, biting back a smile. "Oh, this is no time for jokes!"

No matter his condition, Gustavo was happy to get along with me again. That almost made me cry.

I followed his eyes tracking someone behind me. Val approached us. She knelt at my side, studying Gustavo with care. My brother noticed the way I looked at her with love unbridled. I only wished she would turn to meet my stare. Something held her back.

"Lord Gustavo," said Val. "I must thank you... for saving Lucrezia earlier. I didn't know what to do."

"I woke up," he responded. "I... had to do it."

Val's voice sounded heavy as she asked, "What made you accept her as a sorceress?"

"I knew all along. Heard her and Xavier... talking one day. It scared me. I blamed her... for our parents leaving. But… when there's a war threatening to take your sister away… your perspective… changes."

I looked to Xavier. He nodded, as if to say Gustavo had told him the same thing. It *was* my fault that our parents abandoned us. I'd had no idea that my brother knew for certain. By the pain in Val's eyes, I knew she worried for her own brother. I couldn't imagine Lord Yosef understanding her decision to stay with me after everything. Val likely felt the same about her twin. Seeing my brother accept me helped her to deal with that disappointment, unconfirmed as it was.

Gustavo gripped Val's hand nearest to him. "Take care of my sister," he ordered. "Lucrezia's stronger than… anyone I know. Still… protect her. Keep her safe. This world is unkind to her now… I heard the tales of your ruthlessness… Put it to good use for her."

Val placed her other hand over his, firm. "I will, my lord," she promised.

I adored that Val meant her words. Even after her soldiers turned on her, because of me, she found her resolve in this promise.

Elysia requested that Val and I join her by the barrier. I kissed Gustavo's forehead and told him we would speak again soon. Raj and Videl were there with Elysia, smiling as they held one another. The four of us stood together as we listened to Elysia's explanation about the key we needed. I was surprised to learn just what this key was.

"A sentry," said Elysia. "One that will guide us through Valdivia and keep us in good health. But first—I must create her with your aid. I must transpose one strength and one weakness from each of you in order to create her. She will serve as our protector."

"She?" I asked.

Elysia smiled. "I wish for my daughter to have a loyal, younger sister," she supplied. She raised her staff to the air. "Ser Videl, if you will place your hand just above mine." Videl did so; the same vibrant light surged from her, into Elysia's staff. "Knightly devotion from the world's legendary paladin, and her willingness to sacrifice for her loved ones—no matter the cost." She looked to Raj; following suit, Raj held Elysia's staff. "Endless compassion from the scorpion's empress, and the myriad of demons that haunt her." By Elysia's cue, I held on this time. "The magicks of the Shadow of Venus from our most veritable ancestor: let our sentry live in her likeness, by her eyes, by her face; by her coldness and her secrets as her lifeblood." And Val, for the last. She held the staff, serving as the tip of our hands linked together, touch by touch. "Androgyny as Valerie's social camouflage as she hides in plain sight for her own protection, and the strength of valor that she fights with; let our protector speak with her voice, her pain, her ruthlessness; with her heart locked firmly with those who share blood with my North Star."

Crystal rain of our strengths sprouted from Elysia's staff, forming, morphing into a human body shadowed by our weaknesses. As tall as I, as lean as Val, the sentry landed on the ground before us. Armor covered her from the neck down: the dimmest violet fitting for a dark knight. Long, stylized spikes decorated her shoulder plates, her armored sleeves and her shin guards; flowing up, shaped like embers. Her thigh armor was made of white cloth, ending right at her knee guards. And her chest plate curved just enough to blur her gender. Any onlooker could have assumed she was male or female.

Our sentry appeared as a grown woman. My hazel eyes, with her facial features like mine, like Elysia's; she shared her mother's long, dark hair, flowing straight down to her lower back; her mother's radiant, olive skin that marked their multiracial heritage. Her posture was as proud as Val's. Her knightly servitude showed in her eyes just as it radiated from her aura. Her compassion shone through her expression as she looked upon us, recognizing us as friends, as family.

Our protector was a mix of our traits, yet she was herself. Her own person. Unique.

"This crystal rain," noted Elysia, staring up to the light above. "I shall call you Raine, then. Raine Azrith."

Raine bowed to her mother. She could not yet speak. That was something she had to pick up over time, much like any other newborn. As strange as it was to think of her as such, it only made sense.

Raj handed Raine the long, curved sword at her hip. "I reckon you'll need this," she said. "If you're as powerful as I think you are, it'll be better off in your hands."

Videl approved of Raine accepting her old sword. "Is she a dark knight?" she asked.

"Indeed," replied Elysia. "Lucrezia's skills overrode your paladin magicks, I'm afraid. As I cannot create another sorceress in her likeness, a dark knight was as close as I could get. Her powers will rival the Archangels who originally created this world in Venus and Nyx Vevina's images." She pondered over how to best handle this barrier. "Raine, let us test your might. Deactivate this obstacle, if you please."

Raine looked over her *Mutsunokami*. With one hand, she gripped the hilt with all her strength and thrust the blade into the barrier. She cut through the magic fighting against her. Upward she lifted her blade, keeping it there as a slit, as an opening.

Elysia smiled in satisfaction. "We are ready to set off," she said.

Raj hailed over her people. "Hey, let's get a move-on!" she called. "Everyone inside!"

We allowed Elysium's citizens to enter first. They passed through to the misty lands of Valdivia. As the hundreds of people walked by in groups of three or four, Lee joined us.

"Where exactly are we supposed to come out?" he asked.

"In all honesty," replied Val, "I'd like to go to Eidos. I must visit Gabrielle. I need to know she's safe."

"You're in luck," said Elysia. "The entrance to our new world is beneath Eidos' temple. The Twin Goddesses meet there at the Edge of Reason. It is where Venus sets the day and Nyx Vevina rises to the night. There is an exit in Valdivia that will take us to that very location in the village."

Lee nodded in agreement. "Yeah, I remember where the exit is. I can lead us. It's a whole continent away. All the way to the far west."

"It will take us some months to arrive, yes. We must also mind the mirages in this land."

"I'll head in, then," said Lee. "I wanna see if I recognize anything."

Xavier carried Gustavo in his arms. "May we pass?" he asked, at the tail-end of the long line of Raj's people.

"Go ahead," answered Raj, gesturing for him to enter. "We'll be right behind you."

I smiled at my brother as Xavier followed Lee inside. Gustavo returned my gesture. Having this peace with him gladdened me. It felt as if I could get to know him again—or for the first time.

Just as Elysia was about to enter Valdivia, a sudden force cut down Raine's sword. Steel clanged against the stone ground. Raine staggered back, gripping her wrist in pain. The entrance to Valdivia sealed itself anew. Lee and Xavier spun around just as the magicks locked them on the other side.

Val lunged toward the entryway, smashing her fist against it. "Lee!" she shouted. "*Lee!* Damnit!" She stared at the shadows sealing the door shut. "What the hell is this?!"

An armor-clad figure appeared high above, eclipsed by the crystal light.

Videl recognized who it was. "Vespair!"

"Fuck," cursed Raj, turning around. "This ain't good..."

Sounds of steel footsteps echoed through the passageway. Dozens upon dozens of imperial soldiers charged toward us, swords drawn. Several oracles followed after them, staves drawn; readying their incantations to kill me. We had no time. *I* had no time to think, to decide. I made a split-second decision. I had no choice but to teleport us away. All of us—Val, Elysia, Raine, Raj and Videl.

I abandoned our friends to their fate. The oracles could have reversed Vespair's enchantments. Entered straight through to Valdivia; killed the thaumaturges and sorceresses that had been under Raj's care. *We had to go.* I could only hope that our comrades would persevere.

A coward's hope.

***

I teleported us far away from Eden, out to a beaten path in the night. After wandering westward for a while, we found a carriage on the side of the road. The pair of horses ate the grass until Raine took their reins at her mother's request. The rest of us sat inside the carriage. Raj and Videl sat across from Val and me during the ride. By Raj's silence, she didn't blame me for my decision. I watched her as she came to terms with everything. She leaned on Videl, looking at me with empty eyes, her face full of understanding.

We passed by nothing but trees as we journeyed northwest. As Elysia was from Eidos, I trusted her to lead us back to her island. She knew her way around the world far better than the rest of us.

Val sat away from me, staring out the window. I worried that she would change her mind about me now.

She'd had Lee before. She dealt with losing her soldiers by sticking close to him. Now that he was gone—out of our reach—she only had me. I wasn't sure if that comforted her or not.

Videl lowered her head. "This is my fault," she admitted. "All of this. Everything that happened. I took a stand to protect Raj from Vespair. It's me she should torture, not the rest of you."

Such a quick glance from Val to Videl with the utmost contempt; if I'd blinked, I would have missed it.

Raj held Videl's hand in both of hers. "Don't say that," she insisted. "We're in this together. I thought I'd never see you again... If I've gotta suffer to keep you by my side, then fine. I'll deal with it. At least until we take care of her once and for all. No matter how long it takes, that's what I'll do."

"Raj," I said. "Are you not a ghost? Vespair's spirit is all that keeps you here. When we defeat her, won't you disappear?"

"Guess so," answered Raj, shrugging. "The new world we're headin' to is part of the underworld. Even if we're over there when we kill Vespair for good, I'll probably disappear anyway. I'd have to get back home, somehow..." She gave Videl a fond look. "Like you did. I'll find a way."

The energy Val gave off was filled with hatred. Pure, unadulterated loathing and disdain. She hid it well from Raj and Videl. They were too oblivious to notice. They didn't know her like I did. I recognized this aura about her from many months ago. Back when I'd found her after her terrible meeting with the Privy Council, I'd sensed this same anger from her.

She needed someone to blame. She refused to blame me for what happened.

Videl was to blame for everything. Her and Raj. Their love. Their sacrifices.

The only thing keeping Val quiet was her logic. She knew that if our roles had been reversed, and if it had been my safety on the line, that she would have acted as Videl had done. She would have crossed Vespair and caused this mess for our families. Without hesitation.

Sometime later, we stopped to rest for the night—far enough away from Eden that no one around would recognize us. Tzalieri was a remote musician's village hidden in the woods. Small houses of wood populated the area. Violinists played outside their homes in the dead of night. The largest building around was the tavern, still open for business at this hour.

We took three rooms and paired off. None of us had an appetite after what happened. While Val went to wash before bed, I wandered along the narrow wooden halls. I knew I wouldn't sleep. The bed in the room Val and I shared was nothing like the one I'd left behind. I couldn't stop worrying about Gustavo, about Xavier, about Lee, about everyone.

The door to Elysia's room was open. I heard the water running in the adjacent washroom. I saw Raine sitting at the foot of the single bed, staring at her sword. It hadn't cut in half from Vespair's disruption, but it was damaged nonetheless. By the guilt in Raine's face, she blamed herself for losing the others.

"Raine," I said gently, approaching her. "Are you all right?"

Raine stood up out of respect. She looked around, caught off-guard by my entrance, and bowed.

"You needn't bow to me," I told her. "We're family. You are not my servant. I wish I could say the same about your relationship with your mother... Do you enjoy serving her?"

She didn't know how to answer. Instead, she only looked at me, feeling at a loss. Raine had yet to pick up on any speech or body signals. I found it endearing.

With Gustavo gone, I felt his absence in my heart. We were so close to having a relationship again, only for Vespair to cut that possibility down. I had no idea where he was, if he was safe; if they were on the run from the soldiers and oracles. Now that Raine was here instead of Xavier and my brother, I felt myself growing attached to her already. Her child-like stare reminded me so of Xavier. Her quiet admiration for me helped me to forget my troubles, if only for a moment. She was meant for such power over time, and yet here she was, happy to spend *this time* with me.

I held her in my arms. When Raine returned my embrace, I sighed in relief. Even with her armor in the way, her hold felt gentler than I expected. Already I felt a familial bond with her. As untraditional as her birth was, I cared for her as if she were my sister. As powerful as she was, I had no fear of losing her.

After I bade Raine good night, I returned to my room. Val had changed into her night things. She sat on the bed, facing away from me; staring out the window this time as she listened to the violins playing in the near-distance. Her sniper rifle sat upon the single surface in the room. Some of the clothes I'd packed away by magic for us lay folded nearby.

I went over to Val and touched her shoulder. She didn't acknowledge me. Her distance pained me... but I understood. I didn't hold it against her.

When I finished in the washroom, I found Val still sitting in the same place. She hadn't moved at all.

"Val?" I said.

She ignored me once more.

In more pain than before, I lay down in bed. These sheets and blankets were thinner than I was used to. The pillows held memories from the heads of other people who had slept here. I couldn't care about that... I was exhausted.

The night's events hit me hard as I stared at Val's back, at her long hair.

I wanted to tell Val that I loved her. I wanted to say it then in the hopes of bringing her back…

I said nothing for fear that she wouldn't say anything in return.

The weeks passed. We passed by more towns; stayed in more taverns, some more run-down than others. Still I said nothing. Val died a little more on the inside each day that went by. The distance between us was worse than the four years we'd wasted not *knowing* one another. Val would not kiss me. She would not speak to me. She would not look at me, or anyone, except for Videl, to glare at her on occasion, and then go back to blending in with the carriage we sat in.

We passed the world by in the back of this carriage. Val passed me by. She was too far away from me and I didn't know what to do.

The only comfort Val gave me was sleeping in the same bed. Some nights, she let me hold her from behind. She let me speak to her, begging her to come back to me: emotionally, physically. But it was no use. She wouldn't come back.

I didn't know if I should pull away. Staying in this moment for her, filled with so much love—it brought me such agony. As much as my heart swelled for her, it decayed whenever Val ignored my questions. I wilted next to her each night in bed. If she didn't know, or if she did, and she ignored it, that only made this worse. I wished she would talk to me about whatever was on her mind, no matter how terrible it was. I knew—*I knew*—what she wanted to do. I knew why she wouldn't tell me; why she refused to explain anything to me. I understood…

I wished Val would do whatever she needed to do. Whatever was necessary for her to heal. Whatever she felt she had to do to mend her spirit. So long as she didn't push

me away completely, I would stand by her—no matter
what. I hoped that Val knew this by the devotion I gave her.
And yet the way she ignored me… I couldn't stand it.

As we exited the carriage one late night, I told Val
as much. "I'm here for you. I wish you would act on what
you hold back. Don't fear my disapproval, love… I will
always be by your side. Even if you grow to hate me for
what I am, for what I caused."

Val widened her eyes in shock. She didn't expect
me to say such things. By her surprise, that was exactly
what she needed to hear. What she needed me to say. She
knew that I meant it.

Once again in our room, with the door closed, with
both of us in our night clothes, Val stared out the window. I
assumed my words earlier had been mere drops in the
ocean for her. Perhaps they hadn't affected her in the way
I'd hoped.

Those thoughts vanished when Val turned around.
She moved the sheets aside, the blanket; settling closer to
me to escape the chill in the room. She buried her face into
the crook of my neck, hiding from me. I held her, rubbing
her back with one hand; glossing my nails along her shirt
with the other. Slowly, Val clung to me, tighter and tighter.
She dug her fingertips into my bare shoulders, trying and
failing to stop her body from trembling. From the stories
she'd told me, she had never done this with her father.
Never allowed him to nurse away her emotional wounds.
And her mother had committed a horrible sin against her.
She had been isolated for too long.

I had to tell her.

"Val," I breathed into her ear. She tensed,
controlling herself. "You needn't hold back your emotions
with me. I know… it's difficult for you to lean on anyone.
Your soldiers broke your trust because of me. As terrible as
this is, I am forever grateful that you *chose me*." Val
gripped me harder than before, on the verge. "… I love

you." She broke against me, into me. She broke down, hot breaths blowing against my neck; warm tears flowing down my skin. How I *needed* this from her. "I love you, Val... *so much.*"

No one had ever held me with such need. She was as frustrated as she was hurt. I felt it all from her. Her beating heart against mine. Her clinging hands holding onto me, completely.

"I love you, too..."

Val's frustration washed away for the night. She allowed me to see her core. Stripped-down and vulnerable, just as she made me feel whenever I gave into her, physically.

"I can't lose you, Lucrezia," she worried, holding onto me more. "I don't like these thoughts. I don't like what I want to do... You and Gabrielle are all I have left. I don't know if she's alive. If I lose you, I'll..."

"I'm right here, love," I said, soothing her to sleep. "I'm right here."

Feeling the slope of her neck relax, and her hold over me loosen, I knew Val took comfort in my words. I whispered to her again and again that I was here; that I would always be with her. For as strong as Val was, her strength was dependent on my well-being now. She'd taken that plunge, whether she'd made the decision on her own or not. I had done the same. I held her in this free-fall of emotion, of a future uncertain.

We stayed in this relative position throughout our days, our rides in the carriage. Our journey to Eidos carried on. I rested my back near the carriage door, the chill of the icy wind fogging the window just by my shoulders. Val kept her body over me, resting her head over my chest. She looked so peaceful in my arms. Her body moved back and forth with the movement of the carriage. I ran my hand along the sniper rifle holstered over her back, intrigued by its make. Val had stopped glaring at Videl during these rides. Even if she hadn't, Raj and Videl would have been none the wiser. The two of them kissed and shared soft conversation, oblivious to us at times.

For all this time we had spent on the road together, forced to stare at one another from across the carriage, I still knew little about them. Instead, Val and I had gotten to know Raine better over meals in the taverns. She had a fondness for horses now that she had spent so long driving our carriage with her mother. No matter how intimidating Raine appeared, she was still a child in many ways.

The horses treaded through the early-November snow, taking us further to the port city of Indra, capital of trade in the empire. From there we would take a ship across the Eidos Sea to the archipelago. If I were better versed in Tynan's landscape, I could have teleported us there and saved us this trouble.

I enjoyed this adventure. We had escaped the news of what happened to Eden. No one outside the city seemed to care much about the state of the Empyrean Palace or the empire's leadership. They were more focused on their individual countries, their own politics and their own problems. I suspected the oracles would find a way to take over. I didn't want to live in a world with them as the new self-appointed leaders.

Leaving to this new world couldn't have happened at a better time.

Sudden panic from the horses; the carriage stopped. Explosions from outside startled us all. Screams pierced the winds. The village we passed through erupted in black and blue flames. Coincidence or not, this was Svärd—Sebastian's hometown. I hurried out of the carriage. As I stepped down to the snowy ground, I saw how trapped we were. The flames encircled the village, freeing this blank space for us to cower and fear. Raine and Elysia looked around in shock, not knowing what to do. I went to the centermost point of our arena in the snow. I stared up at the cloudy sky, narrowing my eyes against the light sleet.

Vespair hovered down from overhead, her boots landing evenly along the ground. She was but a spirit, except her place in this world was almost real. Black steel crushed the snow underfoot as she walked toward me. Any other time, I would have been afraid. Yet I sensed no hostility from her. Not toward me.

Toward Raj and Videl behind me—certainly.

"How good to see you again," said Vespair. "Are you enjoying your journey? Getting to know each other more? The four of you are only bound insomuch as you *choose* to stick together."

Videl moved a few paces in front of me, just off to the side. "Why won't you leave us alone?" she demanded to know. "Doing this won't take back what happened. It won't fix the bond you and I had! Val and Lucrezia aren't part of this, either..."

Though our guest was unreachable in this spirit form, Raine made to draw her blade. Elysia held her hand out, stopping her; whispering something to her.

Vespair laughed softly. "It's interesting, really," she remarked. "I warned that Raj would ruin you. Though it wasn't by her hand, the decisions you made for her ended up destroying you. Now the world fears our kind: thaumaturges and sorceresses. Sheer anarchy reigns in the Kingdom of Tibor without their queen. The clerics who feed off the public's ignorance will soon rule this empire. Isn't it amazing how protecting the wrong person can lead to such terrible consequences?"

I barely heard the sounds of Val's boots in the snow. She walked away, toward the hill on our left.

"That was what *you* did!" accused Raj. "*You're* the one who poisoned everyone's heads! You wanted this shit to happen! All 'cause you couldn't handle Videl not followin' your word as law no more."

Vespair shook her head. "Quite the contrary," she countered. "As Archangel of the Excalibur, I was one of the few voices that kept such bile from spreading to the masses. I once killed the oracles who attempted to spread the current Anathema doctrine. I had trained other dark knights to follow in my stead, such as you. They faltered without my leadership. Without me around, those foolish oracles had the freedom to speak their minds. And this was what happened as a result. The parasite I planted in Jyrn's head only hastened the inevitable."

Raj and Videl stared at one another, stunned. If not for Videl's actions, I would have been free to practice magic as I pleased. My parents wouldn't have been alarmed to discover what I was. I would have still had my brother. I might not have met Xavier… or Val for that matter. But the Empire of Tynan wouldn't have existed at all. Perhaps I could have met Val some other way. We could have had a peaceful life together.

"You ruined their lives, Videl," said Vespair. "You did this, not me. The oracles who raided Elysia's village did so because of you. They killed her because of you. She died protecting her husband and daughter—because of you. The masses who fear Lucrezia for her powers condemn her because of you. Her parents abandoned her because of you. The ignorant citizens who made Valerie's life hell—they hate her because of you. And her soldiers who betrayed her… they despise her loyalty to Lucrezia because of you… If you would be Raj's slave, then you will take responsibility for your actions."

"Haven't I suffered enough?!" shouted Videl. "I couldn't know I'd cause all of that! Raj and I were separated for over two hundred years! What else do you want, Vespair!? Tell me!"

"I want you to understand how I felt that evening, in the church. I want you to know what it feels like to have your own comrade turn against you… I want you to feel the same pain I felt."

"Raj would never turn on me. You won't get what you want."

Vespair sounded like she spoke with a smile from behind her visor. "You forget that you aren't the only one who possesses such knightly devotion for your woman. There are others in this world who are smarter than you; more capable than you. All they needed was a little… *pull*."

Loudness from a single, precise gunshot exploded through the area. A bullet from afar pierced Videl's head. Blood followed the bullet's trajectory. Videl collapsed to the snow on the ground, dead on the spot. I stared at her, emotionless. Val had pulled the trigger. The gunshot had scared me more than anything. I knew to expect this. As did Raine and Elysia—they, too, looked on with blank faces, unsurprised.

Raj screamed in terror, in agony. Vespair disappeared as a shadow of laughter. A second shot fired, precise—right through Raj's head as well. She didn't die. She fell to the snow, almost consumed by black wisps of Vespair's vengeful spirit. She stayed there, helpless, as Val returned from the nearby hill, sniper rifle in hand. When Val approached her, Raj tried to scramble away. Fear and guilt filled her eyes.

"Vespair is right," said Val, kneeling at her side. "I knew she was. I knew for weeks. I wanted to kill you the moment I figured it out. But I stayed my hand, because we were supposed to be *comrades*. '*We're in this together*!' you had said. That was a lie. All to cover up your remorse. Videl's love for you ruined me… Worse, your fairytale love ruined Lucrezia's life. She suffered needlessly… because of you."

Val grabbed Raj's collar through the lancing shadows, watching her blood taint the pure white snow underneath. She watched Raj cry of a broken heart as her knight lay dead next to her. I noticed Elysia and Raine watching this exchange with fascination.

Raj coughed, "How could you—?"

"Don't waste your breath," spoke Val. "We will see you again in the new world. I'm certain of that. Eventually, Nyte and Stella will find you once more. They may not remember you, but they took part in your foolishness all the same. Vespair will want to hurt them, somehow... and it will be up to us to protect them." She glanced at me, at Elysia, at Raine. "They are family, thus I will do what I can to aid them. So long as you and Videl stay far away from me, we won't have any problems."

At last, Vespair's spirit consumed Raj fully. As she dissipated into the earth, the flames surrounding Svärd disappeared. Videl still lay dead in a widening pool of crimson. I sensed Raine soaking up the implications of what happened. I felt Elysia's relief and appreciation over Val doing what she couldn't.

I placed my hand over Val's shoulder, activating her innate element. Aspected fire flamed along her palms. She used the embers to cremate Videl's body. As an unusual sign of respect, we watched the fires burn until Videl turned to ashes.

Chapter Ten

Tyrannous Devotion
(Val)

Since that day in Svärd, I couldn't sleep without getting stuck in my dreams. Lucrezia had to force me awake almost every morning. I wasn't lost in guilt over what I'd done. I was instead lost in my absence of guilt. I felt justified. If I had to go back in time, I wouldn't change my decision.

That terrified me. It shook me more than mere guilt ever could.

This was only a dream, and yet it felt so real.

Asleep over my back, I couldn't breathe. My eyes shot open—something was over my face, smothering me. I almost shouted in panic until someone removed the pillow. The surface I lay on felt shallow, soft. I looked around; I was over a thin mattress and pale pink sheets. The white bars of wood surrounding me felt like a prison cell. I was in a crib. One long enough to fit me. I was in my room, back at home in Eden. The walls had blackened with soot. The windows glowed crimson from the fires that had overtaken the city beyond. I didn't feel at home at all. This place was much too dark, too sinister.

Lucrezia stood over me, holding the pillow in her hands. She stared at me with such concern.

"You shouldn't still be sleeping, Val," she worried. "This isn't normal."

"Why am I here…?" I asked.

"You mean you don't know? The home is where the heart is, or so they say. Your heart is trying to tell you something. If it will help you wake up, you should listen. Even if you don't like what it has to say."

There was an opening in this crib. Wooden bars splintered beside me. I stepped out and onto the floor. Creaking floorboards made my home feel older than it was. Older; abandoned. I followed Lucrezia down the dilapidated hall. Withered walls and bloodstains set me on edge.

Near the front door, I found my father and twin brother. They argued with one another. I couldn't hear their words. Furious knocking at the front door only escalated their anger.

Father answered the door. He trembled in shock at the sight of my soldiers.

They aimed their weapons right at him; demanded to know where I had gone. This was right after they betrayed me.

When he refused to answer, Sebastian shot my father to death.

Yosef stumbled back, screaming.

Lydia was kinder. She asked him where I might have gone. She promised to spare his life if he gave them valuable information as to my whereabouts.

"Eidos!" he cried. "That's where Gabrielle went... I—I know she did! Val went there to see her!"

"They'll have to pass through Indra to get to Eidos," noted Lydia. "I'm sorry, Yosef... I truly am. You won't see us again."

Yosef sat curled upon the floor, sobbing, shaking. He stared at our father bleeding out. I saw enough anger pass my brother's eyes to know where he stood.

He resented me for all of this.

He believed it was *my fault* that Sebastian killed our father. That was why he hadn't hesitated to rat me out. That was why he picked up my father, carried him outside; dug his grave with such ferocity, he couldn't contain himself.

He only calmed down to bury Father properly.

Yosef said a prayer and retreated back inside.

And then his ire resurfaced.

He threw a fit in my bedroom, smashing everything to bits. He grew angrier when he saw that none of my clothes or other belongings remained behind. He knew that I'd planned on leaving. He called me all sorts of names for siding with Lucrezia. He, too, despised what she was.

I went back outside.

I had seen this in my dreams too many times.

There was nothing new here.

Vespair appeared in front of me, just as she had before. "Do you not care that they killed your own father?" she wondered. "You could have gone back for him. Instead, you had Lucrezia take you to your soldiers' safehouse. You could have saved his life had you come here instead. Why didn't you? Why did you let Raj *convince* you that it was a poor idea?"

"I don't know," I said, not recognizing my own voice.

"I think you do. He was a busy man, Magister Pathos. Too busy to spend time with his own children. After your many scuffles and brawls, he was not there to tend to your wounds. He was not there to hold you, to fuss over you as a parent should. It's quite amazing how his emotional absence caused you to simply not care."

Of course Vespair was right. She knew me, somehow. She knew me well.

In the far distance, the city burned on. I'd heard no word in my waking hours of anything happening to Eden. Nothing on this scale. This was but a reflection of what I wished would happen. I didn't need Vespair to say it. I already knew. I despised everyone in Eden for villainizing Lucrezia for no real reason. She was a perfectly good woman, no matter what powers she possessed. Their ignorance caused such hatred to fester within their hearts. It was the same ignorance that they had used to make me suffer—until I grew strong enough to rise above it all.

And yet I'd had too many reminders that I had a long way to go: how the Privy Council had laughed at me that spring morning; the bigoted stranger who had almost granted Lee his death wish; even Lieutenant-Colonel James and his chauvinism, his homophobia.

My heart beat slower from those reminders. All along on this journey to Eidos, I feared what would happen if I slipped up. If someone recognized us. If an oracle found us and killed Lucrezia before I could draw my sniper rifle. If my soldiers found us again... I was afraid I would hesitate and let them hurt her.

I felt Lucrezia behind me. She held me around my waist just as I was about to falter. She gave me strength. She made me believe that my life was worth living. She helped me to see that I would've been a fool for giving up long ago. Lee and I weren't so different once upon a time. I had almost given into the beatings, the verbal abuse... their blind hatred. All because of things that were out of my control. Things that I couldn't choose at birth. Things that I could not help and would not apologize for.

Fresh tears welled up in my eyes. I held my breath and held them back. I shouldn't hate. I didn't have the energy to hate. I couldn't fear those people anymore. I hated this rippling; this snowball effect that Videl had started by ending the work Vespair and her fellow dark knights had accomplished in their time.

"Speaking of apologies," said Vespair, "I must apologize to you. To the both of you. I underestimated you. I assumed you would side with Raj and Videl. I thought you wouldn't see past the consequences of their actions; that you would excuse what they did to me. You are far more capable than I had imagined. I wish to extend my gratitude to you—if you would allow it."

As difficult as this was to believe, I wanted to know more. "I'm listening," I replied.

"Xavier, Gustavo and Lee are all safe. I will allow them—and only them—to pass to Eidos from Valdivia. They will be on the island waiting for you when you arrive. Further, I will allow Raine's *Mutsunokami* to open the portal within the Edge of Reason to your new world. I won't hinder your journey anymore."

That sounded too good to be true. "There must be a caveat to this."

"None at all."

"None at all," I repeated, unconvinced.

Vespair laughed a little. "You will do as you please, Val," she went on. "My battle is with Raj, Videl, Nyte, and Stella. Not you and Lucrezia. Certainly not the two of you. I misjudged you. As for Elysia and Raine... time will tell."

"And what of the threats you made?" I recalled. "Lucrezia told me the words you uttered to her. You called her a corrupt noble, all because she couldn't enact the legislation she wanted for the poor and underprivileged. Did you misjudge *that* about her as well?"

"I did. I blamed her for not doing enough. The Privy Council had clipped her wings. Yet I know what's soon to come. She will redeem herself, as you have."

"Fine, then," I conceded. "What do you plan on doing now? When the time comes for Nyte and Stella to find one another again in their respective times, what will you do? Will you let them find you? Will you let them defeat you?"

"They are welcome to try! In fact, I *want* them to train. I *want* them to have their life together, and to challenge me when they feel they are ready. My hold over Raj would disappear if they defeated me... as I am all that maintains her spirit as the ghost she is. I will have the last laugh in the end. That is all I want."

Vespair's sadism was clear in her intentions. I didn't want to be on the receiving end.

"You promise you'll not harm Lucrezia in the future?" I said. "Or me…"

"You have my word. You know you can trust me. We are not so different, you and I. This has nothing to do with good or evil. You are aware of the dangers of ignorance, bigotry, xenophobia. How people allow their fears to rule them; to condemn those who do not deserve it. Those ignorant fools created a beautiful work of art: the pain in your heart from years of abuse. You are a dangerous woman indeed. I would be a fool to cross you. Thus we have our truce."

"… you say that as if I am more dangerous that you are."

"Oh, Val. *You are*. You see, I act alone. I act for myself. But you? Everything you do is for Lucrezia. She deserves your devotion, as tyrannous as it is. I will rue the day you wake up to your full potential. Still, whether you help Nyte and Stella or not… I *will* have my victory."

***

Fresh ocean breeze drifted through my senses, stirring me awake. The morning sun made the softest, warmest memory along my face; the brightness washed over me, reddening beneath my eyelids. Crisp wood from the furniture around me acted as a reminder of where I was. Lucrezia's natural, breezy scent had burrowed into my pillow and into the sheets rumpled over my bare shoulder. She held me from behind as we lay in bed in our room, in the latest tavern we'd stopped in. Lazy, affectionate, she ran her long nails down my arm, stopping longest along the tone of my bicep and my shoulder, boyish as it was.

I remembered where we were—Indra, the center of trade and culture in the empire. Fruits, spices, and other valuable foods and materials from the myriad of islands along the archipelago crossed through here on their way to farmers and traders across the mainland. Cultural traditions from the islands also passed through the trade lines. Those who lived in the west of the empire were far more easygoing than those of us from the heart of Tynan. The scattered towns and cities along the archipelago had no need for the likes of Eden's coldness—doubly so.

The morning wind wafted through the open window. I was used to snow by this time of year. Indra's perpetual summer was much nicer than Eden's bleakness. From the third floor of the tavern, I heard vague shouts from sailors along the promenade; the striking of iron as the blacksmiths plied their trade; skilled bartering from the buyers at the shops beneath the tents. Despite the noise, there was an easiness to this city that I'd never felt elsewhere. I could stay here in bed with Lucrezia for days and not worry about a thing. There were no imperial oracles here. Simpler temples had replaced the grandeur of the cathedrals. Their temple oracles didn't spend every waking hour vying for power. Life in this city was better because of that lack.

Lucrezia kissed the nape of my neck, her breath warming me. "Good morning, love…"

I moved into her more, wanting more. She was as bare as I was beneath the sheets. The smoothness of her skin met mine, and her curves welcomed me. Yet I sensed Lucrezia's weariness. Her hold over me relaxed once she knew for certain that I was awake. She'd had to forego her own sleep to watch over me in my dreams. She must have been exhausted.

I turned around and propped myself up. Lucrezia burrowed her face into the bend of my arm, ready to doze off at any moment. I pressed my lips to hers, lost in her serenity.

"You seem tired," I noticed.

"Mmmh…"

I smiled over her care for me. "Thank you, darling… for watching over me. I would have been lost without you. I'm all right now. Why don't you get some rest? Our ship to Eidos won't be ready until nightfall."

Lucrezia allowed me to tuck her in. For her emotional perseverance with me, I appreciated her limits. Seeing her sleep so peacefully reminded me that she *was* human, no matter what powers she possessed. If only the people who hated her could see this. Perhaps they would understand that she was no different than them. I went to take a quick bath, thinking all of that over. The ones we ran away from were too far-gone in their hatred... we had no choice but to leave. This new world that awaited us sounded like a far-fetched dream, even now—even today, now that we were so close to Eidos.

This was all we had to look forward to. A hope. A wish. A dream.

As I looked ahead to celebrating the New Year aboard our ship to the island, I considered so much more. This was an entire world that we would soon have to ourselves. Not in solitude—I expected I would see my father there, and perhaps other like-minded people who had passed away... I knew we would see Raj and Videl there. They would be wise to avoid us. Would Father forgive me for not going to save him? I had no idea. If he did, then I could, perhaps, give Lucrezia far more than I could have ever given her in this world. Maybe—the family she couldn't have before.

Sorceresses didn't need men, or even other people, in order to conceive children. We had been together for over eight months. I knew I had wanted her for far longer than that. Had she thought about any of this with me...?

I surprised myself, thinking of this now.

I put on one of my traditional uniforms—one that Gabrielle had made for me herself. This softer fabric and looser fit reminded me so of her. Each time I thought of her, I remembered how she and Lucrezia had shared a moment at the theater before the play. And her diamond ring… I had it safe here in the inside pocket of my light coat. I had picked this out for her long ago. Not Yosef.

I lingered overlong as I kissed Lucrezia goodbye. Breathing in her softness as she slept, I hovered next to her face. The natural heat from her skin mixed with mine. The rhythm of her deep breaths matched my own. I stayed in her shadow, shielded from the sun shining in across the way. I wanted to ask her… All of a sudden, after not considering it at all, and then now, I considered it, and I *wanted*. I could commit to no other woman. Not after all Lucrezia and I had been through. Not after all fate had done to send us running together in the same direction, side-by-side.

"I want to be by your side," I whispered to her. "Always and forever. If we will have our immortality in the new world, then I will give you all that you deserve. I will carve our new home in your image with my bare hands. I will give you the throne you should have had in Eden. Just a few more weeks…"

***

Downstairs in the common area, I found Elysia sipping her morning tea. She read a book as she drank, having forgotten about the meal on her table. Her oracle's robes made her stand out from the—common—crowd, as they talked and laughed loudly over their breakfast. The wooden walls, tables and chairs; the dirty clothes the fishermen and other workers wore; their crassness; all else faded in comparison to everything about her, just as they did with Lucrezia, wherever we went.

I bowed to Elysia, first. "Good morning, my lady."

Elysia set her book down, smiling gently. "Hello, Val," she greeted. "Please, sit and eat."

She eased her untouched plate across the table, over to me.

"Have you not eaten?" I asked.

"Mmm, I suspect these cinnamon rolls are a bit too sweet for me. I meant to order something else. As you can see, I grew a bit lost in my reading. I've not read this in some time."

I tilted my head to get a better look at the title. "*The Archangels of Creation...* Isn't that a fairy tale?"

"It depends on which version you read," said Elysia, smiling once more as I ate. "In this age and time, I assume the people only know the story of the angels who stopped the terrible sorceresses from destroying the universe in its infancy."

"My father told me a different story. One that revolved around the archangels—Piety and Tyranny both ascending their sorceress wives to godhood in their devotion. In doing so, the sorceresses became the Twin Goddesses, Venus and Nyx Vevina, who created the universe. There was also Envy, who envied the love the other archangels had for their sorceresses. She worked to undermine Piety and Tyranny and their wives. Many of her beliefs created the barbaric superstitions surrounding magic today."

"That is the truest version indeed. You can relate, can't you?"

"Yes," I said. "I find the story very romantic. It influenced me a lot: my values and how I am with women."

I pulled out Gabrielle's ring in my pocket and looked it over.

Elysia raised her eyebrows at the diamond's purity and shine. "My, I'm impressed," she said. "Do you mean to ask her before we set sail?"

"Wait—*what?*"

"Will you ask Lucrezia to marry you today? Why else would you carry such a ring around?"

"Well, the idea only occurred to me a few moments ago... Since we will soon arrive to the new world in the

Beyond, I made up my mind. I want to spend this eternity with her."

Raine bowed to her mother, and sat down next to me. "You should ask her," she said.

This was the first time I had ever heard Raine speak. She sounded like my echo—her voice, her tenor, were the same as mine.

Not for Elysia. "Good morning, dear," she said. "Are you hungry?"

"No, thank you… I've been up for a while, reading a few of your other books. One of them mentioned a tragedy that affected this city. Around this time. The pages didn't detail much. What happened?"

"Nothing all that important," replied Elysia, turning the page in her book. "A calamity struck Indra, interrupting trade throughout the empire. That is why the Eidos from my time is much like the one in this time. Growth stalled, you see. The archipelago's technology remained primitive in comparison to the rest of the world." By Raine's expression, she worried that it would happen while we were still here. Elysia glanced at us from behind her reading. "Oh, Raine. I won't have you fussing over this. Why don't you and Val take a walk around the pier? The fresh air might do you some good. Perhaps it will help you *commit* to a decision or two…?"

I understood her hint loud and clear. I stood with Raine, bowing once more.

"Thank you again for the meal, my lady."

"You are quite welcome, my lord. I expect it will be a few hours yet before Lucrezia joins me. You've such a knack for putting her to sleep for long hours."

I didn't know how to explain that things were different this time. The small smile on Elysia's face told me she was only teasing. I returned the smile, leaving the tavern with Raine. We walked around for a long while, talking together. I learned of how she hoped to protect her sister Stella in their far-off battle against Vespair. Raine aspired to be as strong as the dark knights in the tale Elysia read. As we sat on a bench over the pier, watching the sunlight glitter over the Eidos Sea, I began to appreciate Raine much more. Already I admired her strength. Yet now I learned that she strove for such heights—far beyond what was possible for me as a mere human.

Deep down, I was also grateful that she didn't hold my actions against me. She and Elysia could have sided with Raj and Videl throughout this whole affair. By Elysia's silence on the matter, she had only needed those two for the ritual, for creating her daughter.

"Magic is the same as willpower," explained Raine. "That is why any human has the potential to become a thaumaturge. We merely channel our willpower through catalysts. Even oracles are thaumaturges. The imperial ones don't wish to accept this fact. The archangels and seraphim in the scriptures of creation were human long before they became dark knights and paladins."

I glanced at her *Mutsunokami* sheathed at her hip. "So, in theory, I could become a thaumaturge?"

"I don't see why not. As long as you have something that drives you, anything is possible. I learned that from you."

"That's true... I never considered it before. What about you, Raine? What drives your will?"

Raine stared up at the midday sky; at the clouds roaming in. "I want to keep my sister safe," she said. "I haven't met her yet. In Mother's time today, Stella is four years old. She enjoys dancing, playing with tarot cards with Father, pretending to read encyclopedic tomes, and making up tunes on the piano in Eidos' temple. I *know* all these things about my sister... and yet I don't know her, really."

"Why do you look so sad about it?" I wondered. "You'll meet her in due time."

"My mother said that I must forsake people in order to keep my mind clear. I cannot be slowed down by caring for unnecessary things, she said..."

That didn't sound right to me. "I think you should embrace how much you care for your sister."

"And if I fail? If I lose her? Or if I care too much, and she cares not at all for me, I'll only get hurt."

"Considering her other family members, I believe Stella will care for you very much. Lucrezia is incredibly considerate. She despised her brother for years, and yet she jumped at the first opportunity to save his life in exchange for him saving hers. As for failing... I don't think you will falter. If you love your sister, then let that be your strength. You won't lose her that way. You inherited my supposed valor, after all."

Raine looked troubled. "This is all rather confusing," she muttered. "I understand your counsel, Val. And I will take it to heart. I will protect Stella with all that I am. I am eternally devoted to serving her. Yet I can't help but think I'm not supposed to feel the way I do."

"What do you mean?"

Instead of answering me, Raine smiled and stood up. "Ask Lucrezia to marry you," she said, and left.

She reminded me so of how I felt once upon a time. I had such devotion, yet no one to bear it for. I dreaded waiting for the right person to come along... only to remember how much I wanted Lucrezia, even at a distance.

And then I saw my love walking toward me along the pier. She and Raine exchanged greetings as they passed each other by. I held my breath, enamored by the sight of her. Seeing the authority in her boots, in her walk, and the kindness in her beautiful face marked the wonderful contradiction that only she embodied. Lucrezia found me just as the rain clouds above settled in. I wasn't superstitious enough to take this as an ill omen. I stood for her, respectfully, kissing her hand once she was near.

"There you are," said Lucrezia, glad to see me. "I wondered where you went off to."

"I thought you might've slept a little longer."

"I can sleep more once we're on the ship. Your sleep pattern is a trying thing for me."

I laughed at the poor joke my mind conceived.

Lucrezia put her hands over her hips. "What is it now?" she chided in good-humor.

"Since I am the younger one in our relationship..."

"Choose your words *very carefully*, Val."

By her glowing smile, I couldn't offend her today. Not even if I wanted to.

"You are a woman of experience," I evaded. "Perhaps you should add less sleep to your bag of tricks...?"

She pushed me lightly. "Is that your way of calling me old?"

"I would *never*! Decades from now, you shall still be the most beautiful woman who ever graced Tellus."

Lucrezia knew I was sincere; I knew she appreciated it. "Mhmm, so you say."

I held her hand, guiding her to the edge of the pier. "Come here. I've something I wish to ask you."

She walked with me at an easy pace. We were isolated here. Lucrezia let me toy with her hand, enjoying every moment. My uniform sleeve caught on my wrist. I still had the cuffs she'd given to me, mostly so that she could always know where I was. If for some reason Lucrezia could not use her magic—if there was an oracle nearby, if she was wounded or worse—the spells in this steel would ever point her to me. Whenever they were warm like this—and I wasn't distracted—I knew that she was nearby.

They also served as a reminder of how we came together months ago. Because of their usefulness, and the sentimentality, I never wanted her to remove them.

Saying this to her was as simple as breathing. "Ever since you gave me these, I've felt bound to you in more ways than one. I think... I was lost before that night. Lost, and angry. I dislike those days. I had too much hatred in my heart. Sometimes I fear that my hatred never left me, and yet you don't seem to mind. You know that whatever rage I do have left... I will put it to good use for you."

Lucrezia hummed in agreement. "Of course you will," she said. "I've no doubts whatsoever. Keep in mind that I was no different than you in the past. I merely buried that part of me. If those feelings come up again, you know that I will also put them to good use for you. We will protect one another."

"I'm relieved to hear you say that."

"And I'm relieved to say the words... Now what's this you wish to ask me, hm? I'm curious."

All I wanted was to make her happy.

I reached in my pocket just over my chest, holding the ring there. I moved slowly, down on one knee over the stiff concrete. Lowering my point of view like this; looking up at her with such meaning; seeing the shock in her eyes—it felt right. Everything, all of this, was meant to be. My love for Lucrezia welled up inside of me, swelling to such heights; I couldn't contain it. I had to give this to her.

"Lucrezia, I would have died with you, in my loneliness, in my hatred... That night when you held me, when you told me that you love me, and that you were right here... it locked me to you, infinitely."

I showed her the ring. Her eyes shimmered as she recognized it, brighter than the ocean's surface.

"Will you marry me?"

I curled my wrist just so, pressing my fingers over my heart. She held her hands over her mouth, trying not to cry. I smiled freely in the way she loved most.

Lucrezia lowered her hands enough to tell me, "*Yes*! Oh, Val, of course I will. This is so..."

She lost the rest of her words to emotion, falling silent. Her smile was more than enough for me. I placed the ring over her finger, adoring the slenderness of her hand, and the feminine touch she embodied, everywhere. I only kissed her hand once before Lucrezia pulled me back to my feet. Each time her lips were over mine, it felt like the first time. This one was no different. And yet it *was.* So different.

I had never wanted to give a woman the world in the way I wanted with her. Soon, I could do that. Once we passed through one last barrier into the unknown, I could give her everything she needed. The security that the world wouldn't turn against her. The comfort she'd had back in the Empyrean Palace. The knowledge that she could go where she pleased, and do as she pleased, and not have to worry about anything. She wouldn't have to hide anymore.

We had this happiness as we returned to our room in the tavern. We had it as I carried her up the stairs, mimicking outdated traditions that I could only envy before. We had it as she draped her arms about my shoulders, beaming at me with pure joy. We had it as we fell into bed, fell into each other.

We couldn't even take our clothes off before the moment shattered before our eyes.

Overcast in the skies above soured the mood, first. Panicked screams outside and the sounds of doors slamming shut down the halls worried me more. Lucrezia and I went to look out the window. People in the houses across the way shut their windows instead. Out in the open space along the promenade, hundreds of imperial soldiers marched toward the tavern. Imperial soldiers...

They were *my* soldiers. My old friends.

They stopped just as the front group reached the tavern's entrance. I heard Lydia's voice. Elysia's voice.

Lucrezia shifted us by shadows to the roof of a nearby house, affording us a better look. From here we saw

Elysia, Lydia and Sebastian talking together. Raine stood guard in front of her mother, torn between standing still as ordered and cutting everyone down. Sebastian grew cross with Elysia when she wouldn't tell him where Lucrezia and I were: raising his voice, threatening to shoot her like he did to my father. She remained calm. She looked to us, once, as if asking permission to handle the situation.

There were far too many of them for even Raine and Lucrezia to defeat. I could only kill one at a time, at most, with my rifle. And I had such limited ammunition. I glanced at Lydia, wondering if she regretted her decision. I saw the guilt upon her face at this angle.

When Lucrezia held my hand, I felt her ring nestled between my fingers. *Tighter* as she gripped.

"Val," she breathed in my ear. "Whatever happens... remember my love for you."

"I want you to do the same for me."

Elysia looked to me once more. I nodded to her.

She raised her staff in the air, channeling her most powerful magicks by crystal rain. Her will tore the sky open. Darker, soot black clouds formed overhead, spiraling into a thin opening of purple light. Raine pierced the ground with her sword and knelt down, transforming into a protective wall of shadows. My troops staggered back in surprise, staring at the wall and up at the sky in horror.

From the light emerged an ambiguous being of pure darkness. Feminine form, a sharp vestment of black chrome that guarded a body of ebony-shadowy skin, and absolute power—Elysia called forth God Herself, Nyx Vevina, down from the Black Heavens.

She held in Her left hand the one true *Anathema:* a scepter of gleaming amethyst and onyx, as tall as the Empyrean Palace itself, decorated with the religion's symbolic lemniscate at the tip. Nyx Vevina exuded such an almighty command of the sky around Her; all of Tellus shook beneath us as She amassed but a portion of Her strength at the tip of Her scepter. Such a small amount from Her acted as a hurricane of magic around us, ripping buildings, ships, and the very ground from their foundations. Strips of wood, masts, chunks of the pier and other debris blew through the unstable winds.

Flames burning violet, Nyx Vevina sent a meteor down to Indra, down atop my troops, decimating the city. Death screams sounded all around me as I lost my footing on the roof. As I fell, I watched Sebastian's dead body fall further down into the mass of splintered wood and stone. Only by Lucrezia's saving grace did I avoid the same end. Gravity itself bent in the wake of God's judgment. I landed on the vertical surface of a broken house, somehow, standing up, and yet facing down toward the gaping chasm Nyx Vevina's meteor left behind. Beneath the chasm, the Eidos Sea roared as a wide, raging whirlpool, swallowing the corpses of the ones who had betrayed me. I cared not at all for their deaths.

I looked around, across the mini-waterfalls pouring from the walls, the fractured insides of homes. I couldn't find Lucrezia. The people in those homes hovered just over the whirlpool, or elsewhere in the air, crying out for help. It was as if something—or someone—willed them to stay in place, to not die yet.

Up where the tavern once was, I saw Elysia disappear. She expended all of her energy to save us. Raine fell to her knees as she watched her mother vanish. She needed time to accept this. I didn't blame her.

Nearby, I heard a familiar cry. Lydia had fallen into this same chasm, into the same space. Broken, wounded, she sat against a wall next to a steep fall. I took advantage of the upset gravity, walking over to her at this strange angle.

Lydia's eyes shot open when she saw me. "N-No… no, not you," she stammered. "Not you, no, *no!*" She scrambled further back against the wall. "Everyone's already dead! What else do you want?!"

"And yet, by God's grace, you survived," I mocked. I remembered how religious she was. "Don't you think there was a *reason* for this?"

"Stop it!" she spat. "Just stop, Val! If you wish to kill me... then do it. Go on. Get it over with..."

I stopped, indeed, right in front of her, level with her. It would have been too easy to kill Lydia like this. I remembered how she had merely watched as Sebastian killed my father. The fear in Lydia's eyes goaded me; encouraged me to seek out her death.

But what good would that have done? She wouldn't learn anything by dying today. I wanted her to learn... to fear her own ignorance.

"*Val!*"

Lucrezia's voice snapped my sight up above. There she was at the center of the city, high in the sky. This time, by *her will*, Indra remained in this shattered state. Not falling apart, not mending itself; Lucrezia held the city together with her magicks. The rest of the people who should have died in the blast didn't. They stared up at her in half-dread, half-gratitude, amazed that a sorceress had saved them.

"Lucrezia!" I shouted back, with the full force of my love for her. I knew she heard me. The fear in her eyes, even at this distance, was palpable. She was so high up... That was unwise. She was afraid of heights. I feared she would not move from her place. Not on her own.

Lydia saw her, whispering, "I can't believe... she would do such a thing."

"Why!?" I yelled back. "Because she's a witch? You think her kind only want to *destroy* the world?!"

And Lydia had the nerve to scoff at me. "She only did this for you," she argued.

I grabbed her neck. Lydia's breath caught beneath my hand. I felt her throat knot and tighten, fighting back against my bare hand.

"So what if Lucrezia only did it for me?! If she wanted, she could send the rest of these people down to their deaths! Oh, but look! They're still here! She's not a monster; she's not a heathen! She's a fucking person! She loves me... she loves me, and she's terrified of heights... She can't move..."

Lydia understood. She couldn't breathe, but she understood. I threw her back down to the ground. I listened to Lydia sputter and cough, heaving for breath. I imagined how I might climb these impossible heights to reach Lucrezia. To catch her fall as I'd done so many months ago, back when we'd gotten up to trouble at Nirvana in Eden. The broken buildings around me collapsed in on themselves, falling down to the raging ocean beneath me.

When Lydia at last caught her breath, I found the words I needed to say.

"You and I should be the last people to judge anyone," I spoke. "I fought to earn the imperial uniform you wear—that you bear against me, against my love. I cannot count how many people looked down on us for loving women, for dressing the way we do, for living the way we do... And you dare to do the same to Lucrezia because of her blood. Because of something she never asked for. You sicken me."

Lydia nodded in understanding. "I know, Val," she said, surprising me. "You're right. I knew when you said it the first time months ago. I didn't want to accept it. But seeing Nyx Vevina come down to *protect* a sorceress from us..."

I knelt down before her, searching her eyes for the truth. "If your Anathema clerics told you outright that loving women made you an abomination, like they do with sorceresses, how would you feel?"

A long pause as she thought it over, and then, "I wouldn't feel at all... If they said that about me, then I—I would have killed myself."

"I know the scriptures helped you deal with the worst of your troubles... But you also know deep in your heart that you are not an abomination. No matter who you love or what powers you possess, you are the same as everyone else. I appreciate what they teach about kindness and forgiveness, but that doesn't mean everything they say is right. Let this go, Lydia."

As emotional as she was now, I knew I got through to her. Lydia only nodded, unable to speak or make a sound. I let out a sigh of relief. I wished my words could have gotten through to more people like this. I wished I wouldn't have had to fight in the past—to defend myself, to enact change. The scars from those battles had hardened me, made me hate. I was glad I didn't have to hate Lydia any longer.

I had to get to Lucrezia, somehow.

When I climbed the wall, Lydia called out to me, "Val, what are you doing?!"

"What does it *look* like I'm doing?"

"Are you mad!? You'll fall! These walls aren't stable!"

"*Yes,* I'm mad!" I shouted back. "I thought I'd made that clear months ago!" Despite her wounds, Lydia climbed after me. "What the hell is wrong with you, woman?"

"I was jealous of her, you know!" she yelled. I smirked over her confession, climbing higher. "Maybe I still am. I know I mentioned something like this before... But I didn't really explain! You always reminded me of the Archangel... Tyrant. How you would do anything to fight for our rights... even if it landed you in trouble. I knew you'd do the same for Lucrezia..."

I spotted Lucrezia up above, still far too high for me to reach. I wished my will would reach her. I wished she could sense me through her dread as I climbed this wreckage to get to her. And yet fate spun a terrible tune. Gravity shifted; the walls around us twisted. I fell again; Lydia caught me by my arm. I hung at her mercy, swinging as a pendulum in the wind. As she stared down at me, I saw not a hint of malice in her eyes. Only fear that I might slip and fall once more.

The ledge she held onto cracked in half. A sudden, jarring split, and gravity overtook us both. Free-falling through the winds, I had nothing to hold onto. Lydia suffocated her screams. This rushing feeling in the pit of my stomach fought against me. Shouting was the only way to let it out. I refused to make a sound. I stared down at the whirlpool as it grew closer, nearer, louder, more powerful; powerless, I glared at the rushing blue and white, the jagged spirals filled with debris, daring it to swallow me whole.

My pride was with me even to the last.

One last tip from gravity turned me over on my back, facing the sky. I held onto Lydia's wrist, borrowing her spirituality for one near-death wish. My free hand, my left, reached out above, eclipsing Lucrezia's body as she held Indra together in her fear of heights. Her name over these cuffs was clearer than ever.

My body stopped. I froze in place, with Lydia hanging in my hold. A second wish I didn't know I needed: rushing shadows headed straight toward us. I sensed Raine in that darkness. She reformed, recognizable as she jumped from ledge to ledge in seamless, swift parkour. Raine embraced us in her very spirit just before the chasm around us collapsed.

Chapter Eleven
Edge Of Reason
(Val)

Fresh ocean air, light rainfall and the smell of damp sand eased me from my sleep. I had passed out after Raine caught me, overwhelmed by the sheer magic she had depleted to carry Lydia and me through the sea. All the way across from Indra—a journey that should have taken a whole day by ship—we had reached Eidos' shore by sundown on this side of the world.

I lay just next to the ebbing low tide with a view of the island's highest peak. Lydia sat next to me, staring off at the water. Raine lay on my other side, exhausted, but still alive. Scores of ships traveled toward Indra's broken state. At this distance, I saw the city lit up at night as a storm of lights and magic. Lightning, wood and stone spiraled around Lucrezia at the city's core, glowing a pale green. Those ships…

"They mean to apprehend her," spoke Lydia, quietly beneath the tide. "A bunch of oracles from the islands nearby are on those ships. I've no idea if she'll have enough energy to get out of there in time."

Raine grunted as she turned over on her back. "She won't."

"She won't?" I repeated, jumping to my feet. "Then *why* did you bring us here?!"

"I wasn't strong enough to pry Lucrezia from her fortress… I'm sorry. There is only one way to save her."

Raine struggled as she untied her sword from her hip. She handed the sheathed weapon to me, instructing me on how to fasten it around my own waist. I felt terrible of a sudden for snapping at her. She could hardly breathe; harder still was it for her to speak or make the slightest movements. I feared she would disappear at any moment, like Elysia who had done everything in her power to save us.

"Use the sword… to open the way to the Beyond. Beneath Eidos' temple—at the island's zenith. The energy from the portal will reach her through your bond. She will use that energy to teleport to you."

Again I cast my eyes to the very top of the island. I feared I would not make the journey in time. Not by walking—not without proper knowledge of the terrain. Whenever I had come here with Gabrielle to visit her family, I had followed her without taking scope of any directions. I recalled it took hours for us to reach the village where the temple was.

"You needn't worry, Val," said Raine. "I memorized the directions my mother gave me. She made me recite them many times… in case we were separated. I will guide you… I will lend you my strength."

She dissipated as a shadowy pool, joining with my faint shadow across the sand. As a sundial with no sun, Raine pointed me further down the shore. From there began the winding road that wrapped around Eidos' peak.

"You'll have to go without me," noted Lydia, gesturing to her injuries. "I'd only slow you down."

I shouldn't have felt sad about leaving her. After everything that had happened…

"Tell you what," she went on. "When I get to the village, I'll tell everyone what happened. I'll tell them that Lucrezia saved the city from being completely destroyed. She saved the people there. She saved you… I'll make sure the truth gets around. I'll do all I can to change the world's mind about magic."

"Thank you…"

Lydia beamed. "Go on, then," she encouraged me. "Mind your asthma if you run, Val. I know how important she is to you. Just—don't kill yourself trying to save her, all right?"

I wasn't sure what to say. The reality of the situation hit me at last. Lydia offered to hold onto my sniper rifle and my uniform coat, as they would only slow me down. I didn't have time to explain exactly *where* my destination was, or why I had to go there. She made me promise to come back somehow and collect my things from her. As uneasy as I was about forgiving all that she'd done, I couldn't waste time lingering on it.

I left down the shore, along the dry areas of the sand, away from the tide. Walking, first, as I took everything else in, I searched for all the memories I had with Lucrezia. From our terse first meeting almost five years ago, to the moment she had told me *yes* along the pier: every single one sped up my steps. I followed Raine's shadow in front of me—our shadow—visible even in the night; believing in her to guide me without fail. The night breeze blew through my short-sleeved shirt; the tide washed just over my tall boots, reminding me of my limitations.

Limitations or none, I had to do this.

I was Lucrezia's betrothed.

I couldn't fail her.

I ran through the cave-like rock formation before me. Small stone towers lit by torches lit my way. The shallow tide pooled through the dank area, rushing with renewed vigor once I returned to the shore. I passed underneath the resort area: intersecting bridges of fine wood amid mini-islands of extravagant tents, filled with tourists looking out to the sea. None of them noticed me race past so far beneath them.

All the way across the shore, Raine's shadow tilted at last. Up to the grass, to the hanging palm trees, to the single dirt path leading to the ferry. Signposts reassured me that Raine led me in the right direction.

And I could run uninhibited with her strength. I breathed. I sprinted. I followed the road without worrying for my inflamed lungs. Tens more tourists blocked the area by the ferry, causing a queue. I didn't have time to wait. The Ageless River winding through the island was light enough for me to run through. I ran around the people in my way. Through the river I went at full-speed. I went against the current, pushing Raine's will alongside mine. This winding road of rock walls as high as my eyes could see led me straight to the dock on the other side.

The ferry skipper and the dozens of tourists there gaped at me. I jumped onto the dock. Up the wooden stairs I went. Across the roofed wooden bridge lit by decorative lanterns, and uphill I went along another, wider, dirt road. The sheer expanse of this place overwhelmed me. A heavier downpour of rain threatened to slow me down.

Weariness crept up to me at last. I pulled at my mental strength; pushing myself to the edge of reason to run faster. I believed in Raine's shadow as my guide—more, and more, even more.

Further up the island she led me to a span of stone ruins over a majestic lake. Far beyond I spotted a smoking volcano from one of the other islands. Beneath my feet, the water glittered like crystal: a pale green to distract me from my burning lungs, my bleeding throat. I ran by a number of couples enjoying the evening out, oblivious to the emergency across the sea. They stared at me in awe as I went. They pushed me harder without trying; simply by existing. They reminded me that I could have been one of them, with Lucrezia, if we'd had the time, the freedom to be together like them.

I gripped the hilt of Raine's sword, pushing myself more—*harder.*

Higher up the hill I went. I blitzed past the weaving walkways that overlooked the long way down. Palaces and castles that lay in ruin brought back memories of the

Empyrean Palace, of our city. I ran away from the old desires I'd had to place Lucrezia on Eden's throne. Yet as I ran away from it, I only wanted it more. I wanted her more. I had to save her.

Far across the longest stretch of land, I ran toward Lucrezia with my back to her. My limits got the better of me. Raine's limits met with mine.

Along the downward slope leading to the village, I broke down. My body shut down. It couldn't keep up with my heart's need to keep going. I collapsed. I clawed at the soaked ground, willing myself to go on. I couldn't. I grunted in pain; my chest was inflamed; I couldn't breathe; I couldn't think from the white-hot agony that burned in me.

Lucrezia was in far more pain than this... using all of her energy to keep those people alive... to keep them from falling into the sea. I wished she would let them *drown* if it would save her even a moment longer. She would never do that. She was a better person than I was... and that was part of why I loved her so.

I needed her in my arms again.

I chased after that mirage, using my arms to drag myself across the ground. I clawed at the earth with my fists, my forearms. Raine's sword dragged at my side. I pulled myself along, splitting my mind in half again. The weak part of me that wished to give up and lie here—I threw it away, far away. Yet it still weighed me down. No matter how hard I fought to forsake it, this pain wouldn't leave...

My eyes stung in frustration, desperation. I had to get through this. I couldn't move fast enough. I couldn't stop those ships or change everyone's mind about her. Yelling her name did nothing. Cursing my own weakness did nothing. *Nothing.* No matter how loud I shouted, or how hard I loved her, it wasn't enough to save her.

"Val!"

That voice...

Gabrielle hurried toward me. Lee was right at her heel. I almost didn't recognize them in the traditional, flowing vestments they wore. They knelt at either side of me, helping me stand. They supported my weight, my arms draped over their shoulders as they guided me to the village. They'd heard me shouting Lucrezia's name. Lee had already explained everything to Gabrielle; as her father was the baron of these islands, she had the key to the temple doors that guarded the portal I needed.

If he was here... then Vespair had kept her promise.

"Lord Gustavo and the emp—err, *Xavier*—are here as well," explained Gabrielle in a rush. "They're by the temple. I know you haven't the energy to explain what's happened, but..."

"We can take a guess," finished Lee.

I swallowed the blood in my throat, muttering, "I need... to get to the temple. The Beyond..."

"I know, Val—just hold on!" said Gabrielle.

When we arrived to Eidos proper, no one noticed us. The people stood outside their quaint wooden homes, staring out at the sight beyond. They gossiped over what could have happened to Indra. All they knew for certain was that magic was to blame. The tense air about the village served as yet another reason why Lucrezia and I had to leave this world. Lydia had changed her mind for the better, but there was no *reasoning* with most other people. They were set in their narrow beliefs.

And the worst of them had formed as a navy of deadly arrows, heading straight toward Lucrezia across the sea.

"Lord Val!" cried a hooded man. By that voice, it was clearly Xavier. "Is that you!?"

"Are you all right?" worried Gustavo. He was on his feet again, leaning against a cane.

"Yes, it's her—no, she's not all right," spoke Lee for me. "The welcome party we talked about might not happen. She's gotta get to that place now."

Xavier kept up with us. "So, Lucrezia... is that really her out there?"

"It is," I said.

"Gods..."

We passed through to the chill of the temple. The dark surroundings were lit up by the torches along the stone walls. Nyx Vevina and Venus greeted me as statues. Other, smaller statues of lesser gods filled the area. Down the halls we went, into a gated area that was off-limits to visitors. Gustavo and Xavier went to stand watch across the way; Gabrielle opened the door with the key she'd procured from her father.

A pair of pure white wings opened with the door. Blinding light of the Edge of Reason washed over us. A winding staircase of crystal led all the way down to the portal to the Beyond. Those pairs of angelic wings rose up around the staircase, acting as an otherworldly form of railing.

Countless oracles rushed down the hall. They warned us to stop—or else.

"Go!" said Gabrielle, pushing me along. "We'll hold them off!"

"Gabby, wait!" I shouted, just before she shut the door. "I promise we'll come back for you all once we know it's safe. Remember that, please. And—thank you... for everything."

"You know I'll always support you, Val. We'll wait for you."

She gave me one last smile as she closed the door. I had my confirmation at last that Gabrielle didn't judge Lucrezia for what she was. I already knew she wouldn't. Knowing for certain still affected me, deeply. I wore my heart on my sleeve, for once, as I limped down the staircase.

Almost there.

I leaned against the hardened wings at my side to help me along. My footsteps resounded as wind chimes, leaving prints of pale blue from where my boots had been. Lucrezia had to know where I was... She no doubt sensed me by our shared consciousness in this steel around my wrist. I gripped my cuffs with my other hand, drawing strength from them.

Somewhere far above, I thought I sensed Vespair watching me.

When at last I reached the glowing white door of the portal, I drew Raine's sword. This whole journey, all we'd had to go off was Elysia's word. *Her word* that we would find our greener pastures here. And now all I had was Raine's word. I had to believe that this would work. Just as my friends had found me when I thought it was over.

"The energy from the portal will reach her through your bond."

I thrust the steel through the door, as Raine had done at Valdivia's entrance. The power was almost too much for me to bear. I held the hilt with both hands, my stance wide for support.

"She will use that energy to teleport to you."

I needed more to hold onto. I was no thaumaturge; I couldn't handle this energy. I clung to my memories with Lucrezia, again, forming my last bastion. My last resort. I looked deep inside of myself for introspection. I focused my growth into this sword.

No longer did I feel the need to change the world. No more did my anger rule me. My impulses. My needs for revenge and ruthless justice. My inexplicable need to *destroy* in retaliation of everyone who had ruined me. Those were gone amid the light that Lucrezia had given me. They were mere shadows in my heart now. All I wanted was this one thing. To take care of Lucrezia, forevermore. Even in this uncertainty we faced, of the true forever that awaited us in this new world, I wished to be her strength. Even if we grew apart, and she fell in love with another... I would always protect her.

I fell to my knees. The white light within the door disappeared. Raine's sword lay in front of me, just through the entrance to this new world. The memories of my ancestors who had lived through Tellus' apocalypse shone across the endless space. A narrow stone bridge formed before me, rising high above the many waterfalls beyond. A metropolis of glass and chrome from the past appeared there over the water, shining in the sunlight. Buildings higher than Eden's had ever been splayed out across the city, forever and ever, with space enough to fit the millions upon millions who had died over the centuries...

The city was empty. And I was still here, alone.

Was I too late...?

My weakness had delayed me. Slowed me down. I couldn't accept it, and yet it all made sense. Now that I had found the pure simplicity in life; now that I loved my one and only... *No.* I couldn't believe that I had failed. To punish myself, yes, I *could* believe it. If this was penance for all the terrible things I'd done in my life, then it was only logical. Only right that a tyrant such as I should end up defeated this way.

"Lucrezia... don't leave me. If you didn't make it, then I will search across heaven and hell until I find you again. *I must.* But it would be so much better if you—if you appeared here. I love you. Please..."

Raine's shadow pointed behind me.

Wind chimes sounded behind me. Clicking heels. Familiar heels.

Kneeling down behind me. Warmth and compassion behind me. Wrapped around me—her arms, her comfort. Feeling her again revitalized me.

"I'm right here, love," spoke Lucrezia, just as she had so many nights ago. "I'm right here."

I turned around in her hold. I knew for certain, again, that it was her when I felt her lips over mine. I breathed hot and hard into her mouth. This didn't feel real, and yet it was. The softness of her hands along my face was hers. The meaning in her touch—it was hers. Everything— how she felt, how she smelled, how she looked, how she smiled—was hers. This brilliance in her eyes was new. This happiness was new, because nothing was in the way. No worries about the wrong person finding us here. No concerns about the masses who didn't understand her, or my love for her.

At last, Lucrezia was as pure as I was; as pure as our feelings for one another.

"It's all right, Val," she said, caressing my face. "We've nothing to fear anymore. We can finally go home."

I smiled with her. "Yes... we can."

By my shadow, Raine reappeared at our side. She helped Lucrezia and me to our feet. I returned her sword and sheathe to her.

"Thank you, Raine," said Lucrezia, embracing her. "I can never thank you enough, really..."

A world of weight had lifted from Raine's shoulders as well. "This is what I'm here for," she replied, bowing. "I enjoy helping when I can."

"Did your mother find her way here?" I wondered.

"Let us find out. This world is yours now."

"The world needs a name," noted Lucrezia.

"Elysium," I said.

We recognized the irony, fitting as it was.

Raine gestured for us to pass the bridge first. Hand-in-hand, Lucrezia and I walked beneath the clear skies. The waterfalls across the way made this world as majestic as I'd imagined. Far beyond, I saw more cities, more towering buildings and vast locations. This would be our own utopia for like-minded people. For the dead; for our living friends and family in Tellus. I hoped to see my father again. I wished to speak with him… to find out how he viewed me now. If he approved of Lucrezia or not. And perhaps I would find my mother and at last have an explanation, in her words, as to why she tried to kill me so long ago.

Infinite possibilities that I had dismissed in Tellus were now in my reach. In my reach, as Lucrezia was; as this ring was, laced between my hand again. As Raine led us to the palace in the heart of the city, we marveled over the sights around us. Clear blue canals stretched across the city, beneath bridges linking boroughs together, and hidden tunnels that acted as shortcuts.

Wide open plazas decorated the city's surface, filled with vast fountains, and masonry that celebrated the archangels and seraphim who had protected the Twin Goddesses. The glass buildings all around us scraped the sky itself: asymmetrical, experimental, beautiful.

Within the palace, the floor shone black and silver. The walls rose higher than those in the Empyrean Palace had. More space, more comfort. And in the throne room, we found simplicity there. A long, white room leading to a single throne: an open canvas for Lucrezia to enchant as she wished.

Raine watched us enter the room, a hint of melancholy in her eyes, and closed the double doors behind us. I wanted to ask what troubled her, but Lucrezia had already led me halfway to the throne. The lancet windows along the wall opened the room up to the sunlight, the perfect weather.

Seeing Lucrezia sit upon this throne was just that— perfect.

"Such meaning," she spoke softly. "I took Xavier's throne for granted. He insisted it was more mine than his… Did you see him in the village?"

"Yes, and your brother, along with Lee and Gabrielle. They're doing well."

Lucrezia beckoned me with her finger. "Come here, love…"

I stood before her, uncertain of what to do, what to say now. She pulled me over her lap; had me sit there. I wrapped my arms around her neck. I relaxed, resting my head over her shoulder. I felt cradled by her in the way she held me. Lucrezia wanted to say something. She couldn't find the words. I was no different.

Being here together defied the limits of what we'd believed before. This was our world. We would have our own rules, our own way of living. No longer did we need to deal with the realities of someone *telling us* that our dreams weren't possible. I worried for but a moment that that lack might inspire complacency in us. I soon dismissed the thought. Not having such obstacles in the way would remind us that this Elysium was paradise. Once the matter of Vespair, Raj, Videl, Nyte, and Stella found us again, we would have to make a decision, together, on what to do. We weren't involved anymore, and yet we cared for Raine and Elysia. They were family, as was Stella. And Nyte. I wanted to protect them. And yet I had a distant respect for Vespair now. I also didn't want to jeopardize this strange bond we shared.

Persevering through hardships wasn't unique to Tellus' surface. We would have to do it again, and again, in some way, in some form through our immortality here.

As long as I had Lucrezia with me, I knew everything would be all right. And even if I didn't…

"I thought of something earlier," I told her. "When it seemed like you wouldn't find me at the entrance… I surprised myself. I considered—I made up my mind. Even if you grow to love someone else in this eternity, I will forever be bound to you. I will be here to protect you whether you want me or not. It is dangerous for me to feel this way… I feared it for the longest."

"And yet here we are now," said Lucrezia. "I cannot speak for the future, as fickle as that sounds. But I've no doubts whatsoever. The moment we passed through this world together—*that* felt like our wedding ceremony. At least to me."

"I love that, actually. Don't you still want a more traditional one?"

"Mmm, I do. Once we've the people to invite to celebrate with us. It will take some time."

"We have all the time in the world now," I reminded her.

Lucrezia held me tighter, sending me soaring in place. "Yes, we do…"

I lost track of how long we spent sitting like this. This time without end held me as Lucrezia did. This was a safe space. I couldn't free her from the shackles of ignorance that had chained her in Tellus. We had Elysium instead. We had this solitude, this silence, this sanctuary.

We were the ones who dared to dream, to believe in a place such as this. With but a hope and a prayer, we found our way here. At last, we were free from the ones who judged us. At last, we had not a care to worry over— not now, not in the immediate future… not until the time came for us to decide between despair and duty. At last, we were free to have anyone, and everyone here, as our comrades, as diverse as this world's terrains and cities, who came from all walks of life; who required spiritual shelter from the ones in Tellus who had wronged them for their differences, as Tellus had done to us.

I would do everything in my power and beyond to keep Lucrezia on this throne. Years we had ahead of us. Decades, centuries, millennia of love: the eternity only literature conceived of, by its declarations of forever, by its permanence of ink on page. As hard as I had fought against my despair; as deeply as I had resisted the slurs and fists of everyone who despised me, I persevered, and found my permanence. Here. Lucrezia was forever here. I was forever hers. She was my smile, my fear, my heartbeat.

Whether this infinite time changed our relationship for the worse; whether she could not weather the storm of what awaited us in the future, my heart was rooted to her existence, to her skin, to her blood, to her bones, linked, inextricable. Locked to her and needing this, I loved her.

We were free at last.

End

About Yushiyuki Ly

Yoshiyuki Ly was born in San Diego, CA. She lived there until moving away to college. In high school, she began writing fanfiction as a serious hobby. Her pen name represents her multiracial heritage and a unique, diverse outlook that reflects in her work. She is a writer and a gamer.

Social Media Links:

Amazon Author Page: Author.to/yoshiyuki_ly
Twitter: https://twitter.com/LyLikeLee
Facebook: https://www.facebook.com/yoshiyukily/
Live Journal: http://yoshiyuki-ly.livejournal.com/
Fan Fiction: https://www.fanfiction.net/~yoshiyukily

If you enjoyed this story, check out these other Solstice Publishing books by Yoshiyuki Ly:

The Scorpion's Empress

After years of serving a corrupt government, Ser Videl, an idealistic paladin, learns that her younger sister is tangled in a dark scheme against Raj Mangala, the compassionate yet troubled empress of the city's oppressed lowtown; the two women meet and are deeply drawn to one another, finding a shared sanctuary in their violently-divided city.

Videl's loving devotion is just what Raj craves, but Raj is wary of letting her guard down while protecting her throne. Determined to prove her worth, Videl chases after Raj and works to unravel the mystery of the plots against the empress. Raj wants Videl to serve her emotional and sexual needs, and the two explore a meaningful relationship of dominance and submission that delves fully into their deepest wants. When the conspiracy against Raj comes to a head, Videl's loyalties are tested when she is forced to choose between her past and her empress.

http://bookgoodies.com/a/B01G4GO5PE

CPSIA information can be obtained
at www.ICGtesting.com
Printed in the USA
LVHW03s1813151018
593654LV00012B/1073/P

9 781625 265241